KT-558-625

Praise for The Cut

'Pelecanos is incapable of writing a book that isn't gripping, and the dialogue is of a brilliance comparable only with Elmore Leonard and George V. Higgins' *The Times*

'A bloody, brooding thriller of rare authenticity'
Evening Standard

'Expertly crafted writing . . . and a plot that keeps twisting to the dramatic finale' *Shortlist*

'The language, like the action, is brutal, fast and hard . . . *The Cut* certainly marks him out as a name to watch. In fact, he may just come to give Ellroy and Leonard a run for their money in the hard-boiled stakes' *Daily Mail*

'Pelecanos keeps readers on their toes with a series of twists that confound stereotypes, drilling the plot along with breakneck prose, sassy dialogue and even shifting into a serious analysis at modern society in all its flawed glory. Exceptional' *Big Issue*

'This is gold-standard character-driven crime writing that few will ever match. I can't wait for the sequel' *Financial Times*

'Pelecanos, heir to Elmore Leonard's throne, has landed another short, sparkling masterpiece. What's more, *The Cut* is just the beginning of a planned series for tough, streetwise, mother's boy Spero Lucas' *Mirror*

'George Pelecanos writes hard-boiled fiction with heart'
Sunday Telegraph

By George Pelecanos

A Firing Offense
Nick's Trip
Shoedog
Down By the River Where the Dead Men Go
The Big Blowdown
King Suckerman
The Sweet Forever
Shame the Devil
Right as Rain
Hell to Pay
Soul Circus
Hard Revolution
Drama City
The Night Gardener
The Turnaround
The Way Home
The Cut
What it Was
The Double

George Pelecanos is an independent-film producer, an essayist, the recipient of numerous international writing awards, a producer and an Emmy-nominated writer on the HBO hit series *The Wire*, and the author of a bestselling series of novels set in and around Washington, D.C. He is currently a writer and producer for the acclaimed HBO series *Treme*. He lives in Maryland with his wife and three children.

THE CUT

GEORGE PELECANOS

An Orion paperback

First published in Great Britain in 2011
by Orion Books
This paperback edition published in 2012
by Orion Books,
an imprint of The Orion Publishing Group Ltd
Orion House, 5 Upper St Martin's Lane,
London WC2H 9EA

An Hachette UK company

3 5 7 9 10 8 6 4 2

Copyright © George P. Pelecanos 2011

The moral right of George Pelecanos to be identified as the author
of this work has been asserted in accordance with the
Copyright, Designs and Patents Act 1988.

All rights reserved. No part of this publication may be
reproduced, stored in a retrieval system, or transmitted, in
any form or by any means, electronic, mechanical,
photocopying, recording or otherwise, without the prior
permission of the copyright owner.

All the characters in this book are fictitious,
and any resemblance to actual persons, living
or dead, is purely coincidental.

A CIP catalogue record for this book
is available from the British Library.

ISBN 978-1-4091-0967-9

Printed and bound in Great Britain by
Clays Ltd, St Ives plc

The Orion Publishing Group's policy is to use papers that
are natural, renewable and recyclable products and
made from wood grown in sustainable forests. The logging
and manufacturing processes are expected to conform to
the environmental regulations of the country of origin.

www.orionbooks.co.uk

THE CUT

ONE

THEY WERE in a second-story office with a bank of windows overlooking D Street at 5th, in a corner row house close to the federal courts. Tom Petersen, big and blond, sat behind his desk, wearing an untucked paisley shirt, jeans, and boots. Spero Lucas, in Carhartt, was in a hard chair set before the desk. Petersen was a criminal defense attorney, private practice. Lucas, one of his investigators.

A black Moleskine notebook the size of a pocket Bible was open in Lucas's hand. He was scribbling something in the book.

"It's all in the documents I'm going to give you," said Petersen with growing impatience. "You don't need to take notes."

"I'd rather," said Lucas.

"I can't tell if you're listening."

"I'm listening. Where'd they boost the Denali?"

"They took it up in Manor Park, on Peabody Street. Near the community garden, across from the radio towers."

"Behind the police station?"

"Right in back of Four-D."

"Pretty bold," said Lucas. "How many boys?"

"Two. Unfortunately, my client, David Hawkins, was the one behind the wheel."

"You just have him?"

"The other one, Duron Gaskins, he's been assigned a PD."

"Duron," said Lucas.

Petersen shrugged. "Like the paint."

"How'd David get so lucky to score a stud like you?"

"I'm representing his father on another matter," said Petersen.

"So this is like a favor."

"A four-hundred-dollar-an-hour favor."

Lucas's back had begun to stiffen. He shifted his weight in his chair. "Give me some details."

Petersen pushed a manila file across the desk. "Here."

"*Talk* to me."

"What do you want to know?"

"How'd they do it, for starters?"

"Steal the vehicle? That was easy. The boys were walking down the street, supposed to be in school, but hey. It's early in the morning, cold as hell. You remember that snap we had back in February? This woman comes out of her apartment, starts her SUV up, and then leaves it running and goes back into the apartment."

"She forget somethin?"

"She was heating up the Denali before she went to work."

"Insurance companies don't like that."

"She left the driver's door unlocked, too. So naturally,

being teenage boys, they got in and took the SUV for a spin."

"*I* would have," said Lucas.

"You *did*, I recall."

"What happened next?"

"From Peabody, David went south on Ninth to Missouri, then drove east. He caught North Capitol along Rock Creek Cemetery and took that cutoff street west, the stretch that goes by the Soldiers' Home."

"That would be Allison," said Lucas, starting to see it, like he was looking down at a detail map. He had a cop's knowledge of D.C. because he was out in it, street level, most of his waking hours. When he didn't have to drive his Cherokee, Lucas rode his bicycle around town. At night he often walked.

"Here's where they got in trouble. David, keep in mind he's fifteen, no significant driving experience far as I know, he loses control of the SUV. Sideswipes a lady in a Buick, which knocks her out of her lane and into a couple of parked cars."

"By now they'd be on Rock Creek Church Road."

"Yeah, there," said Petersen. "The woman in the Buick? Claims she's got neck injuries."

"That's not good."

"I'm gonna work something out with her attorney."

"This kid's father must be flush."

"He is."

"This where the police come in?"

"Happens to be a patrol car, coupla uniforms idling nose out at Second and Varnum see this collision."

"And the chase is on."

"Took the police officer a half minute to put his coffee down and flip on the siren and light bar. By that time, David knew he'd been burned, and he jumps the sidewalk and cuts right onto Upshur Street."

"Driving on the Sidewalk, that's a good one."

"Fleeing and Eluding, Leaving the Scene of an Accident, Auto Theft..."

"Kid's got a rack of problems."

"He fishtails when he hits Upshur. Comes out of that and pins it. You know Upshur going west there—"

"It's long and straight. Downhill."

Petersen leaned forward, getting into it. "This boy is screaming down Upshur, Spero. Blowing four-ways, Wale or whatever coming loud out the windows."

"Nah," said Lucas, chuckling.

"What?"

"Now you're making shit up. You don't know what they were listening to."

"True. They're coming down Upshur, the patrol car, pretty far back but gaining ground, in pursuit. Eventually our boys hit that commercial strip getting down toward Georgia Avenue, at Ninth."

"I know the spot," said Lucas. He was drawing a rough map, very quickly, in his notebook.

"And there's another cop car," said Petersen, "parked right there on the street. The driver is waiting on his partner, who's getting a pack of smokes in a little market they got in that strip."

"What market?" said Lucas.

"I don't know the name of it. Spanish joint, eight hundred

block, north side of Upshur. Beer and wine, pork rinds, like that. It's in the file, along with the address. What happens next is, David sees this police car, and I guess he panics, and here's where he makes the last mistake. He cuts a sharp right into an alley, right before Ninth."

"And?"

"A car is parked in the alley, blocking their way. The boys get out of the vehicle and run; David Hawkins is apprehended on the street. The other boy, Duron, is caught a little while later, attempting to hide in the bathroom of an El Salvadoran restaurant around the corner."

"Who arrested David?"

"The officer waiting in the patrol car. A Clarence Jackson. By then the car in pursuit had arrived on the scene."

"How'd Officer Jackson know that David was one of the boys in the car?"

"In his report, Jackson stated that he observed two boys exit an SUV that they had driven into the alley. Jackson got to David first. The arriving officers arrested Duron in the restaurant."

"Where was Officer Jackson parked when he saw this?"

"It's in the file."

Lucas sat still for a long minute, looking at nothing. He closed his notebook and got up out of his seat. He stood five-foot-eleven, went one eighty-five, had a flat stomach and a good chest and shoulders. His hair was black and he wore it short. His eyes were green, flecked with gold, and frequently unreadable. He was twenty-nine years old.

Petersen watched Lucas stretch. "Sorry. That seat's unforgiving."

"It's these wood floors. The chair sits funny on 'em cause the planks are warped."

"This house goes back to the nineteenth century."

"Your point is what?"

"Ghosts of greatness walk these rooms. I start messing with the floors, I might make them angry."

A young GW law student entered Petersen's office and dropped a large block of papers on his desk. She was dark haired, fully curved, and effortlessly attractive. Tom Petersen's interns looked more or less like younger versions of his knockout wife.

"The Parker briefs," said the woman, whose name was Constance Kelly.

"Thank you," said Petersen. He watched Lucas admire her as she walked away.

Petersen stood and went to the eastern window of his office. Below, on the street, lawyers pulled wheeled briefcases toward the courthouse, uniformed and plainclothes police bullshitted with one another, mothers spoke patiently and angrily with their sons, civil servants took cigarette breaks, and folks of all shapes and colors went in and out of the Potbelly shop on the first floor.

"Life's rich pageant," said Petersen.

"That's a rock record from back in your day, right?"

"Inspector Clouseau, originally."

"You got me on that one."

"I have twenty years on you. At times the perspective is obvious. Other times, no." Petersen looked him over with the respect that men who have not served give to those who have. "You've seen a lot, haven't you?"

"It's been interesting, so far." Lucas slipped his notebook into his jacket and picked up the David Hawkins file off Petersen's desk.

"Bring me something back I can use," said Petersen.

Lucas nodded. "I'll get out there."

THE NEXT morning he stopped by the Glenwood Cemetery in Northeast to see his *baba*. Glenwood was an old but well-kept graveyard, acres of rolling, high-ground land holding plots with headstones memorializing lives going back to the 1800s. His father was buried here, beside his own parents, on the west side of the facility, which bordered dead-end residential streets stemming off North Capitol in a neighborhood called Stronghold. Past this last section of graves the land dropped off and there went Bryant Street, its short block of row homes in a neat descending line. Lucas looked down at his father's marker and placed a dozen roses on his plot. He said a silent prayer of thanks for the granting of life, did his *stavro*, and got back in his four-wheel.

He drove a 2001 Jeep Cherokee, the old boxy model with the legendary in-line 6. The model had been discontinued years ago, but because it was sturdy and reliable there were many of them still on the streets. In that respect it was the aughts version of the old Dodge Dart. With his black Jeep, empty of bumper stickers or decals, and his utilitarian clothing, Lucas was unmemorable by design, a tradesman, maybe, or a meter reader, just another workingman quietly going about his business in the city.

Lucas went up to Peabody and began to drive the route of David Hawkins and his friend Duron. Missouri, North

Capitol, Allison, and then Rock Creek Church, where it had begun to go wrong. He recalled the adrenaline rush he had experienced the day he and a couple of buddies from the wrestling team had stolen a car, back in high school. It didn't matter who suggested it; they had all participated with enthusiasm, and all had been caught, arrested, and charged. They pled down, and, because they were white and came from stable families, they had pulled community service and loose supervision. There were no further problems; Lucas's mistake was a one-shot deal, and he did not want to shame his parents in that way ever again. By the time he entered the Marine Corps, his conviction had been expunged.

He understood why David and Duron had stolen the SUV. Teenage boys did stupid things; their brains were wired for impulse and fun. Wasn't but a little more than ten years back that he had been one of those reckless boys, too, before September 11 and his tour of Iraq. A sobering decade, a decade that stole his youth.

Lucas drove west on Upshur. He gunned the Jeep going down the hill and pulled over when he reached the commercial strip, near Georgia Avenue. He saw the alley, cut along a salmon-colored building, currently unoccupied, where the boys had been trapped. He looked at the south and north sides of the strip and he studied the businesses and the layout of the street. In his notebook he drew a map showing the locations of the establishments. On the south side: a funeral parlor, a dry cleaner's, a carryout featuring Chinese/steak-and-cheese, a nail salon, and a hair salon; on the north side: a storefront church, a market selling wine and beer, a furnishings store that seemed too upscale for the neighborhood, a hair salon, a Caribbean café, the alley, the salmon-colored building, another Chinese/American hybrid, a seafood carryout, a beverage shop, and on the corner a shuttered barbershop. Many of the stores had English and Spanish signage in their windows; there were blacks, Hispanics, and a few whites out on the street.

He got out of the car and, using his iPhone, took photographs of these businesses and their spots on the block. No one questioned him or got in his way. He went around the corner and noted the commercial layout of Ninth: the Petworth station of the U.S. Post Office, a private-detective agency, another funeral home, the Salvadoran restaurant where Duron had tried to hide, an embroidery shop, and a corner Spanish grocery store that did not have any English signage and was padlocked shut. Above the detective agency door was a lightbox that read "Strange Investigations," with several letters enlarged by the magnifying-glass logo placed over them. He had heard tell of the man, Derek Strange, and his latest partner, a middle-aged Greek whose name he could not recall.

Lucas retraced his steps, crossed Upshur and stood by the Chinese eat-house, where in his report Officer Clarence Jackson stated that he had been parked, and saw that indeed it afforded a direct view of the alley. He took a photograph from that perspective. He looked across the street to the market where Jackson's partner had bought his smokes, and he saw that there was a fire hydrant in front of it. That would explain why Jackson had parked across the street. It would have explained it perfectly, except for the fact that Jackson was police.

Lucas crossed Upshur once again and entered the beer and wine market. It was clean, well stocked with alcohol and food packaged in bags, its walls lined with steel shelving and reach-in coolers. Behind the register counter was a man in his forties, round brown face, white shirt open at the neck revealing a gold crucifix in a thicket of black chest hair. By his bearing and the gold-and-diamond ring on his finger, Lucas surmised that he was the owner. When questioned, the man confirmed this. Lucas gave him his name and identified himself simply as an "investigator." He asked if the owner, who called himself Odin, recalled the day of the arrest, and Odin said that he did. He asked Odin where the officer had been parked when his partner had entered the market to buy his smokes, and Odin said, "He park out front." When Lucas noted that there was a fire hydrant out front, Odin, who like many hardworking Hispanics was a law-and-order man, said rather defensively, "But he is police; he park where he want!"

Lucas got the man's contact information, thanked him, and made a note in his book regarding the pronunciation of Odin's name. He left the store and took multiple photographs of the alley from the point of view of the empty parking spot. He framed these so that the fire hydrant was in the foreground of the shots.

THE NEXT day, Lucas was sitting on the edge of Constance the intern's desk, trying to talk her into something, when Petersen called out to him from his office.

"We should continue this conversation later on," said Lucas.

"You think so?" said Constance, a strand of dark hair over

one eye, light freckles across the bridge of her nose. She reminded Lucas of one of those J. Crew girls. There was no trace of a smile on her face, but there was a light in her eyes, and Lucas knew that if he wanted to be in, he was in.

Petersen was behind his desk, loud striped shirt untucked, his blond hair shaggy around his face, looking like an aged Brian Jones. He was checking out photos on his computer screen, displayed from a disk that Lucas had burned from his iPhone.

"These are interesting," said Petersen, Lucas now standing beside him.

"The ones with the hydrant in the foreground? That would approximate the sight line of Officer Jackson. From where he was actually parked, as opposed to where he *said* he was parked."

"He couldn't have seen deep into the alley from there."

"He could only have seen the head of it, and a small piece of it at that. The report says the Denali was found at the back edge of that salmon-colored building. So, from that perspective, there's no way Jackson could have observed David and Duron get out of that SUV."

"Can anyone testify that Jackson was parked in front of the market?"

From his back pocket Lucas produced his notebook and opened it. "The owner. His name is Odin Nolasco." Lucas spelled it and Petersen wrote it down. Lucas said, "It's pronounced Oh-deen. I don't think he'd willingly discredit a police officer's official report. You're going to have to subpoena him. When you get him on the stand you might have to treat him as hostile."

"Thank you for the legal advice, counselor."

"I'm sayin."

"The visual ID, the link of the boys to the SUV, that's the prosecution's case right there."

"Weren't the boys' prints on the Denali?"

"Their prints were all over it. But that's less significant than what we have here. I was weighing a plea, but now I want this to go to trial. You put it into a D.C. jury's head that a police officer gave false testimony to make a case against a juvenile, nine times out of ten that jury's going to acquit, even in the face of damning evidence."

"Well, there's your ammunition." Lucas held up the notebook. "I've got street maps I drew, right in here, if you need them."

"The Book of Luke."

"Yes, sir."

"Good work, man."

"Thank you."

Lucas began to walk from the office, and Petersen stopped him. "Spero?"

"Yeah."

"Don't bother Constance. She's a nice girl."

"I like nice girls," said Lucas. He meant it, too.

IT WENT the way Petersen said it would. A month later, he phoned Lucas and got him on his cell.

"David Hawkins was acquitted," said Petersen.

"Duron?" said Lucas.

"Duron will walk, too."

"Do I get a bonus, somethin?"

"In a way. But not from me."

"That would be out of character."

"David's father, Anwan Hawkins, would like to meet you. I think he has something like an extra envelope in mind."

"Anwan Hawkins the dealer?"

"Yeah. Up on trafficking charges at the moment, unfortunately. He's currently in the D.C. Jail."

"He wants me to come there?"

"Uh-huh."

"Visitation days are set by the first letter in the last names, right?"

"That's for social visits; the prison makes audio recordings of those conversations. You should go in as one of my official investigators. Those conversations are confidential."

"Got it."

"I'll put a letter in to the DOC. It takes twenty-four hours to clear."

"You know what Hawkins wants?"

"I believe Anwan is going to make you some sort of a proposal. But I can't have you taking on any side work for a week or so. You've got those interviews to do for me on that Southeast thing. I'm defending Reginald Brooks, the shooter. Remember?"

"I do."

"So what should I tell Anwan?" Petersen got no comment from Lucas. "Spero?"

"I'll meet with him," said Lucas. "See what he has to say."

Which is how Spero Lucas met Anwan Hawkins, and the truck began to roll downhill.

TWO

LUCAS HIT "end" on his iPhone and placed the device on the nightstand beside his bed. The stand held a digital alarm clock, a lamp with a pillowcase thrown over its shade, his Bible, and a couple of other books. Lucas kept two, a fiction and a nonfiction, going at a time. He rolled over and got up on one elbow. Constance Kelly was beside him, naked in the bed.

"That was your boss," said Lucas.

"Yours, too."

"I don't have a boss."

"Neither do I, technically. I'm an intern, remember? At least you get paid."

"Fifteen an hour."

"It's folding money."

"Don't forget about the meal plan. Horace and Dickies, Litteri's..."

"Tom does like to feed his troops."

Lucas leaned into her. They kissed.

16

"Why'd he call you on a Monday night?" said Constance.

"He had something for me."

"A case?"

Lucas shook his head. He ran his hand down her neckline, her breast, her ribcage. The inside of her thigh and between her legs.

"I'm not on the stand," said Lucas.

"You do side work," said Constance. "Isn't that right?" In the low light of his bedroom lamp she looked very young.

"Something like that."

"That's how you have all this." She meant his spacious apartment. His bicycle, his car, the kayak hung on hooks on the back porch. In terms of Washington, it really wasn't much at all. But from her perspective, living on a tight budget, it looked like a lot.

"All this," said Lucas, finding a spot she liked.

She gasped a little and arched her back. She sucked at his lip and he pulled away, looking down at her, admiring her.

"I guess you think you're pretty smart," said Lucas.

"Just observant."

"And lovely."

Her chest blushed pink and he laughed.

"Stop it," she said.

"Stop what?"

"Talking."

"What's the rush?"

"I mean it," she said, her eyes slightly gone.

She tugged at him and he fitted himself between her, lifting one of her legs. It was slow at first. They searched for it and then they found it and soon it became something else, and the bed moved across the floor. Constance's hand twisted the sheets, her pupils dilated, her hair fanned out about her face. She was the quiet type, but he felt her tense beneath him, and when she made it, Lucas let go and shot a hot river.

They lay there quietly, the sex smell heavy in the room. She liked him to linger. When she was ready she pushed at him a little and she made a small sound when he pulled out. She rolled off the mattress and stood. He watched her cross the room slowly, deliberately, so he could take her in. She was proud of her body and rightly so. He listened to her in the bathroom, washing herself, and then the sound of water drumming in the sink. Thinking, This is what I dreamed of when I was overseas: a nice big comfortable bed in a place of my own, money in my pocket, good-looking young women to laugh with, sometimes just to fuck, sometimes to make love to. God, what more do you need?

Fifteen minutes later, she was dressed and by the front door. He was beside her, shirtless and shoeless, in his 501s.

"You could stay," said Lucas.

"I want to wake up in my own place. I have class in the morning and then I'm doing some work for Tom."

"I feel used."

"No, you don't. You're happy and grateful." She touched his chest, lifted his crucifix, and handled the pendant of blue glass and silver that hung beside it on his chain. "What is this?"

"A *mati*. It means 'eye.' "

"Like an evil eye?"

"The opposite. It reflects evil back on the onlooker."

"I'm evil." She moved her hand to one of his nipples and pinched it.

Lucas smiled. "Don't I know it."

"I hope we didn't wake up the woman downstairs," said Constance.

"She lived here with her husband for over fifty years. I reckon they christened every room in this house, one time or another. Miss Lee understands that I'm a healthy young man."

"I'll say."

He walked her down the stairs that led to the separate entrance to his place. He had the entire second floor of a four-square colonial on the corner of Emerson and Piney Branch Road, in 16th Street Heights. This wasn't the Piney Branch that ran deep into Maryland, a street commuters knew well, but rather a short stretch of road running from Buchanan up to Colorado Avenue, in a country-style atmosphere of quiet lanes and alleys that felt bucolic and was only fifteen minutes north of the White House and deep downtown. A brief bike ride down Colorado to Blagden could take Lucas into Rock Creek Park. Nearby 13th Street was within pedaling distance of the places he needed to go. He had lucked into the spot when Miss Lee, a septuagenarian with a prunish face, a thin cap of cottony hair, and beautiful and wily black eyes, had advertised the apartment the old-fashioned way, with a handbill stapled to a telephone pole. He spotted it one day while cruising through the neighborhood on his Trek. When she interviewed him, she explained that the house was paid for, that she didn't need a tenant for the rent money and was only looking to feel secure with someone in the house. He mentioned that he was a veteran and a marine, and that, coupled with the fact that he repeatedly addressed her as Miss Lee and not by her Christian name, Willie Mae, closed the deal. Given the size of the place, the low rent, and the location, he knew he'd scored.

"Come back," said Lucas to Constance, outside the first-floor door to his apartment.

"I will."

He kissed her and watched her go to her car, a '99 Civic that might as well have had "student" imprinted on its plates. When she was safely in and her engine had turned over, he went back inside. He had things to do in the next couple of days before he went to visit Anwan Hawkins. For one, he needed to get to the library, check out the newspaper morgue material on the man, and gather any intel on him from Petersen. He also had plans to meet his brother for dinner, down around U. Visit some of the soldiers up at Walter Reed, drop off some books. And he needed to get by his mother's house in Silver Spring to cut her grass. Matter of fact, he thought as he went up the stairs, I should call Mom soon as I get in my room.

Tell her I love her, tell her good night.

ON DETAIL maps it was identified as the D.C. Central Detention Facility, but locals — citizens, inmates, and law alike — called it the D.C. Jail. The holding facility sat at 19th and D, in the Southeast quadrant of the city, on acreage that included the old D.C. General Hospital and RFK Stadium. The jail complex was large, ugly, and bleak. Inmates liked to say that they lived on waterfront property, as several of the east-facing cells gave to a view of the Anacostia River.

In the security area, Lucas signed the book, gave up his driver's license in exchange for a pass, went through a metal detector, and was patted down and wanded. He was the only male visitor who wasn't obviously an attorney or some kind of police. Mothers, grandmothers, aunts, girlfriends, and one nun waited in line. The younger women were led into a closed room where they were instructed to shake out their bras. One woman, wearing shorts and a scoop-necked shirt showing ample cleavage, a double violation of the dress code, was turned away. She exited loudly.

Now Lucas sat on a plastic chair in the visiting room, among women visiting men and several guards. Across from him, behind glass, sat Anwan Hawkins, wearing orange. Hawkins was very tall, lean, and freakishly broad shouldered. He was in his thirties. His long braids framed a chiseled face. One of his front teeth had been capped in gold. His facial hair was haphazardly arranged and ungroomed. It stayed where it grew.

They were speaking into telephones. Though they were spitting distance from each other, the telephone connection made them sound continents apart.

"Thank you for helping my son," said Hawkins, his voice low and husky.

"I did my job."

"Mr. Petersen said you do it well."

"He must like my work. He keeps me around."

Hawkins appraised him. "You look like you can handle yourself out there."

"I just try to show people respect."

"I feel the same way." Hawkins dipped his head. "My man said you fought in the Middle East."

"I was there."

"You kill anyone?"

Lucas did not reply.

"Okay, then," said Hawkins. "I understand."

Lucas waited.

"My son David is no gangster," said Hawkins. "Nothin like that. What he did, taking that vehicle, that was just a crime of opportunity right there."

"It seemed that way to me."

"Incarceration wouldn't have taught David nothin he didn't already know. He was raised right."

"By you?"

"His mother did all the heavy lifting. I'm not proud of that. I never intended to have a baby and not be there in his life. I *wanted* my marriage to last. But sometimes a man and a woman just can't make it." Hawkins chucked his chin up in Lucas's direction. "You married?"

"No."

"His mother and I don't stay together, but I always gave her support. I feel like, now, it's extra important that I get out of here, so I can be there for him, to set the right example."

"I can't help you there, Mr. Hawkins."

"I got the best criminal lawyer in town. I don't need more legal help."

"Well?"

"You wanna get to it."

"We only have a half hour. We've burnt a piece of it already."

"How you say your name, exactly?"

"Spero."

"*Spee*-row. We gonna speak freely, right?"

"Yes."

"Mr. Petersen told you about my charges."

"He didn't have to. You were involved with one of the largest marijuana seizures in D.C. history. I read about it in the paper."

"Damn right you gonna read about it. Over a million dollars, wholesale. You *know* they gonna try and put me away for a long time. Actin like I'm Rayful Edmond and shit. But I never sold cocaine or heroin. I wouldn't."

"In the eyes of the law it's all illegal."

"And it's gonna stay illegal. 'Cause that's how they fill up the facilities and generate the construction of more jails. Hire more guards. More administrators, guard unions. The aim is to keep this big prison industrial complex rolling. When I was a kid, the majority of people in lockup was in for violent crime. Now most of the people in prison are in for nonviolent drug offenses."

"There's violence attached to it."

"Don't I know. That stash you got up in your bedroom drawer, somewhere down in Juarez they be cutting someone's head off behind it. If it was legal, that shit wouldn't be happenin." Hawkins leaned forward. "It's a prop, man. Don't matter what the thing is, exactly. You make, I don't know, possession of milk against the law, you gonna give birth to an underground economy where people be sellin milk on the corner or behind closed doors. And some people gonna kill behind that carton of milk. But not me. I'm not about that."

Lucas looked into his eyes. "Say why I'm here."

"I lost something," said Hawkins. "I understand you specialize in recovery."

"Tell me about it."

"Do you know how I used to bring in my product?"

"Mexicans out of California drove it into D.C. in tractor trailers. They'd stop on the side of the road and transfer it into your own trucks. Sometimes they'd even stop on the Beltway or the B-W Parkway."

"You did your homework."

"Again, I read about it. That's a story you don't forget."

"Sounds bold or stupid, depending on how you look at it. But actually it worked out fine for a long time. Thing is, we didn't get busted out on the highway. Someone weak got put under the hot lights and snitched me out. Doesn't matter who. In my line of work you know that day is gonna come. Once I became a person of interest, it was just a matter of time. The police didn't want my shipment, they wanted me. The law GPS'd one of my trucks, let it make its run, and followed it back to my storage facility. I had this spot off Kansas Avenue, up there by Lamond, where they got a whole rack of warehouses."

"I know the area."

"I was there the day the truck rolled in. And now I'm here."

Hawkins folded his hands on the table, paused for effect. He was a showman.

"Go on."

"Even though I got locked up, I couldn't close my business. I mean, I got employees to take care of, not to mention my legal fees. My second, a young man name of Tavon, continues to bring in product, only now he's doing it in a different way. You know about the FedEx method, right?"

"Yeah," said Lucas. "And so do the police."

"Even with that, it's hard to stop it. The supplier FedExes a bunch of packages to residences that we identify as unoccupied during the day. We track the packages on the Internet so we know damn near when they're about to arrive. We intercept the pickups and no one's the wiser."

"Except that it's been in the news lately, in a big way."

"Uh-huh. First you had that incident out in Maryland where the SWAT boys shot the dogs of those suspects who turned out to be innocent. And then that article they had in the *Post*, where those people took in that package and discovered it was multiple pounds of weed. Made it sound like it was some kind of new phenomenon and shit."

"Kids were shipping weed back and forth like that when I was in high school."

"It *is* tried and true."

"Not exactly," said Lucas. "Someone took you off, right?"

Hawkins nodded with embarrassment. "I lost one. More than one, actually."

"When?"

"Three weeks ago, somethin like that. A thirty-pound package got stolen off the steps of a house in Brookland. And then a box holding another thirty pounds of my property got boosted off someone's porch just last week."

"That's money."

"Sure is." Hawkins shook a ropy forest of braids away from his face. "Funniest part of that article was, po-lice said the dealers don't bother with retaliation when that kind of thing goes down. Said the economics was such that the dealers could afford to be philosophical about that shit and absorb the loss. That's some bullshit right there. Don't get me wrong; I'm not lookin to do any kind of violence to no one. Like I told you, I'm not about that. But I can't be philosophical behind it, either. Situation I'm in right now, I need the money. I paid for that product and it's mine. I want it back."

"You want me to recover your lost packages."

"Or the cash, if they done offed it already. I'm not lookin for any muscle here, Spero. Just get me back what's mine. No one I got has your skills. I seen what you did for my son. Got to say, I was impressed."

"What's the value of the product?"

"Wholesale?"

"Retail," said Lucas.

"Roughly one hundred and thirty thousand a package."

"I'd get forty."

"Thousand?"

"Percent," said Lucas.

"That's fifty thousand and change."

"Fifty-two. Per package."

"How you come to that?"

"Forty percent's my standard fee."

"Your cut," said Hawkins.

"That's right."

Anwan Hawkins sat back in his chair. He stared at Lucas, and a glint of gold showed as he nearly smiled.

"Where'd the second package get took?" said Lucas.

"Why the second?"

"Most likely the trail on the first theft is cold by now."

Hawkins gave him an address. Lucas said, "Do you know how to get in touch with me?"

"Tell me your cell number. I'll get it to Tavon."

"Don't communicate with Petersen about this again."

"Understood," said Hawkins. "Your cell?"

Lucas said it and repeated it. "You're gonna remember that?"

"Sure."

"I don't do trades. I take my fee in cash."

Hawkins looked him over. "You're on the cocky side. You know that?"

"It serves me well in my line of work."

"Don't go spending that cash just yet," said Hawkins. "That kinda money you chargin? I ain't quite decided whether you and I are gonna do business."

Lucas said, "Neither have I."

THREE

SPERO LUCAS had two brothers and a sister, but only one sibling he was close to. This was the brother who was a year older than him. His name was Leonidas, but everyone, except for his mother when she was being stern with him, called him Leo. Leo's birth name had been Nigel, but Van and Eleni Lucas had changed it, in the same way that they had changed Spero's name from Sean. Spero and Leo had come into the world from entirely different places and had wound up brothers. Both felt blessed.

"What do you think?" said Spero, talking on his cell, sitting in his reading chair by the window that gave to a view of Emerson Street. "Should I take the job?"

"*I* wouldn't," said Leo, speaking from his basement apartment in Logan. "But I wouldn't do half the shit you do."

"Because he's a dealer?"

"Because someone with a defective personality probably stole that weed. Because someone like that might not like you looking into it, and they *might* go and blow your pretty head off."

"Hawkins doesn't seem to play in that kind of arena."

"Oh. He deals marijuana as opposed to the hard stuff, so he's cool."

"I'm not claiming that. But he is smart and practical. Not practical, exactly. He looks at his situation from the practical tip based on the facts at hand."

"He's pragmatic," said Leo.

"Thanks, teacher. My impression was that he isn't the violent type. He seems like a straight-up businessman who lost an item out of his inventory."

"And *you* seem like you already made up your mind."

"Unless you talk me out of it."

"What for? You've gone ahead and rationalized it, so there it is."

"I'm not trying to judge my clients."

"Not even a little bit."

"It's work," said Spero.

"Someone's got to do it," said Leo. "Et cetera."

Spero heard a female voice, deep in the background. She was saying Leo's name in a singsong way.

"You've got company?" said Spero.

"No," said Leo softly. "That's only a kitty cat."

"A talking kitty cat?"

"Like in the cartoons."

"They say it purrs if you scratch it."

"Now you goin somewhere you shouldn't."

"It better be a woman, dude. 'Cause if you're sticking an

actual cat, even one that can say your name, I'm gonna be very disappointed in you. And Mom is not gonna understand."

"I gotta go," said Leo, and hung up the phone.

Spero Lucas sat in his chair, alternately reading a book and looking out the window as darkness caressed the street. He had hit a little herb and was listening to his Trojan Dub Box Set on the stereo. Soon he felt a familiar desire. He wanted the company of a woman, but it would be discourteous to phone Constance or anyone else now, the moral equivalent of a drunk call, and he was not about to troll the bars, something he had always been loath to do. He had already had a good bike ride that day to Hains Point, ten miles down, ten miles back, most of Beach Drive a slight uphill grade on the return. But he wasn't tired, and decided to go for a walk. He could have gone east into Crestwood, the fine neighborhood across 16th Street, where the mayor lived and where there was little incidence of crime. But when he left the house he headed to 13th, walked in the night through the weedy field of Fort Stevens Park, crossed the dark parking lot of Emory Methodist Church, and went down steps to Georgia Avenue. He found a bar and nursed a beer, then another, sitting quietly among mostly quiet types in their thirties and forties, listening to tunes from a jukebox stocked with deep-soul hits and rarities, not knowing the names of the songs but liking what he heard. Thinking, My brother was right; I've decided to take the job. I'd already rationalized it before we spoke. I need the work, I like the money, I like the action. This is what I do.

When his second beer was done, he settled up his tab and left five on eight.

The bartender thanked him and said, "You parked on Georgia?"

"No."

"I was gonna warn you, we been had kids breaking into cars lately."

"I'm on foot."

"Mind yourself out there."

"Thanks," said Lucas. "I'm good."

LUCAS DID the Reginald Brooks job for Petersen, extensive witness interviews related to a shooting in Ward 7. It was roughly a week before he could get to the Hawkins matter. He cleared the decks and got to work.

Lucas met Tavon Lynch and a young man named Edwin Davis at the Florida Avenue Grill, at 11th and Florida, for breakfast. Locals called it the Grill, as if there were only one, and in their heads it was so. It was the old city's soul diner, the warmest spot for a real southern breakfast, owned and operated by the son of the original owners, in business for almost seventy years. Autographed head shots of former mayors, movie stars, comedians, Howard Theater headliners, and singers, many in Jheri curls, lined the walls. Customers typically wore Redskins gear, bled burgundy and gold, had deep knowledge of high school sports, worked every day, spoke of their mothers with reverence, attended some kind of church, listened to HUR, PGC, or WKYS for their music and John Thompson's show on 980 AM for sports talk, and would have elected 88.5's Kojo Nnamdi for mayor if only he would run. The people behind the counter were friendly if you wanted them to be but not intrusive or overly familiar. The conversations were spirited and often poetic. Some came here for the atmosphere. For Lucas, that was a part of it, but he returned repeatedly for the value and the food.

He normally sat at the counter, but because they were three they took a booth. Lucas had a plate of grilled half-smokes split under onions, grits, two eggs over easy, biscuits, and butter. He'd work that off later on his bike. Tavon had been served pork chops and eggs, and Edwin ate eggs and corned beef hash, hot apples, and toast. Only Lucas was drinking coffee.

"This is good right here," said Tavon, using his fork to point at his plate.

Like his boss, Tavon wore his hair in braids. He was around twenty, had sensitive eyes and an open manner. He wore a T-shirt showing Bob off the cover of *Kaya* and white perforated-leather Lacoste high-tops. Edwin Davis was around the same age as Tavon, average height, with prominent cheekbones. He rocked LeBrons and a Rapteez T. His ears were almost comically elfish, softening the effect of his muscular build. Edwin was soft-spoken to the degree that Lucas could barely hear him. They seemed tough enough, but neither of them were thugs, nor did they pretend to be. Lucas imagined they liked girls, fashion, cars, video games, sports except for hockey, and getting their heads up. They were typical urban young men who happened to make their living in the marijuana trade.

"You got the bomb breakfast," said Tavon.

"I been dreamin on these half-smokes," said Lucas.

"Them shits repeat on me," said Edwin, breaking one egg and letting its yolk run into the hash.

"Everything you put in your mouth does," said Tavon. "Stinkpot like you."

They ate for a while, grunting and sighing in pleasure but barely speaking. Lucas didn't feel the need to rush into their business and he believed that meals were close to sacred. When he had sopped up the last of the egg with his biscuit, he pushed his plate aside and let the waitress refill his coffee mug.

"Anwan said I'd be meeting with you," said Lucas, looking at Tavon. "He didn't say you'd be bringing anyone along. I'm not being confrontational. I just want to know who I'm dealing with."

"Understood," said Tavon, glancing at his partner. "I don't know you, either, but I got told to be straight with you."

"You can be."

"When Anwan said you'd be seein me, he meant me and Edwin, 'cause that's how we do. The two of us are, like, equal. If we had one of those organization charts, Anwan would have a square at the top, and then, under him, there'd be lines to me and Edwin. Us alone, on the same level, and everyone else below us."

"I get it."

"Anwan tells us what we need to know," said Edwin. "But it stops there."

"You must have security," said Lucas.

"We don't need it," said Edwin.

"You sayin this is the inner circle right here?"

"You gotta understand how our operation works," said Tavon. "This ain't no corner thing. We got no turf or real estate to protect. We're all over the city. In the clubs, in the workplace, in all kinds of neighborhoods. Selling to all different kinds of people. Customers who don't have jobs and some who make six figures. But not selling direct. Got a network of people who move it for us just so they can have some walkin-around money and free weed to smoke. Once we repackage it and move it on to our dealers, we don't even touch it."

"Repackage it how?" said Lucas.

"We dime it out," said Tavon. "That's where the profit comes from."

"Lotta work."

"Lot more upside, too."

"You sound confident," said Lucas.

"We are," said Tavon.

"You know the law's gotta be watching you."

"No doubt," said Tavon. "But me and Edwin take precautions. We got no use for guns. We won't even get near 'em. No landlines, either, and we only use disposable cells. Every time I go to my car, I check underneath it for tracking devices before I get in. Drive around for a while, take our time, before we even start to go to where we need to be at. We know what we're doin."

"So did Anwan," said Lucas.

"Someone snitched him out," said Edwin.

"Ain't a whole lot you can do to stop that," said Tavon.

"Cost of doing business," said Lucas.

"Right," said Edwin, missing Lucas's edge.

Tavon worked a toothpick into his mouth and gave Lucas

a long go-over with his eyes. "Anwan said you were some kind of badass marine. I was expecting...I don't know *what* I was expecting, exactly. But it wasn't you."

"I feel the same way about y'all," said Lucas. He signaled the waitress for their check.

Lucas settled up at the register. Out on the street, Tavon pointed to his car, a black Impala SS with 22s, custom rims, and extended pipes. It was the kind of ride that would be remembered.

"You or me?" said Tavon.

"Me," said Lucas.

THE DROP-OFF spot was up on 12th, a one-block residential stretch between Clifton and Euclid. Nine brick row houses on each side of the street, eighteen houses in all, close to the local public high school. On the east side, alleys ran along the end homes. The houses all had porches set on brick bases, some with round columns, some with square. Concrete steps and stoops, painted metal awnings. Several had District-signature turrets and pronounced window boxes. Blue trash cans and recycling bins sat on many of the small front lawns. Some of the houses needed paint. Some were clean and maintained. A couple of them had been completely refurbished and lovingly detailed.

Lucas was behind the wheel of his Jeep, parked on 12th, facing north. There were few other cars parked on the street. Tavon was beside him in the shotgun bucket, Edwin on the rear bench. Lucas had his hands out the window, taking preliminary photos of the houses.

"Which one?" said Lucas.

"Across there, halfway down," said Tavon, pointing to the east-side row of homes. "One with the green trim."

Lucas saw it, a house trimmed in lime green with a white metal awning over the porch and a lime-on-white window box. It was set in the middle of the twenty-five hundred block. Even numbers on the east side, and he counted back from the southernmost home and noted the address, recording it in his phone's voice memo app. He then entered into the record the number of every house, east and west sides, in succession.

"Twenty-five twelve, twenty-five fourteen, twenty-five sixteen..."

When he was done, Tavon looked at Lucas's iPhone and said, "That your main piece of equipment?"

"It is now. I used to carry a camera and a tape recorder, but I don't need them anymore. I have a notebook I use for sketches. Got some tools in the back of the truck as well."

"Low overhead," said Edwin.

"Uh-huh," said Lucas.

"Notice how this street be real quiet?" said Tavon. "I mean, you don't see no one walkin around, right? That's why we picked it. This time of day, before noon? It's a dead zone, man."

"Folks on this street go to work," said Edwin.

"Not all of them," said Lucas.

"Nah, not all," said Edwin. "But me and Tavon sat here a coupla days and just, you know, checked out the situation. Even knocked on a few doors where there wasn't no action at all."

"That house there?" said Tavon. "A lady left for work about seven thirty in the morning, on foot. After that? No one came in and out it, not once, till she returned about six at night. During the day, no one ever answered our knock."

"This the first time you had the package shipped to this location?"

"We used this house three times," said Edwin. "It got good to us, man."

"When'd you lose the package?" Tavon told Lucas the date. Lucas said, "What time?"

"In the day? Right about now."

"So you tracked the delivery time on the Internet," said Lucas. "If you knew it was coming, say, around eleven, how long from the time the delivery was made to the time you picked it up off the porch?"

"Say, five minutes," said Tavon. "I was parked over there on Kenyon, beside the elementary school."

"You had a laptop in your car?"

"I tracked it on my phone. You ain't the only one got a handheld computer."

"The elementary school would be Tubman," said Lucas. "Near Wonderland, right?"

"Yeah, that bar y'all got," said Tavon, and in the rearview Lucas saw Edwin grin.

"So, from the time the package dropped, in the five minutes it took for you to get to the house, someone else stepped in and took it off the porch."

"Seems that way," said Edwin.

"Was it both of you doing the pickup?" said Lucas.

"Just me that day," said Tavon.

Lucas turned his head to face Tavon. "Any idea who took it?"

"No."

"Edwin?"

"No, *sir.*"

"Could your source be involved in this?" said Lucas.

"Huh?"

"Is it possible the people you're buying from are stealing it back from you?"

"We don't know who the connect is," said Tavon. "Only Anwan does."

"For real," said Edwin.

"Okay," said Lucas. "Let's check out the back."

He ignitioned the Jeep and turned it around. Across Clifton Street the high school, Cardozo, took up the entire block.

"It takes hair to choose this street."

"Why?" said Tavon.

"Squad cars are parked in front of that school often," said Lucas. "MPD uniforms are inside, working security every day."

"How you know all that?" said Edwin.

"My brother teaches there," said Lucas.

"Well, we never had no problem," said Tavon.

"Until you got boosted," said Lucas.

He entered the alley that cut west to east on the Clifton end of the block and drove very slowly. The passage was narrow and widened considerably as he turned right and went behind the houses on 12th Street. Many cars were parked in driveways and in the open garages of the backyards. Lucas stopped, took photos, and proceeded to the end, where he hung a right and passed through another narrow alley, landing once again on 12th.

"All right," said Lucas. "I'll drop you guys back at the Grill."

"That's it?" said Tavon.

Lucas nodded. "I'll be in touch."

FOUR

LATE IN the afternoon, on the way out to his mother's house, Lucas drove over the District line and stopped by the Safeway on Fenton Street, where he said hello to his friend C.J., who was stocking canned goods in the soup aisle, and bought some vitamins. In the parking garage he ran into Cory Wilson, a guy he had wrestled with in high school, and they talked for a while about where guys they had known were at in their lives, and then Lucas headed off in his Jeep.

He lived in the District, but in his head he was never far from his boyhood home, just over the line in Maryland. He ate and drank here frequently with his brother, dates, and friends, and took his coffee at Kefa Café on Bonifant because he liked to visit with the lovely sisters, Lene and Abeba, who owned the shop. Wasn't ever a day he came out here that he didn't see folks he knew, the barbers up at Afrikuts; the Hispanic men standing beside their beloved 4Runners; the Wanderer, a guy who walked with a staff and wore a flowing robe; and the women who stood at Silver Spring Avenue and

Thayer and yelled at passing cars. He'd see dudes he'd played basketball with at the courts on Sligo or more serious hoops on the Chicago Ave courts, over by Montgomery College. And there were those people he didn't see but were spoken of, young men and women who had gone off to college, become professionals of some sort, and never returned; others who were in lockup in places like Clarksburg or, if they had done their dirt in D.C., prisons in North Carolina or Illinois.

The moving pictures flickered through his mind constantly when he walked and rode these streets. He saw his brother Leo in his red vest, working his first job with the Gross boys up at the hardware store; and his brother Dimitrius, on his skateboard by the library park, strung out on speed and scary thin; and his sister, Irene, sullen, wearing black, catching smokes with her black-clad friends; and his mom, always gregarious, stopping to talk to neighbors as she walked her dogs. Mostly he saw his father, Evangelos "Van" Lucas, everywhere he looked. In the Safeway, exchanging Christmas cards with the grocery store employee and elder martial artist Mr. Vong; gassing up his Chevy truck outside the Texaco; on Selim, bullshitting with the auto body guys; in the breezeway where the Fred Folsom bust of Norman Lane, "the Mayor," a fondly remembered, now-deceased homeless man, was on display; in the alley behind Bell Flowers where his father had often walked; at the homeless shelter where he had dropped off his old clothing; and on the ball fields where he had watched Spero and Leo compete.

Lucas had been away. Now staying close to home was a comfort.

*　　*　　*

HIS MOTHER still lived in the house in which he'd been raised, a yellow bungalow with a deep backyard, set on the crest of a hill. Lucas's father, who knew many contractors, had blown out the back of the house and raised its roof as their family eventually grew to six. The home's renovation had rendered it architecturally incorrect, but it suited their needs.

Lucas parked and walked toward the house, noting that Leo's car, a Hyundai something-or-other, was on the street. Two dogs, Cheyenne and Yuma, began to bark exuberantly behind the screen door as Lucas approached. Both were mixed breed, short haired, and on the large side, with tan-yellow coats. Cheyenne had a Lab's head on a boxer's body; Yuma was mostly Lab. Eleni Lucas had adopted them at the Humane Society on Georgia at Geranium, against Van's fake protests. Shilo, now gone, a yellow Lab-pit mix, had been their first. Eleni was the type to bring in anyone, human or animal, who needed a home. Despite his mostly feigned gruff exterior, Van Lucas had been that kind of person, too.

"Out the way, dogs," said Lucas as he entered the house, nudging Yuma, the younger and more boisterous of the two, aside with his knee. He patted them and rubbed behind their ears as they flanked him, their tails wagging and windmilling as they walked into the small living room. On the mantel above a brick fireplace sat photographs of their large and scattered family: Irene, now an attorney in San Francisco, the Lucases' oldest, their sole biological child, distant geographically and emotionally; Dimitrius, a longtime drug addict and thief, in and out of lockup, who only called his mother when he needed cash, currently in the wind, location unknown; and Leo and Spero, the two siblings who had stayed nearby. Their photos ranged from toddler to adult: Leo in a basketball uniform, Spero in wrestling singlet, Leo with his students, Spero in his dress blues. Scattered among photos of their children were those of Van and Eleni: shaggy haired and pink-eyed in the seventies; Van leaning on the bed of his Silverado at a job site; the two of them walking arm-in-arm out the doors of St. Sophia after their wedding ceremony, smiling, ducking rice; and the various group family portraits, the frames of the photographs progressively crowded as new babies and dogs arrived, the parents looking increasingly older, tired but happy, an odd-looking bunch to outsiders but perfectly normal to them—two Greek American adults, two black kids, two white kids, and various yellow mutts.

"Everything's all right now," said Spero, walking into the kitchen. "I'm here."

"The prodigal son," said Leo.

Spero noticed a bunch of white and yellow daisies that Leo, no doubt, had brought lying on the counter. Eleni was standing before the island Van had promised and delivered when he redid the kitchen. On the granite surface was a glass of red wine.

"Hey, Ma."

"Hi, honey."

She kissed him on the cheek and they hugged. Eleni was in her early sixties, with dark hair, lively hazel eyes, and a full figure. She had put on ten pounds in her fifties, but it had stopped there. Her neck had begun to turkey. She was a lovely woman, but laugh lines and grief had marked her face, and she looked her age.

"We need a vase for those flowers," said Eleni.

"I'll get it," said Leo. They had only one and he knew where it was. The tallest in the family at six-foot-one, Leo was the go-to guy for items placed on the cabinet's top shelf.

"You boys want a beer?" said Eleni.

"I'm all right for now," said Spero.

"I got that Stella you like."

"All right."

"Leo?" said Eleni.

"He'd prefer a microbrew," said Spero.

"Screw you, *malaka*."

"*Leonidas*," said Eleni.

Malaka meant "jerkoff." It was a noun and oddly enough was used as a term of endearment for Greeks.

"I'll have a Stella, Mom," said Leo.

She got them a couple of beers out of the side-by-side and popped the caps. They could have gotten the beer themselves, but it pleased their Greek mother to serve them. By the time she handed them the bottles, they were commenting on each other's sartorial choices, an inevitable progression of their conversation.

"You didn't have to dress up for Mom," said Leo.

Spero was in his usual 501s, low black Adidas Forums on his feet. He pinched a piece of his long-sleeve Bud Ekins T and held it out. "Johnson Motors," he said, a bit hurt. "Special order out of California."

"Look more like *General* Motors to me. You wear that to the factory? When you're carryin your lunch pail?"

"Least I'm not wearing the tablecloth from an Italian restaurant," said Spero.

"It's gingham, Spero." Leo was particular about his clothing. He favored Hickey Freeman suits and Brooks Brothers casual when he could afford it. He was impeccably groomed and, with liquid brown eyes and an easy smile, handsome as a movie star.

"Last time I saw one of those, it had spaghetti sauce on it."

"You're confusing my shirt with your undershirt."

"Are you two hungry?" said Eleni. "Or do you want to wait?"

"What are we havin, Ma?"

"*Kota me manestra,*" said Eleni.

"I'm ready *now*," said Leo.

"Set the table, then," said Eleni. Before the words finished leaving her mouth, her sons had begun to mobilize.

THEY ATE dinner at a glass-top table on the screened-in porch out back. Golden time had come and gone and dusk had arrived. Eleni had lit candles and the dogs slept beneath the table. The diners were high above the yard at tree level, and branches and leaves brushed at the screen. A half mile over the District line and they were in a canopy of green.

The table was heavy with food. In the center sat a whole chicken roasted with garlic and lemon on a bed of orzo in tomato sauce, a large bowl of salad, bread, and a plate of *tarama*, olives, and feta cheese.

Eleni poured herself another glass of wine. Spero and Leo were still working on their first beers.

"Pass me that *manestra*," said Leo.

"Again?" said Spero.

"I can't stop eating it, man."

"Fas na pachinis," said Eleni.

"He's already grown, Ma," said Spero, passing the orzo to Leo. "He's not gonna get taller if he eats more, he's just gonna get fat."

"Do you see any fat on me?" said Leo. *"Do* you?"

"A little in your *peesheenaw*," said Spero. He was speaking of Leo's behind.

"You were givin it a good inspection, huh?"

"You can't help but see it. It's like a billboard."

"That's all muscle back there," said Leo. "That's why I can't wear those skinny Levi's like you do. I got a man's build."

"Your father used to tell me to buy you Lees," said Eleni, looking at Leo. "And he'd say, get Levi's for Spero."

"Lees had more room in the back," said Spero helpfully. "To accommodate your manly build."

"In the front, too," said Leo.

"Stop it," said Eleni. "More *salata*, Spero?"

"Entaxi," said Spero, telling her that he was fine.

They spoke a combination of Greek and English when they were home. It made their mother happy. Neither Spero nor Leo was Greek by blood, but, somewhat defiantly, they considered themselves to be honorary Greeks. Both were Orthodox, raised in the church. Of the four Lucas children, they were the ones who had attended Greek school, an after-public-school program, when they were young, which they loathed at the time but which paid off with dividends later on. Both had played basketball in the Greek Orthodox Youth of America league as well. Spero had been a wrestler primarily but was a strong athlete and had held his own on the courts. Leo had been a standout point guard in high school, and in the church league he tore it up. He was thirty years old, and it had been twelve years since he had last played GOYA, but in the Baltimore-Washington corridor Greek guys of his generation, even those who had cursed him at one time, and a few who had muttered racial epithets under their breath at him, now spoke of *Mavro Leo* with reverence.

"Your sister called me," said Eleni.

"*Epitelos*," said Spero. It meant, roughly, that it was about time.

"What'd *she* want?" said Leo.

"Just to catch up," said Eleni, noticing the look between Leo and Spero. Irene, the eldest of the siblings, rarely called home and visited even less frequently. She had made her break from the family long ago and had not looked back. As for Dimitrius, their older brother, Eleni knew not to mention his name in front of her younger sons. Leo in particular had no love for his older brother, whom he simply called the Degenerate, and couldn't forgive the stress he had put on their parents. Leo didn't care about his whereabouts or how he was doing. Eleni, of course, had forgiven Dimitrius for everything and would have embraced him without reservation if he were to walk through the front door. She didn't speak on Dimitrius to Spero and Leo, but he was still in her thoughts constantly, and she prayed for him every day.

"What's goin on with Irene?" said Spero, not much caring, appeasing his mother.

"She just won a case. Some corporate thing."

"Big money," said Leo.

"I suppose." Eleni had a sip of wine, looked at the glass, and killed what was left. "How's work going, Leo?"

"Good," said Leo. "I got this class, all boys. I'm really enjoying it, and I think they are, too." He looked at Spero. "You're coming to visit, right?"

"For career day?"

"We don't call it that. I bring in people who have had success, from different backgrounds, to show the boys their options. You got a story, man."

"I'll come in if you want me to." Spero pushed his plate away. "What are they reading in your class, *The Scarlet Letter*, somethin like that?"

"We're finishing up an Elmore Leonard," said Leo.

"Which one?"

"*Unknown Man #89.*"

"Good one."

"Hell, yeah."

"You can do that?"

"I gotta clear it, but I can teach pretty much any book I want."

"You're enjoying it," said Eleni.

"I am," said Leo. "I found my calling."

"Better watch out for the big boss," said Spero. "That superintendent gets a wild hair up her ass and you might be out on the street."

"She's not gonna fire me, man," said Leo. "I *do* my job."

"What about you, Spero?" said Eleni, her eyes slightly unfocused. "How's things?"

"I'm busy."

"Working on anything in particular?"

"Nothing serious," said Spero, not wishing to worry his mother. "A little bit of this and that."

THE MEN had cleared the table and were sitting back out on the porch. Eleni was in the kitchen washing dishes, nipping at another glass of wine. Dark had come to the backyard, the lights from the candles moving across their faces with the passing breeze.

"So who was that woman at your apartment when I called?" said Spero.

"Girl name Kyra. She's all right."

"Stray cat or house cat?"

"Stray."

"What about that teacher at your school?"

"We still hang out," said Leo. "You seein that lawyer?"

"She's not a lawyer yet. I like her."

"How much?"

"We're having a nice time." Spero looked through the open French doors of the screened porch to the kitchen. "Mom's hitting it pretty good tonight."

"She's happy we're here."

"You think it's that? That this is a special night for her and she's having an extra couple of glasses to celebrate? Or do you think that it's like that *every* night for her?"

"I don't know," said Leo. "Gotta be hard for her to navigate her life without Dad. To figure out where it's going next. I think you oughtta, you know, lighten up some. Let her flounder a little if that's what she needs to do. If that means an extra glass of wine or two a night, so be it."

"If Dad was here, the TV would be on right now. Mom would be with him, watching one of his westerns or karate movies, keeping him company. Even though she had no interest at all."

"*Chinese Connection*," said Leo. "*That* was one he liked."

"Pop loved that fight in the yard between Bruce Lee and Robert Baker."

"He was into Baker. Maybe 'cause he looked a little like him."

"But the best fight scene was the locker room fight in *Game of Death*," said Lucas. "Bob Wall played Carl Miller, remember?"

"That picture was some bullshit, though," said Leo. "Bruce Lee was dead when they put that together. Matter of fact, they cut in doubles for most of that movie, man. That's Scott Baio, or whatever his name is, fightin in that locker room scene. It sure ain't Bruce."

"Yuen Biao," said Lucas. "I'm sayin, that was Dad's favorite fight because of what Bruce says after he wastes the guy: 'You lose, Carl Miller.'"

Leo chuckled. "That's right."

"Pop would say that to us when we were playing hoops in the driveway. After he'd score or block our shots. 'You lose, Carl Miller.'"

"I remember."

Spero folded his hands across his midsection. "I went and saw him the other day."

"Yeah?"

"I go by there pretty often."

"Uh-huh."

"I'm still..."

"What?"

"I still struggle with it, man."

"I know you do."

"Him being there and all."

"I know."

"All last winter, when we got those big snows, and I'd think of him buried under it. Frozen. Or when it rains real hard, and I know the ground is full of water..."

"Spero."

"I see him, Leo. Inside that dark box."

"*Stop.*"

"You think I'm nuts."

"No. But you gotta get right with this."

"You never go to the cemetery, do you?"

"I haven't been since the funeral," said Leo.

"Well, I didn't get to go to his funeral," said Spero. "I was in Iraq, remember?"

"Wasn't any way for you to get back. Me and him talked about it. He understood."

"Maybe that's why I keep visiting him. I didn't get to say good-bye."

"Look," said Leo. "Do you know why I don't go to Glenwood?"

"I think so."

"Damn right you do. You been hearing Father John and Father Steve preach about it our whole lives. The reason I don't go to that graveyard is because Dad's not there. I don't stress on him being cold or wet, or his state of decomposition, because that is not my father in that grave. That's just a shell. He went from this good life to a glorious life. Hear?"

"If you say so."

"You can't be beating up on yourself for not being here when he was dying. Dad was proud of you, man."

"I hope so," said Spero, a catch in his voice.

"And you can't undo his death, any more than you can shake the grief out of Mom. You're always trying to *fix* shit, Spero. Like when you enlisted in the Marine Corps, and I asked you why. You said, 'I've got to do something.'"

"I felt the need to."

"But this is not that. And it's not one of your cases that you treat like a puzzle to solve. You can't draw a diagram in that book of yours and fix our mother or your guilt. It's not something you can win. You need to let it work its way out."

"Okay, Leo. Okay."

Cheyenne came back out on the porch, got under the table, and dropped to the wood floor, resting against Spero's feet.

"You know that thing I took on?" said Spero.

"You mean the weed dealer?"

"The guys who worked for him had that package delivered to a home on a street right across from your school."

"On Clifton?"

"Twelfth."

"Odd place for them to do it," said Leo. "All that law around."

"I was thinking the same thing."

"How old are those guys?"

"Round twenty, I guess," said Spero.

"There you go," said Leo.

"What?"

"You're looking for logic," said Leo. "They're still kids."

FIVE

In the morning, Lucas drew a crude sketch in his notebook of the eighteen residences on the 2500 block of 12th Street, Northwest. The row houses were depicted as simple adjoining squares in which he wrote address numbers, leaving room for the names of the owners.

He left his apartment, got into his Jeep, and went up to the Shepherd Park library on Georgia. The computers there were occupied by surfers who did not look as if they would be relinquishing their spots any time soon, so he drove to the nearest big-box office supply store and paid a rental fee for the use of a PC. He typically did the bulk of his investigative work on his laptop at home, using programs like People Finder, but he was about to use a public site and didn't want to leave an electronic trail.

In a private stall, he got to work. He went to the D.C. government website, which was helpfully located under dc.gov. Above a blank box was the question, "What can we help you find?" and in the box Lucas typed, "research real property" and hit "enter." This took him to the Real Property Tax Database Search. In the search box on that page he typed in the address on 12th Street to which the package of marijuana had been shipped. He got the name of the owner, the lot number, the current assessed value of the property, the last sale date, and the last sale price. The owner's name was Lisa Weitzman. Lucas guessed that a person with the surname Weitzman would not be black, though it was possible, or Hispanic, which was even less likely. The last sale date of the property, 2008, told him that she was a newer resident and, in keeping with the recent history of the rapidly gentrified neighborhood, probably on the young side, and white. The assessed value of the house was currently a hundred thousand dollars below her purchase price; she had bought at the height of the market, before property values dipped. What the database did not tell him was whether she lived there; it listed owners, not tenants. But the data was valuable and had been easy to obtain.

Lucas repeated the process for every residential property on the block. As he did, he wrote the owner's name inside the square of each address on 12th Street, along with the last sale date, on the drawing he had sketched into his notebook. When he was done he had a map of the block with each residence assigned an owner's name and an indication of who was fairly new to the block and who was not.

Armed with this information, he left the store, phoned Tavon Lynch, bought a sandwich and a bottle of water at the nearest Subway, and drove south.

TAVON LYNCH and Edwin Davis were on the low end of the Clifton Street slope, down near 11th, sitting in Tavon's Impala, when Lucas passed them in his Jeep. He did not slow down. He parked on 12th and waited for Tavon and Edwin to join him. Soon he saw them in the rearview, coming on foot. Tavon slid into the passenger seat beside him and Edwin got in back. It was close to 11 A.M.

Tavon was wearing a light jacket with epaulets over a Black Uhuru T-shirt, with a different pair of Lacoste sneaks on his feet than he had worn the day before. Edwin wore a UCB Live at the Crossroads T. From the two times they had met, Lucas surmised that Tavon was a reggae man and Edwin was into go-go, but with these guys their choice of shirts could have just been a fashion thing. Edwin had a belt on with a big G buckle, which Lucas guessed advertised Gucci, and he was sporting Ray-Ban aviators. Tavon was wearing, to Lucas's untrained eye, an expensive pair of sunglasses, too. Maybe they were both wearing shades because they were high. They had reeked of marijuana when they got into the Jeep.

"What's shakin, Spero?" said Tavon, and he offered his fist. Lucas dapped him up.

"On the job," said Lucas.

"Us, too," said Edwin, and Lucas saw him in the mirror, studying the screen of the phone in his hand.

"We're gonna have to leave up out of here soon," said Tavon. "Why'd you call us in?"

"I've got names to put inside the houses now," said Lucas, patting his notebook, which rested atop the console on his right. "I was wondering if any of them meant anything to y'all."

"Lemme see."

Lucas opened the Moleskine notebook to the appropriate page and handed it to Tavon. Tavon moved his sunglasses to the top of his head, fitting them into his nest of braids, and stared at the diagram and notations, his lips moving sound-lessly as he read.

Lucas looked through the windshield to the street. An old woman on the even-numbered side stood outside her weath-ered house, staring down at a garden of flowers and ground cover arranged at the base of her porch. She wore a faded housedress and held a trowel. On the same side of the street, farther down, a woman nearing middle age and wearing a business suit left her row house and walked briskly south on 12th. Lucas made voice notations into his phone, noting the addresses so that he could match the numbers to names later on.

Tavon passed the notebook over his shoulder to Edwin, then looked at Lucas. Tavon's pupils were dilated and the whites were pink. "I don't recognize none of the names."

"Not even Lisa Weitzman?"

"Who's she?"

"The woman who owns the house where you arranged the drop."

"If you mean the white girl who left for work each mornin and stayed away all day, then that's her. I didn't feel the need to find out her name."

"That's sloppy, man."

"Ain't like we don't have our operation in control," said Tavon, with a small shrug.

"If you had it under control you wouldn't have lost the package."

57

"We're makin money," said Edwin, by way of rebuttal. He passed the notebook back to Lucas.

"These here are Christian Dior," said Tavon, as if an expensive accessory erased Lucas's criticism. He took the oversize sunglasses off his head and showed them to Lucas. "Three hundred dollars."

Lucas grabbed a handful of his pants leg. "Dickies. Twenty-nine ninety-five."

Tavon laughed, showing a slight overbite. It wasn't that funny, but in his state he found it to be.

"You think we're just dumb younguns," said Tavon, still grinning.

"I don't think you're stupid," said Lucas. "But both of you are baked right now. That tells me you're capable of making bad decisions. And mistakes."

"You don't get high?"

"Not while I'm working."

"We know what we're doin," said Tavon, and he looked over the backseat at Edwin, their eyes meeting meaningfully. Lucas had the feeling that they wanted to defend themselves, give him some kind of explanation or excuse for the loss of the packages. But the moment passed and a tangible silence fell inside the car.

"You into Black Uhuru?" said Lucas, nodding at Tavon's T-shirt, breaking the quiet.

"They're tight," said Tavon. "Don't tell me you know somethin about Uhuru."

"I got some of their music. The Puma, Duckie, and Michael lineup is the best. I'm talking about the records Sly and Robbie produced. The roots stuff. 'Leaving to Zion' is the shit."

"Ho," said Tavon with surprise. "How you up with that?"

"I had a buddy in the Marine Corps who turned me on to reggae."

"Jamaican dude?"

"White dude from Louisiana," said Lucas, remembering his friend, that high-pitched laugh he had, the way he ducked his head when he smiled. Jamie Burdette, buried now in Metairie.

"You go to the dance halls and shit?"

"Nah," said Lucas. "I wouldn't know where to go, and I doubt I'd feel comfortable if I did. There was a place called Kilimanjaro, down in Adams Morgan, when I was a kid. It's been closed for a long time."

"I go sometimes," said Tavon. "They got this warehouse out there in Maryland, off Colesville Road, where they be havin shows? But you need to be careful. The Rastas come to have fun, but then you got the rude boys mixed in the crowd. If things pop off, ain't gonna be just a fistfight. Someone's about to get shot."

"That not your thing," said Lucas.

"I'm a man of peace. A lover."

"They got the best girls at Twenty Four," said Edwin, speaking on the big club off Bladensburg Road, near New York Avenue in Northeast. "Them dance hall girls stink."

"So do your drawers."

"Your father's."

"Edwin likes the VIP room," said Tavon.

"I just like the women."

"You mean, like, the one I seen you with the other night? One they call Precious?"

"That's her name," said Edwin defensively.

"She look like that beast, too."

"Go ahead, Tay."

"Too bad you can't satisfy the girls like I do," said Tavon.

"I don't need to. When I gyrate, they bug."

"You *know* they call me the Cobra."

"Now you gonna brag on your tongue," said Edwin.

"When you break a woman off," said Tavon, "you got to break her off proper."

"If I can't buy it at the Shoppers Food Warehouse," said Edwin, "I don't eat it."

"Look there," said Lucas, stopping them, because if he didn't they would go on. "You guys see that old lady up by her house, with the shovel in her hand?"

"So?" said Edwin.

"That little garden she's got, looks like it's her pride. At her age, you know she's not working. This time of year, I bet she's out there every day, tending to her flowers."

"You sayin she might have seen something?" said Tavon.

"She'd be someone I would try to talk to," said Lucas.

"Don't let us stop you."

"I'm just giving you an idea of how I work."

"We don't need to be schooled on that," said Tavon. "That's your specialty. That's why Anwan hired *you*. We'll stick to our thing."

"Matter of fact, we gotta bounce," said Edwin, seeing something on his phone screen and putting his hand on Tavon's shoulder.

"Y'all got a pickup?" said Lucas.

"A'ight, Spero," said Tavon, pointedly ignoring the question. "You know how to get up with us if you need us."

"You guys be safe," said Lucas.

They left the Jeep and walked back toward Clifton and their SS. Lucas watched them in the side-view mirror, cracking on each other, laughing. He liked them both. He also felt they were in way over their heads.

LUCAS CHECKED his notebook, got out of his Cherokee, crossed the street to the east side of 12th, and walked toward the house where the old woman still stood near her garden. The owner of record was Leonard Woods. The home had been purchased for well under a hundred grand and was assessed at six times that today.

Lucas stood at the foot of the concrete steps looking up at the woman, shapeless in her dress. Her hair was white, thin, and uncombed. Even from this distance he could see that her face was dotted with raised moles.

"Afternoon," Lucas called out.

"Just about," said the woman. Her tone did not invite further conversation, but it did not deter him.

"Nice garden," he said. "Is the ground cover there, the purple flowers, is that phlox?"

"Creeping phlox, yeah," she said sourly. "You selling somethin? Cause if you are, I don't talk to solicitors. I got a sign right up there on the door says the same."

"No, ma'am," said Lucas.

"Well?"

"I'm an investigator. I'm looking into the disappearance of a package from the porch of a home on this street."

"Investigator for who?"

"I represent a client."

"Who is it?"

"Unfortunately, that's confidential."

"Well then, we got nothing to talk about."

"I'm attempting to retrieve my client's lost property."

"An *in*surance thing," she said with something close to disgust.

"Is it Miss Woods?"

"Young man, you don't know me. Don't even be so bold as to call me by my name."

"I apologize," said Lucas, knowing that the conversation was completely blown. "Maybe we'll talk again when it's a better time."

"Ain't gonna be a better time," said the woman. "Go on, now." She made a shoo-away motion with the hand that held the trowel. "Before I call my son at his job. You do not want *that*."

"Sorry to trouble you," said Lucas, bowing his head slightly and walking back to his car. When he got in it, he looked at her house. She had gone inside. He didn't blame her for being ornery. She was somebody's mother, probably a nice person when she wasn't being bothered by a stranger. He was sorry he had spoiled her peaceful day.

SHADOWS SHRANK and disappeared. They grew elsewhere as the sun moved across the sky.

A late-middle-aged man with a large belly came out of a row house. He was wearing old khakis, a long polo shirt, and a Redskins hat. He walked down the sidewalk in the direction of Lucas's Jeep. He was softly singing a song, a slo-jam that Lucas was familiar with but could not identify.

" 'Make me say it again, girl,' " sang the man.

In his notebook, Lucas checked the diagram of the street.

The man neared, and Lucas, his arm resting on the lip of the open window, said, "Mr. Houghton?"

"Huh?" The man stopped walking. He seemed momentarily dazed. Then he looked back over his shoulder at the house he'd come from.

"Mr. Houghton, is it?" said Lucas.

"Nah, that's not me," said the man genially. "Mr. Houghton's deceased. His daughter stays there now. I was just visiting."

"Oh," said Lucas. "Look, I don't mean to bother you, but I'm looking into a theft on this block."

"You police?"

"I'm an investigator," said Lucas. It didn't answer the question exactly, and it wasn't a lie. "A package went missing from the porch of a home across from your friend's house. About a week and a half ago." Lucas told him the exact day.

"I ain't been to this street but twice in the last year. And my lady friend wasn't around then. She just got back from a three-week cruise, no lie."

"Got it." Lucas pointed his chin up at the man's hat. " 'Skins gonna do it this year?"

"Not *this* year."

"I like Donovan."

"The fans in Philly treated him like dirt."

"Yeah, I know. I hope when we play the Eagles we shove it up their asses."

"We'll play up. But we ain't got that full squad yet that can compete at the next level. Wasn't anything wrong with

Jason Campbell. They never did give him an O line. He had heart."

"No doubt."

"I like McNabb, too. But this move wasn't about upgrading the position. It was about sellin jerseys and merchandise. I won't even go out to that stadium and put money in that owner's pocket. I'm a fan for life, but until we get a new owner I'll just watch the games on TV."

"I heard that," said Lucas. In fact, he heard a similar version of that sentiment in D.C. damn near every day.

"Good lookin out, young fella."

"You, too."

The man walked away. Lucas heard him singing the same song as he neared the Clifton Street cross.

LUCAS ATE his sub, a BMT, and washed it down with water. Time passed and he felt the need to pee. He reached into the back of the Jeep and retrieved an empty half-gallon plastic jug he kept there when he was doing surveillance. He urinated into the jug, capped it, and placed it on the floor of the backseat.

Minutes later, an MPD squad car turned onto 12th and cruised slowly by Lucas. Lucas did not stiffen, nor did he eye the officer behind the wheel of the car beyond taking mental note of the driver's race (black), general age (on the young side), and gender (male). Lucas was not breaking any law, but he was not looking for any unnecessary confrontation. The car, affixed with 4D stickers, kept on going, and at the end of 12th the driver turned right on Euclid. Something flickered faintly in Lucas's mind as the car disappeared from view.

The street settled back to quiet. The sun moved west.

TEENAGE KIDS began to appear later in the afternoon. Those who had been visited by a guest speaker that day wore street clothes, as they were allowed to do, but most wore white or purple polo shirts with khakis, the school's uniform. Though there were many white residents in this neighborhood now, the kids coming from the schools were African American, African immigrant, and Hispanic, with a few Vietnamese and Chinese in the mix. The air was filled with their con-versations: loud, boisterous, and laced with profanity. Even as they moved in groups of two or three, they occasionally stared at the phones in their hands and texted as they walked.

A young man walked alone down 12th. Lucas studied him in the side-view: sixteen, seventeen, on the tall side, very thin, dark skin, and braids that touched his shoulders. He was wearing purple over khaki. His lips were moving. He was talking to himself.

Lucas watched him turn up the steps of a house on the odd-numbered, west side of the street, the row house that was left-connected to the house of Lisa Weitzman, where the package had disappeared. Lucas checked his notebook quickly and stepped out of his Jeep. He jogged across the street as the young man neared his porch.

"Hey, Lindsay," said Lucas, using the last name of the home's owner, a woman named Karen Lindsay.

The young man stopped and turned. "Yeah?"

"You got a minute?"

The boy studied Lucas—his age, his build, his utilitarian clothing—and then he looked down the block toward his high school. Lucas's eyes naturally followed. Back on Clifton there remained many students, hanging out in groups, walking slowly; uniformed police officers standing on the sidewalk, verbally moving the students along; an occupied squad car parked nose-east on the street.

"I just have a quick question for you," said Lucas, turning his attention back to the Lindsay boy.

"No," said Lindsay, moving quickly again, going up the steps.

"Hold up," said Lucas.

"*No!*" shouted Lindsay, turning the key to his front door and disappearing inside his house.

Lucas walked back to his Jeep. He had enough experience to know that his time spent on 12th Street had not been wasted. He always learned something, even if that nugget of knowledge was not readily apparent. It was possible that the Lindsay boy distrusted anyone who looked like police, or didn't want to be seen by his peers talking to an authority figure. It was also possible that he had real information related to the theft. At any rate, Lucas knew where this Lindsay kid lived and where he went to school. He would be easy to find.

SIX

The next night, Lucas was buzzed through the camera-monitored security entrance of the American Legion, Cissel-Saxon Post 41, on Fenton Street in Silver Spring. Fifteen minutes later, he sat on a stool beside an army veteran named Bobby Waldron, not long back from Afghanistan. Waldron was stocky, muscled up, heavily inked, kept a military haircut, and had close-set eyes. He lived with his parents in Rockville and worked occasionally as a uniformed security guard. He'd been treading water since his return to the States.

Beers in brown bottles sat on the bar in front of Lucas and Waldron.

"So this guy, the manager of the appliance store," said Waldron, "he decides to give me my instructions. They were about to have a tent sale on Saturday and they needed someone to guard the merchandise they had brought outside on Friday. My orders were to be on the premises overnight. I guess my boss had told him I was a vet, 'cause this dude was trying to speak his idea of my language. *Secure the perimeter. Hold your position,* shit like that."

"You see much action that night?"

"Tons. Those appliance thieves were crawling across the parking lot on their bellies once the sun went down. Had Ka-Bars clenched between their teeth."

"How could you see them if it was dark?"

"I was wearing my night vision goggles."

"I saw those in Call of Duty. They're cool as shit."

"I know."

The room was large, dimly lit, and had no decorations to speak of. It looked more like a rec center than it did a saloon. Unless there was a special event, the bar stayed sparsely populated and was usually patronized by men. One didn't have to be a combat veteran to be an American Legion member. If a person served in the military, they were eligible. Sons, daughters, and spouses of vets were also welcome. Of those who had served in theaters of war, Middle East, Vietnam, and a few Korean veterans were the main customers. Once in a while a WWII man would shuffle in, often accompanied by a relative or a walker. If a woman entered, the drinkers were momentarily filled with hope, even if she was plain or unattractive. If the woman was under thirty, tongues scrolled out of the drinkers' mouths like those of cartoon dogs.

Guys constantly went in and out the side door, which led to a fenced yard with a barbecue grill and patio. Out there they could smoke.

The beer was very cheap. People came here to drink at 1960s prices, but also to be among their own. The post was a place of comfort if you wanted to be around people who understood. Some, like Bobby Waldron, only felt right in this atmosphere. One young Texan, an Iraq veteran, showed up twice a month, driving all the way from Brownsville. He said this was his favorite post. Lucas came here occasionally, and to the VFW Post 350 at Orchard and Fourth in Takoma Park, to meet friends. Today he was waiting on Marquis.

Waldron was in Lucas's ear about his girlfriend, who worked out at the Kohl's off Route 29.

"Ashley's her name," said Waldron.

"Yeah?" said Lucas. He knew it would be Ashley or Britney. He sipped at his beer.

"Nuthin upstairs," said Waldron, himself at the bottom of the bell curve. "But down below? *God*."

Thankfully, Marquis Rollins soon arrived. As he came into the room, a sort of half-assed salute was issued by a couple of the guys at the bar. Rollins was tall and, if not exactly handsome, always well groomed. He was wearing a matching outfit, silk shirt and pants, earth-tone print, looked like expensive pajamas to Lucas, with New Balance running shoes. His left pants leg had little inside it. There was a plastic knee and a titanium shin pole, fitted to one of the sneakers, beneath the fabric. Marquis walked stiffly but more proficiently than many amputees. He said hello to Waldron and eased himself onto the stool on the other side of Lucas. Lucas noted, without saying so, that Marquis smelled nice.

"Gentlemen," said Marquis.

"A beer for my friend," said Waldron.

"Bud Light," said Marquis to the tender. "Wanna maintain my good looks."

"You do look tight," said Lucas. "Where do you get an outfit like that?"

"Nowhere you shop."

"Ali Baba wants to know who stole his shit."

"Ho!"

"Gotta give you credit. I couldn't get away with wearing a getup like that."

"Who don't know *that?*"

The bartender served Marquis his beer. The three veterans tapped bottles.

"Sorry I'm late," said Marquis. "Had to go out to Seven Locks and pick up my nephew. My sister's son?"

"What he do now?"

"Possession with intent to distribute. His second arrest, so it might get serious. The boy stayed overnight 'cause I had to secure the bond. I'm hoping one night in that jail out there was enough to scare him. But who knows? Another baby gangster, thinks he knows somethin."

"They all do."

"And they all get caught. He had to pee in a cup every week since his last conviction. Told me he had that beat, too; something about a syringe of clean urine he taped under his nutsack. Like those parole people ain't seen that trick. They nailed him for that and violated him, and then they gave him another chance. And now he blew that chance."

"How's your sister?"

"On her last nerve. I'm gonna stay on that boy now. Get him involved with my church."

Marquis would get a substantial disability check from the government for the rest of his life. He also had a business, traveling up to car auctions in Pennsylvania and making luxury auto purchases for buyers back in the D.C. area. The savings for the customer were substantial, and Marquis took a flat thousand-dollar fee. He spent part of his free time with community outreach programs, working with fellow members of his congregation, and the rest trying to snake women. At thirty-two, he had the need.

"*I* could do some stuff at your church," said Waldron. He was tapping the base of his beer bottle on the bar. On his left forearm were a multitude of "dots," shrapnel bits embedded under his skin. He had added many other dots in ink. Both his biceps were inked in tiger stripes.

"Like what?" said Marquis.

"Help out, somethin," said Waldron.

"What about your job?"

"I can't stand that security guard thing I got. First of all, there's that stupid uniform. And they gave me a can to hang on my belt—can you believe it? The shit postmen spray at dogs."

"We can't pay," said Marquis. "But we can always use help."

Waldron nodded, a familiar look of disappointment on his face. He stared ahead, then threw his head back and killed his beer. He signaled the bartender and was served another. Then he patted his breast pocket, where a pack of Marlboro Reds showed through the fabric of his cheap white shirt.

"I'm gonna go have a smoke," said Waldron.

He picked up his fresh beer off the bar. They watched him exit through the side door to the backyard.

"You hang with him much?" said Marquis.

"Nah," said Lucas. "Bobby's got a girlfriend."

"For real?"

"She's got the fire down below."

"Like in the song."

"He's there if I need something," said Lucas.

"He still goin to those gun shows?"

"I believe he is. He makes a lot of interesting contacts."

"You can buy damn near anything from those folks."

"Seems that way."

"Your man sure is all wound up," said Marquis.

"He doesn't know whether to shit or go blind. In the Korangal he got up every morning, took orders, and knew exactly what he was supposed to do. Here he's got *nothin* to do. You know what I mean?"

"Yes."

It was a common problem for many of the vets. Overseas, in the thick of it, they talked about going home. What they would do when they got back, the anticipation of their favorite Mom-cooked meal, the Chevy or Ford truck they were going to buy, how high they'd get, which girl they'd fuck first. Once home, some said that their time overseas was the most exhilarating and rewarding of their lives. It felt as if nothing would ever fill them up like that again. So they looked for it. Lucas and Marquis had been lucky to find something. Most did, eventually. The ones who couldn't were in for some long hurt.

"You feeling all right?" said Lucas.

"Better than a year ago. Much better than in the beginning, when they had me in a harness and on a leash. It's no house party, walking on a stilt."

"Looks like you're maintaining."

"Praise God, I'm here."

Marquis Rollins had taken a direct hit from an RPG. It had come right through a doorless, unarmed Humvee that Marquis was driving, ferrying wounded back from a hot spot of houses under heavy insurgent fire near the Jolan graveyard. He knew immediately that it was bad; he could feel the blood pooling beneath him, but he kept driving, weakening by the minute, never once looking down. He had a mission: to get the wounded back to safety. He felt the task would keep him alive. HQ kept him talking on the radio, kept him conscious until he brought the men in. Later, they told him that a piece of shrapnel the size of a cell phone had entered his thigh. The surgeons couldn't stop the resultant infection. Two weeks later they took his leg off above the knee.

Marquis was from Suitland in PG County and had grown up fifteen miles from Lucas, but they met for the first time in the war, both serving in the 2/1, the Second Battalion of the First Marine Regiment assigned to Fallujah. Their shared geographic background had made them close fast.

"What about you?" said Marquis. "You maintaining?"

"I'm fine."

" 'Cause it's hard to tell with you, man. The way you hold all your shit tight inside you."

"What do you want me to do, speak on my feelings about the war?"

"You can, with me."

"Ask me a question. Not any old question. *The* question."

"Okay. You ever kill anyone over there?"

"I did, Marquis. I killed someone."

"More than one, I remember correct."

"Course, they were all trying to kill *me*."

"Pretty simple," said Marquis. "Now, when you get to the *why* of it, that's somethin else. But it's better if you stay with the basics: We fought to win and we fought for each other. That's how we do."

"Except they didn't let us finish it. In Fallujah they sent us in, pulled us back out, and sent us in again. The brass and the politicians played games with marines. They were concerned with perception, all those images on TV broadcast around the world. They let Al fucking Jazeera influence their strategy."

"That's better," said Marquis with a chuckle. "That's my boy."

"Fuck it," said Lucas, letting himself wind down.

"Right," said Marquis. "So I guess you *are* maintaining."

Lucas had a swig of his beer. "I'm keeping busy."

"Anything interesting?"

"Workin on a thing. I need any help, I'll let you know."

They drank slowly. Marquis nodded toward the side door. "Waldo been out there a long time."

"Bobby's gunnin those smokes in tandem."

"He chews, too."

"But not at the same time."

"Yeah, that would be unseemly."

Lucas finished his beer, left money on the bar, and slipped off his stool. "Tell him I said good-bye."

"You gonna leave me here with him?"

"I'm meeting a lady friend," said Lucas.

"That's why you got that shirt on?"

"You like it?"

"Looks like a tablecloth to me."

"It's gingham."

Marquis held out his hand. "Two-One, man."

"Two-One."

They bumped fists. Lucas left the bar.

CONSTANCE KELLY was waiting for him outside his house. She got out of her Honda, crossed Emerson, and walked toward his Jeep. Her hair was down and she walked with energy and looked first-snow clean. Lucas felt a little light-headed, looking at her. Goddamn, she was mint.

"Hi," she said, settling into the passenger bucket.

"Hey," said Lucas. He kissed her mouth. "Hungry?"

"You know it," said Constance.

They drove down to the U Street corridor, where he found a spot on a residential street. Lucas took her into Busboys and Poets, the bookstore and café that was bustling with activity, all sorts of faces and types, the D.C. most folks had wanted for a long time. He bought her a couple of novels: *Lean on Pete* and *The Death of Sweet Mister*.

"Is there a reason you picked these out?" said Constance as they stood before the register.

"You mean, am I sending you a message."

"Yeah, like when a guy makes a mix tape for a girl."

"Good clean writing, is all. I thought you'd like them."

He had a table reserved at Marvin on 14th, but they were early, so they went up the stairs to the rooftop bar. It was warm enough to be outside without the heat lamps on, and not yet summer. The space was crowded for a reason. It had a beach atmosphere and a city vibe. The people were attractive, and that night's music, seventies soul and funk, was bottom heavy and tight. A snaky trombone solo had come forward, and everyone was moving their feet and hips. They couldn't help themselves.

The bar specialized in Belgian ales. Lucas wedged out a spot for him and Constance, ordered her a blonde and a Stella for himself. He left a five on the bar and asked the tender who was on the stereo.

"Fred Wesley and the Horny Horns. 'Four Play.'"

"Righteous," said Lucas.

"You *know* those people had fun back then."

Lucas flashed on images, photos he had seen of his father as a young man, smiling with his friends out in one of the Blackie Auger clubs, his hair longish and curly, stacks on his feet, baggies, an open rayon shirt, a crucifix and *mati* hung on a chain resting on his hairy chest.

"You here?" said Constance.

"Just thinking on someone," said Lucas.

"Think of me."

Lucas felt the vibration of his iPhone buzzing in the front pocket of his jeans. He retrieved it, looked at the screen. Tavon Lynch was calling in. Lucas answered.

"Hold up, Tavon," said Lucas. To Constance he said, "I gotta take this, a work thing. I promise, just this one time tonight."

"Go ahead."

Lucas left the rooftop, walked passed the doorman, took the steps down to the main floor, and went out on

14th, where he stood on the sidewalk and resumed his conversation.

"What is it?" said Lucas.

"We lost another one," said Tavon.

"Another one *what?*"

" 'Nother package. Off the porch of a home east of Capitol Hill. More like Lincoln Park."

"Where are you?"

"We're in Northeast right now."

"How much did you lose?"

"Thirty-pound package, like the last two."

"What's goin on?"

"Huh?"

"I'm askin you, what do you think is happening?"

"I don't know, Spero. I don't."

"Somebody knows what you guys are doing."

"That's impossible. Only me and Edwin do."

A crowd of folks approached, loudly, and Lucas waited for them to pass.

"Look," said Lucas, "I'm with a friend right now, about to have dinner. I'll call you first thing in the morning."

"A'ight."

"You guys watch yourselves."

"We're good."

"*Listen* to me, Tavon. Don't go trying to work this shit yourselves. We're talking about some weight now, and big money. Whoever's behind this is not going to play."

"We got it, Spero. Me and Edwin can handle it."

Lucas, exasperated, let it go. "I'll talk to you tomorrow, hear?"

"Is she pretty?"

"Who?"

"Your friend."

"Yes."

"My man," said Tavon.

Lucas ended the call. He stood there on the sidewalk, thinking things over. Something was not quite right.

SEVEN

THEY SAT in a deuce near the large mural of a smiling Mr. Gaye. Constance had ordered the signature dish, fried chicken and waffles with collard greens and gravy. Lucas was getting down on a strip steak with Maytag blue cheese and sauce bordelaise. They had eaten mussels with bacon, apples, and cream to start. The house was lively and packed.

"I don't get the Belgian-food thing," said Constance. "How does it connect with Marvin Gaye?"

"Late in his career, he moved to this place Ostend, on the Belgian coast. He went there to clean up. He did it, too. Claimed it was the happiest time of his life."

Constance picked up a piece of chicken and went at it. She was cleaning it to the bone. He admired a woman who enjoyed her food.

"You're gonna be one of *those* kind of lawyers."

"What kind is that?"

"The ones who eat what they kill."

"I want to be a good defense attorney," said Constance. "Public, at first. Help people who can't afford high-priced representation. That's my goal for the time being. You?"

"Me, *what*."

"What do you *do*, exactly? You didn't get your lifestyle on Petersen wages. You're not even a licensed investigator. I asked Tom."

"Petersen doesn't require CJA training or a license. That's attractive to me. I prefer to work without the ticket in my wallet."

"Well?"

Lucas swallowed the last bite of his steak. He sat back in his chair, had a swig of his beer, and put the glass back on the table.

"I find things for people," said Lucas. "I retrieve things that were lost or stolen."

"And you get what for that?"

"Forty percent. If it's not cash I'm looking for, then I take the same percentage of the assessed value of the item."

"How in the world did you get into that?"

"When I came back from the Middle East, I did a little security work. Limo companies, driving celebrities and dignitaries, like that. I also silent-bounced at a couple of clubs. One night at the bar I met a woman whose boyfriend had stolen her jewelry before he broke up with her. She was a nice person and this guy was a bully; he'd fucked her over, basically, because he knew that he could. I agreed to try and get her stuff back. She asked me what my fee was, and forty percent came into my head. I don't know why. I took the job and I completed it."

"How?"

"It's not important. I've always been aggressive. Make a decision and act on it. I like having a task and solving things, I guess."

"How'd you turn it into a living?"

"Her jewelry was worth a lot of money, and my take was substantial. I thought, I can get used to this. And I was good at it. I did a couple more jobs, one private, one for a small-businessman whose employee was ripping him off, and it got around on the street telegraph that I was that guy. I started getting referrals. Petersen heard about me from a client."

"I get it. What about things like pension and insurance?"

"I can buy health insurance. Far as a retirement account goes, it's not on my radar screen."

"No college?"

"I had a couple of semesters. It wasn't my thing." Lucas leaned forward. "There's a lot of men and women out here like me, Constance. We've been through this war and we just look at things differently than other people our age. I mean, there are certain bars I don't hang in. The people, the conversations, they're too frivolous. I'm not gonna sit around and have drinks with people who are, you know, *ironic*. Being in a classroom, listening to some teacher theorizing, I can't do it. I also wasn't about to take a job in an office and deal with the politics. I woke up one day and knew that I was never gonna have a college degree or wear a tie to work. I was coming up on thirty years old and I realized, I've fallen through the cracks. But I'm luckier than some people I know. I've found something I like to do. My eyes open in the morning and I have purpose."

Constance pushed her plate, now holding only bones, to the side. "You're either the most complicated guy I ever met or the simplest."

"I'm the simplest."

"You're *smart*. You read a bunch. You should try school again."

"Not gonna happen," said Lucas. "Does that bother you?"

"No."

"But it will."

"Maybe." She reached across the table, put her hand over his, and squeezed it. "It doesn't bother me tonight."

Lucas signaled the waitress.

TAVON LYNCH and Edwin Davis drove east over the Benning Bridge in Tavon's SS, passing streetlamps haloed in mist. The Anacostia River flowed darkly beneath them. They were headed toward central Northeast, a part of the city that was largely unfamiliar to them. A Backyard CD, a live at the Tradewinds thing with Big G on vocals, was playing low in the car. As Tavon accelerated, the young men felt the buzz and rumble of the Impala's twin pipes.

"Why'd you have to tell him 'bout the package?" said Edwin.

"We're gonna have to tell Anwan," said Tavon. "And then he's gonna put Spero on this one, too. Might as well be up front about it from now."

"What's his last name?"

"Lucas."

"He don't seem like the type to give up." Edwin rubbed at the whiskers on his chin. "You tell them about him?"

"No need to jam him up. He ain't gonna find anything anyway."

"Had the feeling he was gonna sit out there on Twelfth Street all day."

"Man keeps hard at it," said Tavon. "Got to give him that."

Tavon admired Lucas's work ethic. He believed that he, Tavon, was of the same stripe. He and his boy Edwin were young, but they had been on it for a while.

Tavon had grown up in Chillum, the youngest of a large family, now scattered. He was closest with his eldest brother, Samuel, who had done time in his youth but was now living straight. Edwin was from a smaller family that lived in an apartment in West Hyattsville. Edwin saw his father occasionally and of late had begun to reestablish a relationship with him; Tavon had no relationship with his father at all. Both of them had graduated from Northwestern High School, where Len Bias had played, on Adelphi Road.

They were into watching sports on TV and playing video games, but mostly they loved nightlife. Tavon caught reggae at the Crossroads and dancehall at TNT and Mirage Hall, and hung out with Edwin at the go-go and hip-hop clubs in the city and in Prince George's County. The Ibex had been shuttered long ago, and so had the Black Hole, but shows were live in places like Legend on Naylor Road, Icon in Waldorf, the Scene, D.C. Star off Bladensburg, and 24. Tavon and Edwin beat their feet to Reaction, TOB, Backyard, Junk Yard, old bands like EU with Sugar Bear at Haydee's, and up-and-comers like ABM. They tipped the doormen, the bouncers, and the men guarding the parking lots, and soon they were in the VIP rooms for free and never had to be on the lower floors with those who stood in line. They met a promoter named Princess Lady who got them started on her street team, passing out flyers for a flat fee of thirty dollars a night, then they graduated into real promotion money, creating a guest list for the door that brought in three to five dollars a head. They made up stage names, Young Tay and E-Rolla. They always looked fresh.

In the VIP loft of one of the big clubs off New York Avenue they met Anwan Hawkins, who most everyone knew by sight. He was approachable, an older man who didn't have to front or act hard because he wasn't trying to get somewhere; he was *there*. After several nights partying with Anwan, they began to do a little work for him on the side, keeping their promotion enterprise going all the while. Anwan moved them up quick and kept them busy, and the weed work overtook the promotion stuff and made it seem less important. Soon they were Anwan's seconds and they let their show business aspirations die.

Thing of it was, they weren't making all that much money. Only Anwan was bringing it in big. But the life was exciting, for a while.

The two of them still lived with their mothers. Edwin tended to lead a secret life and never did talk to his mom much; Tavon was close to his. She was excited for him when he first began to bring in dollars, and encouraged his entrepreneurial spirit. Then she found a scale in his room and tiny plastic bags, a ledger book with figures and names. He continued to tell his mother he was working on his music, but she could read the lie in his eyes.

"Why they pick this part of town?" said Edwin, as they turned left onto Minnesota Avenue, passing fast-food chains, Chinese grease pits, pawnshops, high-priced convenience markets, and high-fee check-cashing establishments, the kind of places that kept folks unhealthy, broke, and low.

"Said they was gonna be over here tonight on other business," said Tavon. "They didn't feel like crossing back and uptown just to pay up. Said if we wanted our piece we'd have to go where *they* decided to meet."

"I don't like being off our turf," said Edwin.

"I don't either," said Tavon. "But I like the way money feel in my hands."

Tavon drove a couple of blocks farther and hung a right onto Hayes Street. They went up a rise, crossing 42nd, and there the street ended dark in a court bordered by what looked like a stand of trees and dirt through which ran a narrow creek.

"You sure?" said Edwin.

"This is where he said to come."

Tavon cruised slowly around the semicircle of the court and curbed the Impala, its nose pointed back to the west. He killed the engine. Edwin looked around, at the wooded area on their right, at the little bit of light that reflected off the creek, past the trees to the houses and apartments they had back up there on Hunt Place. It was quiet.

"Man, *I* know what this place is," said Edwin. "One of my uncles used to live over by the Mayfair units, and he would talk about it. This is part of Watts Branch."

"So?"

"They be murderin motherfuckers back in here."

"Not anymore. Your uncle's name must be Fred Sanford, 'cause that was an old man talking about things that happened a long time ago. Neighborhood people cleaned things up back here, Edwin. Got all kinds of government money to do it."

"For real?"

"I read on it, man."

An MPD squad car came slowly up the street. Thirty yards below them, on the rise, it swung to the curb. The driver cut his lights but kept the engine running.

"Here we go," said Edwin.

Another car, a black Chevy Tahoe with factory rims, came up the rise. It swung around the court and stopped behind the Impala. The driver of the Tahoe cut the engine and killed the lights. The driver of the squad car lit his headlamps and turned around in the street.

"He supposed to stay," said Edwin. "Right?"

Tavon squinted, looking hard at the patrol car. His eyes went to the cell phone in his hand. He pondered the situation for a moment. He went to messages, found the recipient he was looking for, and typed in four numbers. He sent a text and slipped the phone into the pocket of his jeans.

Tavon checked the side-view mirror and watched the driver of the Tahoe get out of the SUV. Then in the rearview he saw another man step out of the passenger side. This man held a shoe box close to his side. The two of them walked toward the SS.

LUCAS AND Constance were making it with great enthusiasm, Gregory Isaacs's *Soon Forward* playing loudly in the bedroom, when Lucas's iPhone began to buzz on his nightstand. Neither of them heard a thing.

TAVON AND Edwin sat in the front seat of the Impala, waiting for the men. Tavon's eyes were moving between the two mirrors.

"That our man?" said Edwin.

"Yeah," said Tavon. "He brought that white dude with him, too."

"Why?"

"You holdin that kind of money, guess you need an extra man to guard it."

"What you gonna do with yours, man?"

"Buy things," said Tavon, as the men neared their car.

Buy things. Tavon had been driven to do just that for as long as he could remember. From his first pair of baby Nikes on, his mother had sacrificed and run up her credit cards to see that he had the right labels, especially when he went off to school. Couldn't have those other kids and their parents seeing him in knockoff Timbs. Never mind that his mom was ass broke; working the after care program at the local elementary for next to nothing, she still took care of him, made sure he had things. Bought him the videos for the VCR, his earliest being *Aladdin* and his favorite *The Lion King.* The Spanish people in the apartment next door had the same movie, but theirs said *El Rey León* on the box, and he cried about that, and damn if his mom didn't find one of those for him, too. And then *Space Jam,* with that song his mom used to sing to him at night to make him feel positive, that R. Kelly thing, "I Believe I Can Fly."

Tavon took his mother's buying habits to heart, and when

he was old enough to pick out his own stuff it had to be the best. Or at least it had to look like it. His Gucci belt buckle was fake, and so were his Dior shades and Rolex with cut glass around the face, but the We R One stuff was real, as was his Helly Hansen parka and collection of Lacoste shirts and sneaks, which he wore with the tags still on. He even had a Zegna suit. Man said it was Zegna, anyway, even though the name had been tore out the jacket.

Why spend two, three thousand on a suit when you could buy one just as good for a couple hundred in the back of someone's shop? Why go to community college, with no guarantee of a job after you had put in all that work, when you could make money now? Same thing with Anwan, putting them on, teaching them. Okay, they had been impatient. But why wait for it to come to you in a big way? Why not walk to *it*? It was why he and Edwin had done their dirt.

But even with what was about to come their way, Tavon, at that moment, felt empty. He was thinking on his mother, the way she looked at him with disappointment, the hurt on her face when she found the scale and dime bags in his room. "Didn't I give you everything?" she'd said. "Yes, ma'am," he said, thinking, *You did.*

Tavon was sitting behind the wheel of a dark car on a dead-end street, and in his mind he was seeing his mother, his vision of her as a younger woman, singing to him softly, sitting beside his bed, telling him that he could touch the sky. All that money that was about to come his way. He should have been elated, but he was not.

The two men opened the rear doors of the Impala and slid into the backseat.

The man holding the shoe box was thirty-five, wiry and flat faced and cat eyed. He wore a large wooden crucifix on a beaded chain hung out over his shirt. His name was Earl Nance. The man who had slipped in behind Tavon was also in his thirties, large, stack shouldered, wearing an unfashionable fade, one gold hoop earring, and a jacket too heavy for the weather. His name was Bernard White.

Tavon swiveled his body some and turned his head to look into the backseat. "Y'all got it?"

"It's right here," said Nance, untopping the shoe box and reaching inside.

Nance pulled a .357 S&W Combat Magnum and pointed it at Tavon's face. Tavon said, "Mom," and the interior of the car exploded in sound. The muzzle flash strobed Tavon's death mask as the hollow-point round entered his cheek and exited big as a peach, blowing head stew across the dash and windshield.

Bernard White had drawn the .380 Taurus holstered inside his jacket. In futility, Edwin Davis raised one hand to cover his face. Wilson shot him through his palm, and as Edwin screamed and turned his head, Wilson shot him in the temple. Edwin's last breath was a long exhale. His head came to rest against the passenger window. Blood dripped into his open mouth.

The air was heavy with smoke and the smell of gun smoke and shit. White used the barrel of the Taurus to break the dome light on the headliner.

"Get their cells," said White.

Nance rat-fucked through their pockets, coughing against the stench of Tavon's voided bowels, and found their phones.

White retrieved the two shell casings that had been ejected from the .380. They used their shirttails to wipe the inner and outer handles of the Impala and everything else they thought they'd touched.

Ten minutes later, as White drove west in the far right lane of the Benning Bridge, Nance leaned out the passenger-side window and heaved the two guns over the rail, where they dropped into the Anacostia River, sinking to the bottom to come to rest with countless other murder weapons that would never be found.

"You didn't need to use a cannon in that small space," said White. "Wasn't no need for that big gun. Seems to me you were compensating again for your lack of size."

"You mean *over*compensating," said Nance.

"So you do admit it."

They drove for a while in silence.

"That was easy," said Nance.

Bernard White said, "They fucked with men."

LUCAS, STANDING naked on the hardwood floor, picked up his iPhone off the nightstand. He looked at the text message from Tavon Lynch. It read, "4044."

"What is it?" said Constance, slick with sweat, lying on his bed.

Lucas stared at the phone, then placed it back on the stand. "Nothing I need to worry about tonight."

EIGHT

THE NEXT day, Lucas phoned and texted Tavon Lynch and Edwin Davis but got no response.

There was nothing on his plate for the morning, so he got on his bike and hit Beach Drive north and took it out into Maryland all the way to Veirs Mill Park. The ride back was flat to a subtle downgrade. There was little road traffic and he found his zone, where it was just the motion, his feet tight in the toe clips, the chain quietly running over the teeth, a perfect, simple machine at work.

He carried his bike up the stairs when he returned and put it on the back porch. As he often did after a good ride, he wanted a woman. Instead he did several sets of push-ups, normal and wide stance, and then did chin-ups and pull-ups on a bar mounted inside the door frame of his bedroom.

Lucas took a shower and tried phoning Tavon and Edwin. Nothing.

*   *   *

LUCAS LEARNED of the murders that evening while reading the news on the *Washington Post*'s website. He felt an inner chest-bump at first, seeing Tavon's and Edwin's names as fatal victims of a shooting. That soon passed, and he had no lasting feeling of grief beyond the too-familiar feeling of lament for young lives that had been prematurely terminated. He had willed himself to be unemotional about such events. He had witnessed too much death, and if he got stuck on it he felt he would be frozen and done.

He phoned Tom Petersen at home to tell him that Anwan Hawkins's two top associates had been murdered. He thought that it might have implications for Anwan's trial and that Petersen should know. Certainly the prosecution would try to bring the murders into evidence, if only to tell the jury that Anwan Hawkins moved through a world of extreme violence connected, in some way, to his drug enterprise.

"You *are* working for Anwan," said Petersen.

"He hired me to find something he lost."

"Are these murders related to that job?"

"I don't know for sure," said Lucas. He suspected they were, but the qualifier took it out of the realm of lie.

"Okay," said Petersen dubiously.

There was a silence that was a standoff.

Lucas said, "If you hear anything..."

"I'll check in with my sources," said Petersen. "If you come across anything that might impact my client..."

"Right," said Lucas.

They ended the call.

*　　*　　*

LUCAS GOT up early the next morning and read the newspaper's print version of the Lynch and Davis murders, which held no further details. The story made it inside Metro and had a few more inches than the usual "roundup," due to what was described as the "execution-style" method of the crime, a coded message telling readers that the victims had probably been in the game.

A notable decrease in violent crime in the District had made the murders of young black men and women more newsworthy than they had been in the past. Certain high-profile murders, like the recent shoot-into-the-crowd drive-by that had claimed several victims, and the killing of a DCPS principal in Montgomery County, might have left the impression that little had changed since the dark days of late-eighties Washington. The reality was that homicides were down to a forty-five-year low in the city. The implementation of community policing and more foot patrols under Chief Lanier, the closing and relocation of troubled public-housing units under former mayor Tony Williams, and a genuine shift in the culture caused in part by activist groups within the community had all contributed to the positive developments in the atmosphere and the stats. The *Post* continued to routinely bury the violent deaths of D.C.'s young black citizens inside the paper, telling its readership implicitly that black life was worth less than that of whites, and that policy, apparently, was never going to change. Had Tavon Lynch and Edwin Davis been raised in Bethesda or Cleveland Park, their demise would have been reported on A1. As it was, they made B2, which felt something like progress to Lucas.

When the subject came up at the Lucas family dinner

table, as it surely would, Eleni Lucas would say, "Those young men deserve the same memorial in the newspaper that anyone does," and Spero Lucas would respond, "You're right, Ma." He did agree with her, but he was not a crusader, leaving those kinds of conversations to his mother and others who were more conscientious than he was.

Lucas took a shower and dressed in Carhartt. He had work to do.

LUCAS DROVE down to the holding facility, signed the logbook, and gave the DOC woman his driver's license. He was still on an official visitors list per Petersen's letter. The woman handed him a pass that would allow him entrance to the next step of security. Lucas looked her over in her uniform, a tall woman, broad shouldered and full in the back, like many females who worked security at the jail. They were union, and he assumed their income and benefits package had been well negotiated, but still, for the atmosphere they endured, for the risk, they had to be underpaid. The woman's badge plate read Cecelia Edwards. She had buttery skin, large eyes, and a lot of muscle coupled with femininity. Lucas wondered.

"Have a good one," he said, looking at her the way a man does.

"You have a blessed day," she said, holding the look for the one extra moment that spoke many words. He would remember her name and write it down after he left the jail.

Lucas met Anwan Hawkins in the visiting room. The glass between them was filmy and smudged, their chairs low and hard. Hawkins wore an orange jumpsuit with slip-on sneaks. His braided hair was pulled back, exposing neck tats,

Japanese characters in a vertical formation. His facial expression was serious, his posture all business.

"Talk about it," said Hawkins, speaking into the phone, his voice gravelly and distant. Their connection was as weak as it had been the last time they'd met. "Tell me what happened."

"It was straight murder," said Lucas.

"By who?"

"I know what you know. Less than you, if you're holding out on me."

"Why would I?"

"It's safe to say that their killing was related to your business. Maybe it was a power grab by someone beneath them."

"Wasn't anyone below 'em who knew shit."

"Were you aware that they lost a third package?"

Hawkins did not speak right away. Lucas studied his reaction.

"When was that?" said Hawkins.

"I don't know when, exactly. Tavon told me about it the night he and Edwin were murdered. But I'm guessing it was stolen the day before. I was surveilling the street of the second theft, and they left me to do some business."

"Where was it stole at?"

"East of the Hill. Tavon didn't give me the address. Maybe you can tell *me*."

"I don't know it. Those boys were on their own."

"So I'll just keep working the theft on Twelfth."

"But I don't *want* you workin it, Spero. What I want is for you to drop this."

"Why?"

"This shit's got to stop," said Hawkins. "I don't care about the cash no more. If I get off, then I walk out of here and start new. If I do more time, so be it. Either way, I'm done. I wanna be with my son again, like a regular father. I want to live a long life. "

"That's a lot of money to leave on the table."

"It's mine to leave."

"We had a deal."

"Not the kind you take to court."

Lucas and Hawkins stared at each other without malice.

"You speak to the police?" said Hawkins.

"No," said Lucas.

"You were in contact with the boys by phone, weren't you?"

"I was."

"If the police got hold of their cells, there'd be a record of that."

"Which tells me their cells weren't found," said Lucas. "Otherwise the homicide detectives would have contacted me by now."

"Did the boys, you know, leave you any kind of clue as to what was about to go down?"

Lucas thought of the last text message he received from Tavon Lynch. "No."

"What do *you* think happened?"

"No idea. The police are conducting an investigation. If an arrest is made, I'll hear about it, same as you."

"What about their funerals?"

"They haven't been announced. There've been no obits yet in the *Post*."

"You gonna pay your respects?"

"No. The police will be there. Could be they'll be shooting video footage from vans, taking still shots like they do. I'm not trying to put myself in the mix. Anyway, I barely knew those guys."

"You don't seem too interested."

"And you don't seem all that shook."

"I'm sorry for what happened to them."

"So am I," said Lucas. "But I'm not getting involved in those murders. You hired me to retrieve your property or your cash. That's it."

"You're not even curious?" said Hawkins.

"Homicide police close murder cases. Private investigators never do. I took this on to make money. With this third theft, the pot just grew. I still intend to honor our agreement."

"I guess I can't stop you."

"What do I do if I'm successful?"

"Take your cut," said Hawkins. "What's left, get it to my son's mother."

"Right."

"Watch yourself out there," said Hawkins, looking hard into Lucas's eyes.

"I will." Lucas cradled the phone.

LUCAS WAS not far from Capitol Hill and Lincoln Park. He left the jail and drove west on Massachusetts Avenue, turning to explore the neighborhoods and the streets, doing the same past Lincoln Park proper, the dividing line of sorts that brought him into the eastern portion of the Hill, where the homes were noticeably nicer and the income levels rose. He was looking for a 4044 address. He assumed the text from Tavon was meant to indicate the number on the house where the second drop had been made and lost. He found nothing to match the number, and if he had, he wouldn't have known what to do. He felt lost.

Continuing west, toward his home, he suddenly said, "Yeah," and pulled over to the side of the road, near the St. James Episcopal Church. Something had come to him. He remembered from the newspaper accounts that Tavon and Edwin had been found shot to death in their car, parked on Hayes Street, Northeast. More accurately, upper central Northeast, where the cross-numbered streets were in the forties. Tavon must have been trying to give him the location of the house. That's where the drop was: the 4000 block of Hayes.

He drove in that direction, crossing the Anacostia, and ten minutes later was on Hayes. But the address did not appear to be a good one for the scheme that Tavon and Edwin had cooked up. There was a house there, but it was not the kind of place that you would ship a package to and expect it to go unnoticed. There were folks around, standing by their vehicles, going in and out of their homes, sitting on their porches. It did not look like they were typically away or at work during the day. Tavon wasn't stupid. He wouldn't have chosen this spot to drop the weed.

Lucas continued up the block to the dead-end court that stopped at a thin tributary of creek and woods that was a part of Watts Branch. The Impala was gone. Except for a piece of yellow tape lying in the street there was no sign that a crime of extreme violence had occurred here. The mobile crime technicians had completed their investigation of the scene, and the next task was in the hands of the chief medical examiner's office, where the autopsies of the young men would be performed.

Lucas knew that this area had been murder notorious at one time, but it was quiet now. Serene almost, with the water cutting through the trees. Had to be dark at night back here, but still. It did look cleaned up and relatively safe. Tavon and Edwin could not have known what was coming to them. And then the fear and panic, when they *did* know. Lucas only hoped it had been quick for them. Pain and confusion for sure, but not prolonged.

Darkness, he thought, seeing his father in a box. Lucas closed his eyes.

HE HAD a fish sandwich with hot sauce from a carryout on Benning Road and headed into Northwest, where he found himself once again parked on 12th Street. He was facing north, looking in his side-view at the students walking from the school, the uniformed police ushering them along. Soon the Lindsay boy appeared, wearing a purple polo, his braids touching his shoulders, talking to himself, walking home.

"Hey, Lindsay," said Lucas, from behind the wheel of his Jeep.

The young man recognized him but kept walking without reply.

"Lindsay!"

"It's *Ernest*," he said, without breaking stride, going up the concrete steps and disappearing behind the front door of his house.

At least I know your name, thought Lucas. Progress.

A few minutes later, he phoned his brother, who was no doubt still inside the school.

"Leo."

"It is me."

"Got a question for you, man."

"Where you at?"

"On Twelfth. You could throw a rock and hit me if you had an arm."

"You wearin your decoder ring?"

"Doing surveillance."

"That's awesome! Do you have that piss jug in the car?"

"And my porta-potty."

"Thought you had a question."

"You wouldn't happen to have a student by the name of Ernest, would you? I been trying to get up with him."

"I believe I got a couple of boys named Ernest. One goes by Ernie."

"He called himself Ernest. Lindsay's his last name."

"He's in my all-male class, in the morning."

"What can you tell me about him?"

"He's all right. Sensitive, on the intelligent side. You're not gonna get him in any kind of trouble, are you?"

"I wouldn't."

"Well, why don't you come meet him?"

"Huh?"

"I been asking you to talk to my class."

"Oh, yeah."

"Come past tomorrow."

"For real?"

"Why not?"

"I need time to prepare."

"No, you don't. Just come in and be yourself. They don't want to hear about, You can be anything you want to be, or any of that jive. Say what you been doing these last ten years. Be honest and real. That's what the boys appreciate."

"Okay."

"Ten o'clock, Spero."

"I'll be there."

HE WENT home, showered and changed into street clothes, dropped some paperbacks off at Walter Reed for the soldiers and marines, and drove back toward Cardozo. At 13th and Clifton, where he was stopped at the red light, he saw people walking up the long hill, coming from the U Street Metro station in business attire, a mix of Hispanics, blacks, and many whites, all coming home from work. From a local's perspective, it was startling to witness this neighborhood's transformation.

He parked in shadow on 12th, on the east side of the street.

A half hour later, a woman walked down the sidewalk. She appeared to be in her early thirties, with long chestnut-colored hair, a prominent nose, high cheekbones, and dark eyes. She wore a gray business suit, a shirt-jacket-and-slacks arrangement that did not conceal her long-legged, thoroughbred build. She carried a briefcase and walked with good posture and confidence.

Lucas got out of his Jeep as she hit the steps leading to the house with the lime green trim. He jogged across the street and said, "Lisa Weitzman?"

She stopped and turned, cool and unafraid. "Yes?"

"Spero Lucas," he said. "I'm an investigator."

NINE

HE SAT on her porch, on a folding metal chair that was one of two situated around a small round metal table. Lucas had asked for ten minutes of her time. She had agreed and told him to wait outside. She went into her home and when she returned she had removed her jacket. Her white button-down shirt was fitted and served her well. She took a seat in the second chair. Dusk had come to the street.

"I'm afraid I can't help you," said Lisa Weitzman, after he had told her why he had sought her out. He had not been coy. He'd given her the straight information about the package and why it had been shipped to her house.

"You weren't at home that day."

"I don't take time off. If I do go on vacation I leave town. But I'm at work every day, typically, out the door at seven thirty and usually not back here until six thirty, seven at night. So, no, I wasn't aware that anyone had taken something off my porch. Certainly not a large amount of marijuana."

"It was thirty pounds."

"Was it shipped out from Boulder?" said Lisa.

"Huh?"

" 'Packed in coffee grounds and wrapped around in dryer sheets.' "

" 'Multitude of Casualties,' " said Lucas, with a slow, dawning smile. "The Hold Steady. You like them?"

"Oh, yeah."

"I do, too. They burn it down live."

Their eyes met and something passed between them. Lisa pushed a strand of stray hair behind her ear and crossed one leg over the other.

"That's how the dealers pack it, right? The coffee grounds mask the smell from the dope dogs."

"So I hear," said Lucas. "Any of your neighbors mention seeing suspicious activity up here?"

"A few of them certainly would. If they saw someone stealing something off my front porch..."

"Like the old lady across the street?"

"Miss Woods? She'd be one, definitely. She'd probably try to stop the culprit, too."

"Yeah, we met."

"She's sweet."

"To *you*, maybe," said Lucas. "How about Ernest Lindsay, next door?"

"Ernest and I are cool."

"Good guy?"

"Yeah. He has some home issues. I let him hang here sometimes, watch TV and stuff, when he wants to get out. Ernest loves movies. He even watches the black-and-whites on TCM. He wants to be a director." Lisa looked away, out toward the street. Perhaps she felt she had betrayed Ernest's trust. "Ernest would have said something."

"No doubt."

"If I hear anything..."

"I'll write my number down before I go. I appreciate you taking the time."

Lisa Weitzman stood. Lucas did not. He was being presumptuous and somewhat childish. He didn't want to go.

"Anything else?" she said.

"Nope."

She stared at him and he said nothing.

"I'm going to have a beer," she said. "Would you care to join me?"

"Absolutely," said Lucas.

SHE HAD come out with a couple of Dogfish 90 Minute IPAs, candles, and matches. She told him about her work in copyright law, saying with sarcasm that it was "fascinating," and he said that he did investigative work for a private-practice defense attorney who had an office down by Judiciary Square. He told her that he wasn't the office type and that he liked working outside. He listened to reggae, ska, dub, and guitar-based rock and bar bands. He liked soul music when he heard it but was unfamiliar with the artists because they had come before his time. She too liked rock, and a good night out for her was a transcendent live show. She could tell she was going to get along with someone if they were into DBT.

"*Decoration Day*'s the shit," said Lucas.

Dark had come and the candle flames threw a pleasant light on the porch. The beer was good, heavy with malt and alcohol. They were on their second round.

"You're supposed to drink this one out of snifters," said Lisa.

"I wouldn't," said Lucas, and he tapped the neck of his bottle against hers. "Thanks."

"My pleasure." She swigged some beer and put the bottle on the table. "It's Spero..."

"Lucas."

"With a *c* or a *k?*"

"With a *c*."

"I was thinking it was Greek."

"It is."

"But there's no *c* in the Greek alphabet."

"My grandfather changed it. He thought it looked better when he wrote it out in cursive. More American. How did you know that? About the alphabet."

"I took Greek in college."

"Where was that?"

"Stanford." She said, softly, almost apologetically.

"That where you got your law degree?"

"Yale."

"Oh, just Yale."

"How about you? Where did you go to school?"

"The University of Baghdad," said Lucas, repeating a lame joke he had heard many times but had never made himself, up until now. "Stupid, man. I don't know why I said that."

"You're blushing."

"Fuck, I know."

"Army?"

"Marines."

She asked nothing else about the subject and said, "Welcome home."

"Good to be here," said Lucas, taking in the graceful curve of her neck.

"You don't look Greek."

"I'm adopted. I've got a brother, also adopted, who teaches at Cardozo, right there." He pointed his bottle sloppily in the direction of the school. His head was up. The alcohol had given him a kiss.

"You ever wonder, you know, about your identity?"

"No. I know who my parents are."

"That's nice."

"I was blessed. You?"

"I'm from California, a suburb north of San Francisco. Grew up in a nice Jewish home. Progressive parents..."

"Bedroom community."

"Sounds idyllic, I know. Out there the folks like to say that they don't have any racial problems. No black people, no problems."

"Must have been a culture shock, moving here."

"For my neighbors more than for me. They like me now. I think."

"Doesn't matter if the racial makeup changes. This is a black city, far as I'm concerned. Always will be."

"My local friends tell me that it's mostly out-of-town transplants who buy houses in neighborhoods like these. You all can't forget what it was. I don't remember the high crime or the Clifton Terrace apartments when they were HUD, and I sure don't remember the riots, because I wasn't even on the planet. I just saw an affordable house on the edge of downtown with middle-class homeowners tending to their own, and I scooped it up. It's quiet here. I walk up to Thirteenth and Clifton some nights and I sit on the school wall and look down at the city, and I feel like I hit the lottery."

"The million-dollar view," said Lucas. "You walk up there alone?"

"Most times," she said, looking right at him. "Yeah."

She went inside and came out with a couple more beers and a half-smoked joint. Lucas lit the joint off one of the candles and they passed it back and forth.

After a long exhale, Lucas said, "This isn't stuff from that package, is it?"

"Nope. I already told you, I had nothing to do with it."

"Just checking."

"Stop working, Spero."

"You're right, I should."

Lisa said, "Relax."

Her knee brushed against his and he felt an electric current run up his spine.

They talked some more. It was easy. Lisa roached the last of the joint in the pack of matches, blew out the candles, got up, and gathered the bottles off the table.

"You want another?" she said.

"I could."

"It's gotten a little chilly out here." She moved toward the door and looked over her shoulder.

"What?"

"You wanna come in?"

"Yes."

THEY KISSED standing up in her living room. Her mouth was made for it. He admired the curve of her hip as she ran her hand down his biceps. She reached under his shirt and touched the hardness of his abdomen and ran her fingers down the ladder.

"I knew it," she said.

"These are nice," he said stupidly, as he cupped one of her breasts. His finger and thumb swelled her nipple through the fabric of her shirt.

"They hold my bra up," she said.

The two of them laughed.

"I'm trippin," he said.

"Me, too," she said, her eyes alive.

"You know I can't stay."

"Really?"

"I can't stay *long*."

"That's better."

She stepped forward and came into his arms.

LUCAS WALKED out onto the street after midnight, satiated, a cocky lilt in his step. He had no misgivings or remorse. For a couple of hours, he had forgotten about Tavon, Edwin, and death. He had not thought about Constance, his brother's inevitable comments, morality, or anything else. His father had once told him, "Don't let anything walk past you," and Lucas knew well what that meant. There are opportunities and adventures that are there for only a short period of time, and only available to people of a certain age. He and Lisa Weitzman understood. They'd had fun. He didn't want to be one of those sad middle-aged guys who think about the women they should have bedded in their youth, if only they'd been less sensible. He planned to age with good memories.

He started up his Jeep and drove over to 13th Street with the windows down. The ride home was sweet.

TEN

IT WAS known as the high school up on 13th Street with the fine view of the city below. It was designed in the manner of a castle, complete with crenulated battlements and clean-line walls of brick and sandstone. In the distant past, the building had been described as the jewel of the public school system, but few made that claim anymore. Many students thought of Cardozo as a kind of prison, as students of a certain age are inclined to do, wherever they attend school. Because of this, and because of its imposing structure, dramatically set in relief against the high ground, generations of D.C. kids had simply called it the Rock.

The school sat on the steeply graded edge of the Piedmont Plateau, on the south edge of Columbia Heights, straddling the border of an area most still thought of as Shaw. For thirty-two years, when it was filled with whites of northern and southern European extraction, it was called Central High. Numerous generals, successful lawyers, committed educators, local department store moguls, and one famous

FBI director were alumni. One hundred and forty-seven of its former students lost their lives in World War II.

In 1950, four years shy of *Brown v. Board of Education*, Central was declared a school for "Negro" pupils. The city needed the large facility for its black students, as their schools had become severely overcrowded, while the student population in white schools had begun to fall. Central's name was changed to Cardozo High, the moniker of the smaller, all-black high school that had been located down the street. Its white students immediately transferred elsewhere, to west-of-the-park high schools like Woodrow Wilson and uptown schools like Calvin Coolidge and Theodore Roosevelt. After *Brown*, despite the good intent and goal of desegregation, Cardozo stayed black. Central had boasted of graduating J. Edgar Hoover; Cardozo would claim Marvin Gaye and Maury Wills among its own.

Cardozo was not the greatest success story in the D.C. public school system. Its test scores were said to be at the top of the second ladder, behind Wilson, Banneker, and School Without Walls, and its dropout rate was too high. It was a deep-city school, with all the problems that accompanied the social conditions outside its walls. What made the news were the failures and shortcomings. But many students graduated, went on to college and beyond, and became productive and in some cases noted members of society. Their stories, for the most part, went untold.

Leonidas Lucas knew these stories intimately. He taught English up on the second floor.

The route to Leo's classroom, once students and administrators passed through a main-entrance metal detector manned by private-firm security personnel, was via the stone steps in one of several stairwells. Millions of feet had traveled heavily over these steps since the building had opened almost a century ago, rendering the stone concave. Leo's classroom windows were covered in heavy-mesh iron screens, allowing fractured, dim sunlight to enter. The room's sole computer, donated years earlier, was ancient; its printer did not print. Pencils were hard to come by. Some of the desks and blackboards looked more than fifty years old.

Leo didn't think too hard on the lack of supplies, the missing ceiling tiles, the bathrooms with no doors on their stalls, the stopped-up toilets, the grim, barely lit halls, the students who did not listen, or the few students who were dangerous among the many who were basically good. He thought about his kids and why he was there. Leo was only in his third year as a full-time teacher, and he had not yet lost his enthusiasm for the job.

He stood before the class, his ID badge hanging around his neck, pacing slowly like a yard dog on a chain, a paperback copy of *Unknown Man #89* in one hand. Leo had a desk, but he rarely sat behind it during class.

"Okay," said Leo. "I assume you've all finished reading the novel. You should have, by now."

Leo looked out at the all-male group. He had classes with girls and boys together, but this one was newly instituted, modeled after parochial and private school setups, part of a growing public school trend. It was thought that a good deal of the misbehavior and non-participation in classrooms on the part of boys was due to the mixing of sexes. Boys had to show off for female students, or they were just distracted in their presence. Boys didn't want to give up too much of themselves in front of girls for fear of appearing weak.

Leo had come to feel that all of this was true, as this class was the liveliest in his schedule. The boys spoke freely here, with enthusiasm, and he allowed them to do so, for the most part, uncensored. They were seniors, and most were seventeen or eighteen years old. Men or close to it. Unless the conversation crossed a line, and all sensed where that line was, Leo let it roll.

No one admitted to finishing the assigned pages, nor did they admit to not completing the assignment. Leo had not expected them to answer.

"I'll start the discussion," said Leo.

He talked about the author's use of dialogue, how it illustrated character and moved the plot forward; how the central conflict of the novel was set up economically in the early chapters; how the protagonist, Ryan, struggled with alcoholism, and how his problem was handled with subtlety and grace. This led to a few of the boys talking about experiences in their family lives involving alcohol and drugs. Leo let them go with it. Inevitably this was followed by a discourse on the sexual relationship between Ryan and a character named Denise, also an alcoholic.

"The scene where they split a bottle of wine," said Leo, "and then they leave an inch or so in the bottle? Neither one of them has the need to finish it. It means they're making progress with their recovery through the vehicle of their relationship. Great scene, right?"

"Yeah, but after? You think he's gonna do her. You *want* him to hit it. I mean, they been leading up to it."

"They're taking their time," said Leo. "It's going to happen, and both of them know it. But neither one of them wants to rush it."

Many boys began to talk at once. They had landed on a subject that they all felt they knew well.

"That right there wasn't realistic. He would've banged that trick right after dinner."

"She wasn't no trick. Denise was cool."

"She wanted it, didn't she?"

"*All* of 'em want it."

"Mr. Lucas is sayin, it was more special to them 'cause they took their time."

"Why would you wanna take your time?"

"You don't know nothin."

"I know more than you."

"How you gonna say that?"

"Cause I *get* more than you."

"Since when?"

"Last night."

"Yeah? What was his name?"

The space filled with taunting "ah-has" and laughter. A balled-up piece of paper flew across the room.

"All right, that's enough," said Leo. He nodded to Spero Lucas, who was seated in a student chair in the back of the room. "Come on up here, Spero."

Spero got up out of his chair and walked to the head of the class. As he passed Ernest Lindsay, he made brief eye contact with the young man, as he had done when he'd first entered the room. Ernest had recognized him immediately, shaken his head with mild annoyance, crossed his arms, and looked away. Now his eyes tracked Spero as he threaded his way across the classroom.

Spero stopped beside Leo, rested one hand over the other below his belt line, and stood straight with his legs comfortably apart. He wore jeans and a clean, fitted T-shirt bearing a winged wheel. His veins were wired out on his biceps and forearms. He knew that young men of this age would respect him as much for his build as they would for any of his accomplishments. It had certainly been that way with him when he was in his teens.

"Want you all to welcome Spero Lucas," said Leo. "My brother."

Spero could see the confusion that was plain on some of the boys' faces.

One young man who could not hold it in said, "That's your brother, for *real?*"

"Yes," said Leo. "All my life. We shared a bedroom for almost twenty years."

"Separate beds," said Spero, which got some chuckles.

" 'Cept when you had nightmares," said Leo, which was true.

Leo let the murmurs die down. He wasn't about to explain the color difference between him and his brother. It was more fun to let the boys wonder.

Leo addressed the class: "This is part of our Reach for Success speaker series. Spero's gonna tell you what he's been doing since he got out of high school."

Spero said, "Thank you, Mr. Lucas," and began to talk about his life. He covered high school athletics, his stint in the Marine Corps, boot and overseas duty, and his work as an investigator for an attorney who defended homicide and high-profile drug cases. Because they were young men and the subject matter touched on danger, crime, and violence, he had their attention from the start. He told them that he had not graduated from college, but that didn't mean that he had given up his intellectual curiosity. He stressed that the physical was as important to him as the mental. He told them, with honesty, that many of them were not going to be rich, famous, or wildly successful, and that the years ahead of them would most likely be filled with joyous highs as well as crushing disappointments. That they should try to find work they were passionate about and strive to lead productive lives. The last part sounded like bullshit to his own ears, so he knew it would sound that way to them, but he felt he had to give them something in the way of wisdom, however lame. The truth was, he was still trying to navigate his own path. He had no long-term plans.

"Questions?" said Spero.

"Remember what I told y'all," said Leo. Spero knew then that they had been prepped not to ask the question they were all curious about.

"You carry a gun on your job now?" said Moony.

"No," said Spero. "That would be illegal."

Some of the boys looked at one another and smiled.

Another boy raised his hand. "What kind of gun you carry in I-raq?"

"I carried an M-Sixteen rifle."

"Like my grandfather did in Vietnam," said a boy named Hannibal. His peers called him Balls.

"We had a different version," said Spero. "The A-Two. It

had an improved flash suppressor and better sights. Fired three-round bursts instead of full auto. That made it more accurate, supposedly."

"What about straight machine guns?"

"There were SAWs. Fired seven hundred and fifty rounds per minute."

"No pistols?"

"Some guys carried M-Nines, which are nine-millimeter Berettas. We also had mounted fifty cals, Mark Nineteens, tanks that fired one-hundred-and-fifty-millimeter shells, incendiary grenades, M-Forty sniper rifles...all kinds of cool stuff."

This energized the class and caused more chatter.

"What about knives?"

"Yeah, but not standard-issue. Guys bought their own."

"What the enemy have?"

"The insurgents had AK-Forty-sevens," said Spero.

"Dag."

"Pretty much indestructible," said Spero. "You could pull 'em out of a sand dune and they'd still fire. And they had these rocket-propelled grenades, which we just called RPGs."

"I seen this one video," said a boy named Mark Norman, "where these soldiers are in the desert, and they call in the place, on the radio, where the enemy is located at..."

"The coordinates," said Spero.

"Yeah, and they just vaporized 'em with bombs and stuff. Is that what it was like?"

"Depends on where you were," said Spero. "There was that kind of conflict. But where I was, in a place called Fallujah, it was a more direct kind of engagement. Straight-up combat. What they call house-to-house fighting. It was..."

Spero stopped himself. He felt he had said too much. A rare silence fell on the room.

"Why they call y'all marines," said a young man named Marcus Murray. "I mean, *marine* means the ocean or somethin, right? Seems like the navy guys should be called marines."

"We're called marines because we come in from the oceans and the seas. The navy *delivers* us to the battlefields."

Ernest Lindsay raised his hand. "Why'd you join up?"

Spero cleared his throat. "Well, first of all, personally, I think I was a good fit. I already told you that I wrestled in high school. Wrestlers who are serious about what they're doing, they don't want to just win on points. They want the pin. They're competitive and focused, and they've got a deep need to win. The recruiters targeted me, man. But I didn't get tricked into anything. I *wanted* to enlist. I saw some of the guys in my neighborhood goin, and a lot of them didn't have many other opportunities, and I thought, why should it just be them and not me? I guess what it comes down to is, I know it sounds corny, but I wanted to do my part." Spero looked directly at Ernest Lindsay. "All the decisions I've made, what I can tell you is, I did what I thought was right."

"He's not suggesting you go out and enlist, necessarily," said Leo, looking at Spero out the corner of his eye.

"Course not," said Spero.

"*I'm* goin to college," said a young man.

"That's excellent," said Spero clumsily. "Anyone else?"

"How much money you make?" said Balls.

"That's not an appropriate question, Hannibal," said Leo.

"Do marines get much?" said another young man.

"Okay," said Leo, "I think we're about done. Let's give my brother a round of applause."

The students clapped for him. It wasn't thunderous but it was respectful. He felt he'd done all right. At least he hadn't shit the bed.

On the way out the door he got close to Leo and grabbed his forearm.

"It's a good class," said Spero. "I'm proud of you."

"Proud of *you*," said Leo.

GETTING INTO his Jeep, parked on 11th, Lucas got a call on his cell.

"Where you at?" said Leo.

"Still outside the school."

"Ernest Lindsay would like to speak with you."

"Now?"

"It's lunchtime, so I'm headed to the teachers' lounge. You two can use my classroom."

"What, I gotta go through security again?"

"Stop acting like a little girl."

Spero got out of his vehicle and headed back toward the school.

ELEVEN

SPERO LUCAS and Ernest Lindsay sat at one of the long tables in Leo's classroom. Ernest had begun to eat his lunch from a paper bag. His mom had fixed him a tuna fish sandwich and had included Cheetos, a bottle of water, and an apple she had cut into slices.

"Thanks for coming back," said Ernest.

"No problem," said Lucas. "You know I been tryin to get up with you."

"Sorry. I was kinda rude when I saw you on my street."

"That's all right."

Ernest shifted his weight in his chair. "Did you read that book we were talkin about?"

"I read it a while back. Good stuff."

"That thing teacher said, about the book being a Western in the *dis*guise of a crime story?" said Ernest.

"That's right."

"Works that way in movies, too."

Lucas remembered that, the night before, Lisa Weitzman

had mentioned that Ernest was a movie lover. He did not know that Leo was pushing him to go to college, get his needed education, make contacts, and move ahead from there, possibly to grad school. Ernest's grades were excellent, but he was reluctant to leave home, so Leo had suggested he apply to the University of the District of Columbia. It was a start.

"How so?" said Lucas.

"You know that first Man with No Name joint?"

"*A Fistful of Dollars.*"

"That was based on a Japanese movie about a samurai. And *that* one was taken from an old crime story. That Hamlet dude—"

"Hammett. You're talking about *Red Harvest.*"

"They made a rack of movies based on that book. Not a one of them gave credit to Hamlet."

"Hammett."

"Right."

"You're pretty smart, Ernest."

Ernest smiled shyly. "I'm gonna make movies, Mr. Lucas."

"Call me Spero."

"Sayin, I'm *going* to."

"No doubt. But you need to get your undergrad work done first. Get yourself a base."

"I picked up an application from UDC a few days ago."

"There's plenty of scholarship money for minority students. It's lying around, waiting to be used. I bet my brother will help you fill out the forms."

"My mother will help me."

"Great."

"I'ma drop the form back off next week."

"Do it," said Lucas. "Don't wait."

The room became uncomfortably quiet. A failing fluorescent bulb buzzed steadily overhead. Ernest withdrew the apple slices from his bag and handed one to Lucas. As Lucas ate it, he noticed Ernest staring at him.

"What's up?" said Lucas.

"I was just wondering. About when you were overseas, in the war."

Lucas sat back. Instinctively, he folded his arms across his chest. "Yes?"

Ernest shifted his weight in his chair. "You hear all kinds of stuff about what got done over there. By our soldiers, I mean. Things that got done to, you know, the people that lived in that country."

"The civilians," said Lucas.

"People that weren't the enemy or terrorists."

"It happens. Especially in wars that get fought today. Generally you're not fighting men and women in uniform. Mistakes are made involving citizens. What's called collateral damage."

"So you saw civilians bein killed in Iraq?"

Lucas did not answer or gesture with his eyes.

"If you saw something like that," said Ernest, "would you turn the soldier in who did it?"

Lucas shook his head. It was not a no. He was telling Ernest that the question was unanswerable and maybe out of bounds.

"Okay, then," said Ernest. "Let me ask you this: You know that soldier who got killed by his own men? The one who played football in the NFL? They got a word for what happened to him."

"Friendly fire. His name was Pat Tillman."

"Well, it wasn't just the generals and the politicians who knew what happened. Some of his friends, the other soldiers, they had to know, too. So why didn't anyone speak out? Why didn't anyone come forward and say what went down?"

"It got told eventually."

"But everyone tried to cover it up at first."

"I don't know about that, Ernest. I can't speak for those who were there."

"You're not helping me out here much."

"Helping you out with what?"

"You're an investigator. You tried to talk to me, and I think I know what it was about."

"Well?"

Ernest looked toward the windows and gripped his legs above his knees. "Man, I don't know."

"What's going on with you?"

"I got a problem," said Ernest.

"What is it?" said Lucas.

Ernest leaned forward. "I *saw* somethin."

"I WASN'T at school that day," said Ernest, after Lucas had helped himself to a couple of water bottles from Leo's desk drawer and returned with them to the table.

"Were you sick?" said Lucas.

"Nah. My mother works at the GAO, and all her other kids, my brothers and sisters, are grown and out the house."

"So you cut school. What do you do, bring girls over while your mom's at work, stuff like that?"

Ernest looked away, mildly embarrassed. "I watch movies on Turner, mostly, like if they're havin like a festival. Something I really want to see."

"What were you watching that day? Do you remember?" Lucas wanted to test the young man's veracity. The TCM schedule for the past month was easy enough to check.

"It was..." Ernest's brow creased. "It was called *The Last Hunt*. 'Bout buffalo killings in the West. I hadn't even heard of it, but I got this friend Diego, a movie freak, told me about it. It's not on DVD, so when it got scheduled during a school day, I knew I had to find a way to watch it."

"Go on."

"Way my mom's got our house set up, when you're watching television, you're kind of sittin by the front porch window, so naturally you look out onto Twelfth Street from time to time. I heard a truck come down the street and stop. It was the FedEx man. He got a big package out the truck and carried it up the steps of Miss Lisa's house and left it on her porch. She works during the day, too."

"Lisa Weitzman, your next-door neighbor."

"Yeah. So right after the FedEx man leaves, a black Impala SS shows up and this young dude gets out the car. It was the old-style SS, not that crud joint they got now."

"How soon after?"

"Like, five minutes."

"What'd the guy look like?"

"He had braids. That's all I remember 'bout him, really."

"Anyone else in the car with him?"

"There was someone in the passenger side, but he never did get out."

"Okay."

"So this dude with the braids comes up on Miss Lisa's porch real quick and picks up that box. Must have been kinda heavy, 'cause he struggled with it some."

Lucas's blood was getting up. Tavon and Edwin had been lying to him. The package wasn't stolen. He took a long drink of water and set the bottle back on the table.

"What happened next? The guy put the package in the car and drove away?"

"No," said Ernest. He said nothing else and sat back in his chair.

Lucas stared at Ernest Lindsay. "You didn't tell Lisa Weitzman that a package had been taken off her property. I know that she's been a friend to you. Why wouldn't you let her know?"

"I like Miss Lisa. She's cool people."

"Come on, Ernest, help me out here. What is this?"

"I don't know for sure if I can trust you. You stand up in our class and talk about doin what's right, and it moved me to reach out to you, but I just don't know."

"What's holding you back?"

"It's not just me. I got my mother to think of."

"What are you afraid of? Do you want to bring the police into this?"

"No."

"Do you need protection?"

"*No.*"

"What, then?"

"Police are already *in* it. They *part* of it, man."

Lucas nodded slowly. "Tell me about it."

Ernest exhaled, the air leaving him like he was pushing something away. "When that boy went down Miss Lisa's steps with that box in his hand, a police car turned onto Twelfth and stopped behind the Impala. By then I was standing up in my mom's living room, looking out the window, looking down on the street."

"What happened next?"

"Police officer gets out the squad car and opens up its trunk. Says somethin, just a couple of words to the dude with the braids, and then that dude puts the package in the police officer's trunk. Police officer gets in his car and drives away. Dude with the braids drives off, too. It happened fast, like, *bang.* You know?"

"Was the officer riding alone?"

"Yes."

"What kind of car?"

"You know, a patrol car. Fourth District car."

"And this cop was in uniform," said Lucas.

"Yeah, but not a regular one, though. He had on a blue shirt, said 'Police' in big letters across his back."

"What did he look like?"

"He was kinda skinny, had a long nose, like a beak almost. Hair was cut close, like a reddish color. Dude looked like a big old rooster."

"Black or white?"

"If he was white I would have said so."

"Right," said Lucas. "What else?"

"I think this man saw me."

"You *think*."

"Before he left outta there, he looked up toward my house. I don't know, maybe he had one of those feelings you get, like someone's watching you. When he did, I stepped back, away from the window."

"So you don't know for sure."

"The other day, when you were parked on this street, the first time you called out to me?"

"I remember."

"He was parked over there on Clifton, in front of my school. I felt like he was waiting for me, man."

That's why Ernest had been so uptight that day, thought Lucas. It was the same 4D patrol car, the same officer who had come down the street earlier, driven slowly by Lucas's Jeep, and checked him out. Now Lucas knew why the sight of the car had felt strange to him. The Fourth District's southernmost boundary ended at Harvard Street, several blocks north of 12th and Clifton, which was 3D territory. So this car was out of its district. The officer knew who Ernest was and where he lived. He also knew Lucas's vehicle by sight and maybe had its plates; he'd seen Lucas get out of it and try to talk to Ernest.

"What's wrong?" said Ernest.

"I'm thinking," said Lucas.

"Should I be worried?"

"No. You've told me everything you know, right?"

"Yeah."

"You did right by talking to me. But you're out of it now."

"What's your connect?"

"I was hired to get that package back."

"Yeah? What was in it?"

"It's better that you don't know."

"You sayin this shit is dangerous."

"Nothing's going to happen to you, Ernest."

"I can't lie. I'm scared."

"Don't be," said Lucas. "You'll be fine."

HE WAS riding his bike out along Sligo Creek, away from the city, heading into the woods of Wheaton Regional Park property later that day, when it came to him. He kept pedaling and pushing it, and when he hit the park itself he found a shaded shelter that was cool and unoccupied. He removed his gloves and helmet, then sat on a picnic bench, took a long drink from his insulated water bottle, and wiped the drip off his chin.

He stared out into the trees.

The numbers of an MPD squad car, called the CAD, were printed on its right rear bumper and front quarter panels. The sequence started with the police district's number. So a car from the Fourth District would display a CAD identification that began with the number 4.

The number that Tavon Lynch had sent him through the phone was not an address. Tavon had texted Lucas the number of the squad car driven by the police officer who he was in with or was shaking him down. Sitting on Hayes Street that night, he must have had the feeling that something was terribly wrong.

Car 4044.

Lucas's grin was feral and tight.

TWELVE

In THE morning, Lucas did a circuit workout in his apartment. He showered, changed into clothing that was suitable for a lunch date, got on his computer, and did some research on dc.gov. With time to kill before his lunch, he went out and hit a couple of used-book stores. At Silver Spring Books, in his old neighborhood, he found two nonfictions that he had read and enjoyed: *Kings of the Bs*, by McCarthy and Flynn, and *Sergio Leone*, the massive biography by Christopher Frayling.

He met Constance Kelly at My Brother's Place, at 2nd and C, Northwest, a lunch-and-happy-hour spot not far from the courts and Tom Petersen's office. The bar, dark wood and low lights, was one of the better down-home watering holes in town, a longtime haunt of cops, judges, federal marshals, Department of Labor employees, and college students. Lucas and Constance sat out on the enclosed porch, watching the sidewalk parade. Constance was studying the menu.

"You eat meat, don't you?" said Lucas.

"So?"

"Get the burger. It's Angus beef and they put it on a nice kaiser roll."

"What are you having?"

"The Cubano. They got a kickin mojo sauce here, man."

"What is it with you and food?"

"Part of my culture," said Lucas. "It's a way of life."

"You're not even Greek."

"Want me to prove it?"

Constance looked up from the menu and blushed. The waiter, a young El Salvadoran, arrived and took their order. As he moved away, Lucas reached into his pocket and produced a plastic cell phone, which he placed on the table.

"What's that?" said Constance.

"A gift."

"I have a phone."

"This one's special. It's a disposable."

Constance picked up the phone, examined it, and placed it back on the table. "It's got a drawing of a cartoon kangaroo on its face. And a special button for nine-one-one. Who makes this, Fisher-Price?"

"It's made for kids. And seniors."

"Which one do I look like?"

"I was hoping you'd use it to do me a favor."

"You want me to make some kind of call that's hard to trace or monitor."

"Well..."

"You're asking me to break the law."

"Nope. But I am asking you to lie, a little."

"Why can't *you* lie?"

"This needs the distaff touch."

"That's an antiquated term. Tell you the truth, I'm not all that surprised you're using it."

Lucas pushed the phone in her direction. "I'm trying to find the name of a police officer who was driving a certain MPD squad car on a specific day and time."

"How would a person do that?"

"Call the Office of Unified Communications and ask for a dispatcher. All the cars have a four-digit CAD, which is the Computer-Assisted Dispatcher number. Police officers are required to give the CAD to the dispatcher when they put a vehicle into service. This particular vehicle was a Ten Ninety-nine, meaning it was a one-man unit."

"You want me to call the OUC."

"Now you're getting the hang of it."

"I'm just trying to speak your language. Your knowledge of acronyms and ten-codes is very impressive."

"Thank you," said Lucas, ignoring her sarcasm. "So what I need you to do is give the dispatcher this information right here." Lucas pulled a piece of paper from his jacket pocket and handed it to Constance. On it was written the number 4044, and a date and time. "Ask them who was driving that car on that particular day and shift."

"And they'll just give it to me."

"They're supposed to. But sometimes they don't, for good reason. In that case you have to file a Freedom of Information Act request, which could take a lot of time."

"And you'd have to put your name on the FOIA, which you don't want to do."

"In this instance, that wouldn't work for me."

"You're not telling me much."

"I don't want you to get too involved."

"But you want me involved just enough—"

"Yes."

Constance sat back and stared at Lucas.

"Mo' ice tea?" said the waiter, appearing like a sweaty apparition.

"Yes, please," said Lucas.

"Are you going to give me some kind of instructions?" said Constance, after the waiter had poured and drifted.

"Tell the dispatcher that you had an Officer Friendly experience. That a certain police officer stopped to give you directions, or help change your tire, or whatever. That he showed an unexpected kindness to you and you'd like to send a thank-you note to the station, but you don't recall his name. Or, you know, you wanna put him up for a commendation."

"A laurel and hearty handshake."

"Something like that."

"So," said Constance, "I do this and I get, what, a twenty-dollar lunch?"

"I was thinking dinner, too."

"That sounds nice."

"How about Mourayo on Connecticut? They bake a fish that you'll dream about."

"Always with the food, Spero." She put the toy phone and slip of paper in her purse.

Constance and Lucas walked out of the restaurant and stopped on the 2nd Street sidewalk to say good-bye.

"I've got a full day," said Constance. "Tom's got me running on a case."

"I'm headed over there right now," said Lucas.

"To Petersen's office?"

"Yeah."

"You're calling in all your chits today."

"Thank you for doing this," said Lucas. "I mean it."

He bent forward to kiss her. She gave him her cheek instead of her mouth. Maybe she knew. Some women just did.

TOM PETERSEN was at his desk, eating a Potbelly sub from the shop on the first floor. Lucas was seated before the desk. His chair was wobbling on the rickety wood planks of the ancient floor.

"Where you been?" said Petersen. He was wearing a Ben Sherman shirt that looked as if it had been purchased in swinging London, circa 1967.

"Working."

"I could use you if you're free. The interns I have right now aren't giving me what I need. There's this one young guy, big guy, got a few inches on you, I ask him to go to Southeast to do a witness interview, he starts walking backwards."

"Send Constance, if you don't think it's too dicey. She's got backbone."

"Don't you know it," said Petersen, not looking in Lucas's eyes.

"I'll be around. But I need a little time."

"What can I do for you?"

"I'm looking for a contact over at Internal Affairs. I remembered that you have someone over there who you speak to."

"I do."

Petersen, unlike many other defense attorneys, had a decent relationship with the police. He occasionally defended them, successfully, in misconduct cases and alleged wrongful shootings. Unlike others, he did not take high-profile civil suits against the department. He kept himself in reasonable good graces with both criminals and police. He was a forward-thinking man.

"What happened?" said Petersen. "A police officer fondle you at a traffic stop or something?"

"Nothing that exciting. I just want to know what they have on a certain someone, if anything."

"You're fishing."

"Uh-huh."

"I'm not even gonna ask."

Petersen wiped his mouth with a napkin and reached across the desk. He flipped through the cards of his Rolodex. He was one of a dwindling number of professionals who still used one.

"You ready?" said Petersen.

"Yeah."

"Guy's name is Tim McCarthy."

Lucas typed it into the Contacts section of his iPhone. "Number?"

Petersen gave it to him. "Don't call him, though. Let me. I owe him a phone call on something else anyway. There's no way he's gonna talk to you unless I ask him to. And even with that, frankly, I don't think he's gonna give you jack. Even though he *is* one of your stripe."

"He served?"

"McCarthy, I put him at about fifty-four. He missed Vietnam but served in the Corps stateside. Was a patrol cop in the late seventies through the eighties, then did a long stint as an investigator in Six-D. Here's the kicker: when we invaded Iraq—what was that? two thousand three—he takes a leave of absence from the force and goes over there as a chaplain. He was too old to fight but said he wanted to be with the men. Can you believe it?"

Yes, thought Lucas.

"He's got this photograph of him over there in the desert, got a Bible in one hand and an M-Sixteen in the other, the butt resting on his thigh. McCarthy's the Burt Lancaster of chaplains."

"Why don't you think he'll talk to me?" said Lucas. "He doesn't like investigators?"

"He likes his job. Man's a couple of years from retirement. He could get fired if he gives out classified information to a civilian." Petersen took a last bite of his sub and balled up the white paper on his desk, shoving it into a cylindrical brown bag. "But I'll call him. Most likely, he'll get in touch with you. You'll probably have to meet him somewhere outside of Indiana Avenue."

"Thanks." Lucas got up out of his chair and stretched. "What's going on with the Hawkins case?"

"Preparing to go to trial."

"Sounds like the Feds have him dead to rights."

Petersen said, "We'll see."

LUCAS BOUGHT two bunches of roses from a street vendor, then drove up to 12th Street and parked his Jeep. He crossed the street with a plastic bag in one hand and one bouquet of roses in the other. He went up the steps to Lisa Weitzman's home and laid the roses, heavily wetted, on her doorstep, along with a note he had written in childish scrawl before getting out of his vehicle. The note was corny and obvious, something about how nice it was to hang out with her. He had no plans to try and see her again, but he wanted to do something respectful for her, at least. Flowers had come to mind. He was a resourceful but not particularly original young man.

Lucas then went to the Lindsay residence and knocked on its front door. The door soon opened, and a middle-aged man with a sour face and alcohol breath appeared in the frame.

"What you want?" he said, looking Lucas over in a way that no man likes.

"I've got something for Ernest."

"Who *are* you?"

"Spero Lucas. I'm the brother of Ernest's English teacher over at Cardozo."

The man closed the door without a word. It wasn't quite a slam but had a similar effect.

"Dick," said Lucas.

A short while later Ernest came outside. He had an Oreo cookie in his hand, dripping with milk, and he popped what was left of it into his mouth. Lucas waited for him to chew and swallow.

"Spero."

"Got you a couple of books."

Lucas handed the bag to Ernest, who took it and pulled out its contents. "Cool."

"Thought you'd like them. I know you're into Leone, and *Kings of the Bs* is one of the best film books I've ever read. I was lucky to find it. It's been out of print for a while."

"That's what's up," said Ernest, genuinely touched.

"Read 'em in good health."

"Was that man rude to you?" said Ernest, jerking a finger over his shoulder.

"Who is he?"

"My mother's boyfriend," said Ernest, with unmasked disgust.

"Is your mom home?"

"She's still at work. That man's tryin to stay here all the time."

"If you need me for anything," said Lucas, "you call me, hear?"

Lucas gave him his number and Ernest entered it into his own phone.

"Thanks for these."

"My pleasure."

Lucas walked to his Jeep. Ernest sat on the porch glider and began to look through the books.

On the way home, Lucas stopped at Glenwood Cemetery to see his father. He laid a bouquet of red roses on his grave, did his *stavro*, and said a silent prayer.

LATE THAT night, the phone rang in Lucas's apartment. He crossed the room and turned down the Ernest Ranglin CD he was listening to on the box. He'd smoked a little weed, and the sinewy instrumentals had been doing it to his head.

Constance was on the line. He asked her if she wanted to

come over, and she said that she was tired and was looking at an early day. He reminded her that they had a dinner date in the future, and she said that she hadn't forgotten. She'd phoned him because she had made the call they had discussed. She'd found the name of the police officer who had driven car number 4044 on the day and time Lucas had given her.

"What's the name?" said Lucas.

"Lawrence Holley," she said, and spelled it. "I imagine he goes by Larry."

The name meant nothing to Lucas. But it would.

THIRTEEN

LARRY HOLLEY, in street clothes, drove his personal vehicle, a black Escalade tricked out with aftermarket rims, over the District line into Prince George's County, Maryland. He was on Bladensburg Road, Fort Lincoln Cemetery on either side of him. Then he passed through a low-slung retail strip of barbers, beauty salons, pawnshops, independent eateries, and the usual fast-food death-houses, the town of Cottage City on his right, Colmar Manor on his left. He went over the upper Anacostia River, the Peace Cross monument in sight, and where Bladensburg became 450, which most called Annapolis Road, Holley hung a left onto an industrial-commercial road in an area known as Edmonston. He passed the famous Crossroads nightclub and drove on.

The radio was set on a hip-hop station that often played go-go at night. Because it was lunchtime and an older crowd was listening, the DJ was doing an eighties mix of first-gen rap, heavy on effects. But Larry Holley was paying no attention to the music, which would have sounded corny to his young ears. He had things pressing hard on his mind.

He wore a blue windbreaker. Underneath it, holstered to his belt, was his service weapon, a Glock 17.

Holley drove by legitimate businesses, building suppliers, tire and muffler discounters, countertop makers, parts yards, pipe and steel works, automotive service shops, and electrical supply houses, most surrounded by chain-link fences topped with razor wire. Some of these places were guarded at night by German shepherds and Rotts. He turned off on a cross street, Varnum, and then took another turn down one of the high-forties streets, and at the end of the road came to an establishment, Mobley Detailing, that also had a fence and an open gate and was the last place on the block before woods and wall topped with elevated track. He pulled the Escalade into its lot.

A large one-story, gray-cinder-block building sat back on the property, fronted by several closed bay doors and barred windows. A few young men were in the lot, washing, waxing, rim-shining, and tire-wetting the exteriors of some SUVs. One vehicle's doors were open and an old Rare Essence blared from inside, where a man was applying a special solution that cleaned leather and promised to return the new-car smell. Holley, phone to his ear, walked past the workers without acknowledgment. He told the person on the other end of the line that he had arrived, and when he came to the front door of the building, the door opened and he walked inside. A man was waiting for him.

"Aw'right," said the man, short, well into middle age, still muscled, with an unlit cigar butt lodged in the corner of his mouth. His name was Beano Mobley. His face was compressed and featureless. He wore a cheap guayabera shirt that he had bought at the PG Plaza mall and a Redskins ball cap, the profile with feathers, on his head.

"Where they at?" said Larry Holley.

"In the office," said Mobley, his voice all rasp. He looked over the tall, thin young man with amusement as he followed him toward the back.

They passed Mobley's Aztec gold Cadillac DTS, the black Tahoe owned by Bernard White and Earl Nance, and a '79 Lincoln Mark V, landau roof, double-white-over-blue-velour, opera windows, and wide whitewalls, which was the pride of Larry's father, Ricardo Holley.

The cars took up much of the bay space, lit by fluorescent drop lamps. One tubular light flashed. No one had thought to change it.

In the back of the space was a large office area, previously glassed in, now enclosed in wood panels so that any activity within could not be seen by those out in the work area. Larry Holley came to a wooden door and tried the knob. It was locked. Beano Mobley unlocked it with a key and stepped aside as Larry entered the office. Mobley went in behind him.

It looked like an office outfitted for business, violence, and pleasure. In it were a large desk, several chairs, a green leather couch, and file cabinets against one wall. A calendar showed photographs of women looking over their shoulders, posing in thongs stretched tight over large behinds. There was a bar on a wheeled cart holding a bottle of Popov vodka, a nondescript rum, King George scotch poured into an empty bottle of Johnnie Walker Black, a fifth of unopened Canadian Club, and various cognacs and brandies. Behind the desk, beside yet another door, against the rear wall, was a freestanding steel gun cabinet, eight felt-lined compartments above for pistols, five vertical compartments below for rifles. Each compartment had a lock. Ricardo Holley kept the keys in his desk drawer. The contents of the cabinet changed week to week. Mobley had been in the illegal-firearms business for a long while.

Earl Nance and Bernard White were seated on the couch. Nance's wide-set eyes, psoriatic skin, flat face, and coiled little build gave him the look of a snake. He seemed to lack eyelids, which furthered that impression. He wore his wooden crucifix out over a rayon shirt. Bernard White was large and strong, but his eyes looked passive and he did not appear aggressive. Massive muscles in his shoulders bunched against his neck. When White stood beside Nance he dwarfed him.

Ricardo Holley was seated behind the desk. He wore a lavender shirt buttoned high with a bolo, beltless black slacks, and the kind of sharply pointed dress shoes favored by Africans. On his fingers he wore several stolen rings that featured emeralds. He had cinnamon-colored skin, light eyes, a comically long nose, and reddish hair he wore in an unfashionably puffy, loose Afro. He looked like a pimp who'd stayed too long. He was forty-six.

Larry Holley, with the same skin and hair color, nose, and build as Ricardo Holley, was twenty-five. Larry did not like the curl in his hair and had always kept it close to the scalp. To look at them together was to erase any doubt that they were father and son. But Ricardo had done nothing to raise, support, or nurture Larry. In fact, Ricardo had only come back into Larry's life in the past year.

"My boy," said Ricardo, rising up out of his chair. He crossed the room with a pronounced limp and gave Larry the half-hug-and-back-pound that feigned affection.

"Ricardo," said Larry. He had stopped calling him "Dad" long ago.

Nance and White glanced at each other. Mobley, who had taken a place on the edge of the desk, one foot on the floor, one dangling, shifted the cigar butt in his mouth and stared impassively ahead.

"Why'd you call me in?" said Larry, easing into his cop stance, feet planted comfortably apart.

"Thought it was important we get together in person," said Ricardo. "Talk about where we're at."

"Talk, then," said Larry. "I got my shift to get to."

"You want a drink, somethin?"

"No." *Not with y'all.*

Ricardo nodded his head and returned to his desk. It was uncomfortable for him to be on his feet for too long. Larry remained where he was. He preferred to stand over them.

"So," said Ricardo. "What's the status of the investigation?"

"I don't know," said Larry. "I'm in Narcotics, remember?"

"You can't look into it?"

"Homicide's working outta One-D now. You expect me to walk into that station and start talkin random shit to those detectives?"

"Thought you mighta heard something, is all."

Larry let them wait. He *had* heard things. He knew what was going on because it was easy for any MPD officer to get information on an ongoing investigation without arousing suspicion. At roll call alone you could get up on most any case.

"They got nothin, far as I know," said Larry. "Evidence techs did their jobs. Autopsies been done. Right about now this case is getting cold. If Homicide had witnesses...that is, if they had any idea who the killers were, your boys would be in the box right now." He pointedly did not look at Nance and White.

"So they got jack nothin," said Nance.

"That's 'cause the work was clean," said White.

"Y'all were *paid* to do good work," said Mobley.

Ricardo looked at White. "Beano sayin, there ain't no need to boast."

"When you got a big dick," said Nance, "you wear tight pants."

"Let's cut all this *bull*shit," said Larry to Ricardo.

"What'sa matter, Officer?" said Nance. "You uncomfortable around men who do their jobs?"

"Your ventriloquist dummy better check himself," said Larry, speaking to White.

"All right, Earl," said Ricardo. "That's enough."

Nance and White fancied themselves professional hitters. They were auto service technicians who had met at the luxury import dealership where they both worked. Tired of the economic struggle and grease under their fingernails, they had done a murder-for-hire together, ten thousand dollars each, after reaching out to the minions of a drug dealer, up on homicide charges, who frequently brought his E Class into their shop. Nance and White's first kill was a potential witness. They were thorough and also indiscriminate. They killed women and those outside the game if they were asked to. The fact that one of them was black and one was white was attractive to clients. Either of them could go into certain neighborhoods without arousing suspicion. As their rep grew, they did several murders a year. They had no criminal records and had never been suspects. They thought they were smart and good at their work. They had merely been lucky.

"Sorry, *Larry*," said Nance, and White smiled.

"We do have an issue," said Ricardo.

"Say it," said Larry.

"I think you know what it is," said Ricardo. "Before Earl and Bernard destroyed those boys' cells, they checked their incoming and outgoing phone calls and text messages and they wrote those names and numbers down. The Lynch boy had been in contact with that man Spero Lucas the night we took him out. Tavon texted him the number of your squad car."

"I know that," said Larry. "We been through this already."

"What if Lucas ties you into this? Ties you to *us*."

"He ain't tied nothin yet. I been watching him."

"*Yet*," said Ricardo. "You willing to risk your career on that?" Ricardo made a sweeping motion with his hand. "Willin to risk all this? All I done worked for?"

"Tavon's brother's name was on that call list. His mother. Bunch a girls, too."

"So?"

"What you gonna do?" said Larry. "Kill everyone whose name was on that list?"

"Don't get smart with me, boy," said Ricardo. "I don't like it when you do."

Earl Nance chuckled.

"There's another matter, too," said Beano Mobley. "The youngun on Twelfth."

"What's his name again?" said Ricardo.

Larry didn't say it. He wished he had never mentioned the boy. He knew the young man had seen him the day Tavon had put the package in the trunk of his cruiser. And Larry had seen Lucas trying to talk to him outside his residence. But he wasn't about to encourage any more killing. He hadn't signed up for it. His so-called father had brought him into this, but he hadn't told him they'd be doing this kind of hard dirt.

"It's Lindsay," said Ricardo. "Right?"

"We can take care of it, you want," said Nance.

"Hold up," said Larry.

"Problem?" said Ricardo.

"I need to speak with you alone."

There was a long silence. Larry did not look at the others. He held his gaze on his father.

"In the back," said Ricardo.

Larry followed Ricardo through the door beside the gun cabinet and closed it behind them. They entered a smaller room than the office, one that carried no air of business at all but was rather a play pad that Ricardo and Beano Mobley used for sexual activities with women and, if they could get

147

them, girls. There was another bar on a rolling cart, a stereo, a small refrigerator, more chairs, a table, and two double beds. A coke mirror and photos of women on the wall. Two windows, barred on the outside, curtained on the inside, and a locked door that led to the rear of the building. Outside the door was a small area of gravel and dirt. Past it, weed trees and brush.

Ricardo sat in one of the chairs. He gestured to another. "Sit down, son."

"I'd rather stand."

"Sit. I ain't about to look up at you."

Larry took a seat and spread his legs wide.

"You shamed me in front of my people," said Ricardo. "Talkin to me like that."

"I'm not gonna have a heart-to-heart with you in front of that trash."

"They serve their purpose."

"Trash," said Larry. "I don't even want to be in the same room with 'em."

"Beano's my partner."

"I'm talking about White and his little Jesus freak."

"Far as those two go, I don't see us needing them again. Not for, you know, the foreseeable future."

"You tricked me, man."

"How so?"

"I was supposed to watch the transaction," said Larry. "Make sure no one rolled up on them while they were exchanging the money. It was you who called me on my cell and told me to bounce. *You* said that Nance and White had seen police cruising the neighborhood, down on Minnesota

Avenue. That the situation was too hot. You got me to leave up outta there so Nance and White could murder those boys. You knew I woulda had nothing to do with that."

"You're right," said Ricardo with a careless shrug.

"*Why?*"

" 'Cause you're soft," said Ricardo. There was no malice in his voice, or threat. He was simply stating the fact.

"I'm not about to kill anyone, if that's what you mean. You make it sound like a character flaw."

"Look. A decision was made that required a solution that I knew you wouldn't get behind. So I had to make sure you were removed from the scene. That simple enough for you?"

"Why'd you have to do those boys?"

"Let's just say it was a mutual decision between interested parties."

"Quit tryin to sound more educated than you are," said Larry.

Ricardo's face slackened and his eyes grew hard. He kept his voice level and low. "Those boys were punks playin a man's game. We eliminated the middleman, is all. You prof-ited. We all did. And we gonna keep makin money. I don't need you to do no violence and I ain't about to ask you to. I brought you in to identify persons of interest, seein as how you're hooked into that narco squad. You just keep doin that from time to time and we'll be straight."

"No more killin."

"*I* decide that."

Larry stared at his father with anemic eyes.

Ricardo knew that his son was trapped. To turn Ricardo and his crew in was to turn himself, now a corrupt officer of the law, in as well. Ricardo had reached out to his boy at just the right time. He was vulnerable, eager to please his old man, who'd walked into Larry's world with the promise of connecting and healing wounds. Shoot, the boy had become a police officer, in an act of twisted logic, to honor his father. Ricardo had played him well.

"I don't wanna be in with y'all no more," said Larry.

"You like what you got?" said Ricardo. "You like that pretty Escalade you drivin?"

Larry didn't answer. He stared at the floor.

"You *are* in," said Ricardo. "There's more money on the way, too. You just keep doin your little piece of it. I'll see to the rest."

"Don't be fuckin with no more kids," said Larry.

He got up out of his seat and left the room. Walking through the office, he stayed in stride, said nothing to Nance, White, or Mobley, kept going through the indoor bays, went out into the sunlight and fresh air, and did not even nod at the young men who were detailing the SUVs in the lot. He got into his Escalade and drove away.

Larry Holley thought about his father as he drove back into the city on Bladensburg Road.

He hadn't known Ricardo at all or seen him once throughout his childhood, coming up in the Kennedy Street corridor of Northwest. His mother worked hard, made it her mission to keep Larry in line. She did it, too. He grew up in an area where many boys failed, but he'd stayed straight. Had a half brother fathered by another man who got into some wrong, but he didn't let that boy influence him. Got decent grades, was active in church groups, community outreach, all that. Was tapped to play basketball because of his height, but didn't have the skills. Not a particularly social dude, not real good with women, but he knew that was partly due to his strange looks, which his mother called "unique." She said he'd gotten his nose and coloring from the man who impregnated her. She never called Ricardo his father. As for Larry, he wondered about Ricardo often, prayed to God that he'd come by and take him to a ball game or Six Flags. But he never did. Relatives said the man had been a police officer in his youth and still lived in the city. They hinted that he wasn't all the way right. It wasn't said, as it often is of ne'er-do-well relatives, with affection. In his mind Larry defended this man. He wanted his father to be better than they said he was. Ricardo became an imagined hero.

Larry had a goal. He did his two years of community college and then entered the academy. He became a policeman, like his father. In his fantasies, he would find his pop and, on a day he was wearing his uniform, visit him. His father would be pleased to see that Larry had made it. He'd be proud.

It didn't happen that way. Ricardo had come to *him*.

Larry had always heard, from the do-good types and folks at church, how a boy needed a man in his life to make him whole. But Larry had been doing fine before Ricardo Holley had sought him out. And when he did, it was as if Larry were terminal. He'd been ill since the day that cripple came to see him with his honeyed words and slick grin. It was like Ricardo had pulled him into an open grave. The man stank of death.

FOURTEEN

TIM McCARTHY had short curly hair of ginger and gray, a freckled face deeply lined from age and the sun, and a sturdy build. He sat at a table in a nondescript bar in a large hotel on New Jersey Avenue, not too far from his Internal Affairs Bureau office, located in MPD headquarters on Indiana. He had walked over to the hotel at lunchtime to meet Spero Lucas. Lucas sat across the table from him, his Moleskine notebook and iPhone set neatly before him. Both of them were having iced teas.

"Lawrence Holley," said Lucas.

"Goes by Larry," said McCarthy. "Narcotics and Special Investigations. What's your interest?"

"Just curious. He drifted into the margins of something I'm working on for a client."

"That's pretty vague."

"I can't say more."

"It's confidential, huh?"

"Exactly."

McCarthy laced his finger together and rested both hands on the table. He had a serene, confident way about him, a trait seen most often in military and law-enforcement types.

"Well?" said Lucas.

"I can't tell you anything," said McCarthy. "I agreed to meet you as a favor to Tom Petersen."

"So if you had something on Larry Holley..."

Smile fans appeared at the corners of McCarthy's eyes. "That would be confidential."

"You must have looked into him after our phone conversation."

"Something about the last name was familiar," said McCarthy.

"It rang a bell."

"More like an alarm."

"But you're not going to tell me why."

"No."

"Well, then," said Lucas amiably. McCarthy was one of those people, you looked at him and liked him. Lucas guessed no one had ever swung on this guy in a bar just for fun.

"Petersen said you served in Fallujah," said McCarthy.

"I did. And you went in with the initial wave."

"First Recon Battalion. I was just a chaplain."

"Just."

McCarthy looked Lucas over. "I heard you guys caught hell."

"It was interesting."

"I wish I could help you," said McCarthy.

"I understand."

They shook hands firmly across the table.

*   *   *

HE TOOK a bike ride that afternoon. He rode all the way to Lake Artemesia in Berwyn Heights, Maryland, a twenty-five-mile round trip, some of it into a headwind, on roads and the Northwest Branch trail. His idea was to lose himself in his pedaling and empty his brain to the degree that something new would come to him upon his return. He was pleasantly exhausted and ripped but no smarter after his shower. He sat in his reading chair and looked out onto the street, thinking, I have come to that part of the road that simply ends.

His eyes fluttered. He knew that he was about to drift to sleep. He thought, Maybe it's me. Maybe I'm not good enough for this job. I was a pretty good marine. I came back alive, though that was luck as much as training or skill. I protected my brothers. I killed men who were trying to kill me. But I am not much of an investigator, because I seem to have gone nowhere on this case at all.

His phone rang on the end table beside him. The light had dimmed in the room. He had been asleep for a while.

Lucas looked at the screen, showing a 301 number. He did not recognize the caller's name.

"Yes?"

"Spero Lucas?"

"That's right. Who's calling?"

"My name's Pete Gibson. I think you and I should meet."

"What *is* this?"

"It's about Holley."

"How'd you get my number?"

"Tim McCarthy. We were on the force together, way back in time." Gibson coughed. "I'm free tonight."

"Where?"

"You're over in Sixteenth Street Heights..."

"How do you know that?"

"Let's see, that's near Colorado Avenue....Too bad Cagney's is closed."

"*Been* closed. There's a place up on Georgia, between Geranium and Floral, coupla doors away from the Humane Society."

"Christ," said Gibson. "*That* joint. Give me an hour. I'm coming down from Frederick."

"How will I know you?"

"I'm sixty," said Gibson. "I still look like police."

Lucas ended the call. He got up out of his chair, energized.

LEO'S HAD an oak bar going front to back, twelve stools, and several deuces and four tops. The walls held a poster advertising an old Dick Gregory concert, a signed head shot of Jackie "Moms" Mabley, a Globe poster of James Brown and the Famous Flames at the Howard, and travel posters of little white houses set against the blue of the Aegean Sea. The jukebox was filled with obscure soul singles. The place was owned by a Greek, the bald, eagle-beaked Leo, who, like Lucas's brother, was only called Leonidas by his mother. It was a neighborhood spot that serviced all types, determined alcoholics and casual drinkers alike.

Lucas had spotted Pete Gibson right away when he'd come through the door. Gibson indeed looked like a cop. He had a strong jaw, a neatly trimmed Vandyke beard, pinkish skin, and a clean dome shaved close on the sides. His light blue eyes were intense; his smile was white and tight. He wore neatly creased slacks and a plaid button-down shirt with a pack of Marlboro Reds in the breast pocket. Lucas guessed that the shirt's label read Arrow or Gant.

They were seated at a deuce in the center of the room. Gibson was drinking a Bud Light straight from the neck. Lucas was working on a Heineken. An old song with a female vocalist and big production was coming from the juke, and two guys standing up at the bar were arguing loudly about the singer.

"It's Bettye LaVette," said one of the men, a short guy with a white-man's Afro that looked like a Harpo wig.

"Nope," said the other man, blond, rail thin, with a little beer hump. "It's that chick who did the Stones song before the Stones. What the fuck is the name of that song?" It came to him and he slammed his palm down on the bar. " 'Time Is on My Side.' Irma Thomas!"

"But what's the name of *this* song?"

"Buy me a drink and I'll tell ya."

"Drink this," said the guy in the wig.

"All the Einsteins come in here," said Gibson, jerking his thumb in the direction of the two guys at the bar. "I used to stop in once in a while on my way home. The Greek behind the stick was a kid then."

"When was that?" said Lucas.

"The early seventies, when I was a patrol officer in Four-D."

"You grow up in D.C.?"

"No. I was raised over in Cheverly. You know why I picked the MPD? It paid two hundred dollars more a year than the PG County police. And in the District I could become an officer at twenty years old. They didn't require any college then, either. I wasn't about to sit in a classroom. I was ready."

"So, patrol in the Fourth District," said Lucas, trying to move it along.

"Yep. Worked K-Nine for a while after that. I was good with dogs. Then I moved over to Six-D, where the action was. They made me a sergeant. I worked patrol first, then Tact. Then I got my own investigative squad. Tim McCarthy was one of my detectives. Good guy, real good character."

"You guys were on homicides?"

"No. We investigated crimes that were serious but not homicides. Unarmed robberies, B-Ones..."

"B-Ones?"

"Burglary Ones. Dudes who break into houses. Dangerous guys, much more serious than burglars who do warehouses and commercial properties. We also assisted the sex squad when they went after multiple offenders." Gibson patted his breast pocket, jonesing for a smoke. "That squad I had was a good bunch. This was in the mid to late eighties. The low years. You're too young to remember."

"I know about it."

"Four hundred and some homicides a year, all kinds of violent shit, a big piece of it east of the river. The Mayfair-Paradise homes alone, Christ. The Jamaicans came down here from New York, got off the train at New Carrollton, and took over the crack trade. Auto pistols, Mac-Tens, you name it. That was when the department switched over from the thirty-eight to the Glock, 'cause we couldn't compete with the firepower on the street. Anyway, eventually I made lieutenant, got shipped off to Seven-D, and then Two. That was a cakewalk. That's where I ended my career as an LT. Like, twelve years ago."

"So you couldn't have known Larry Holley."

"You mean the kid. He was a baby when I was in uniform."

"You said—"

"I said this was about Holley. I didn't say anything about Larry."

"You lost me," said Lucas.

"First things first. McCarthy called me to say you two had a meet. But I didn't get any information from him and he doesn't know that we're sitting here. I'm not gonna do anything to jam Tim up."

"I get it."

"I'm not here about the kid," said Gibson. "I'm here to talk about his father. Richard Holley."

Lucas had no idea where this was going, but Gibson had his attention. "Go on."

"Richard came on the force during that hiring binge, when the Feds mandated that the MPD bring on police in numbers because of the crack wars and the homicides. Some of those people turned out to be good police. Some of them were plain unqualified. They must not have background-checked Richard Holley too good, 'cause he was a real cum-sack. Came up with some drug dealers west of North Capitol and south of Florida, down around O and N, the area around

Hanover Place. First time I heard about Holley, a sergeant from Vice came into my office and made some inquiries. Holley was a patrolman at the time. This guy had suspicions that Holley was pointing out vice officers when he was off duty to his little knothead buddies from the neighborhood. After that I had my eye on him."

Lucas had opened his notebook and was taking notes. Gibson stopped talking and watched him.

Lucas looked up. "You mind?"

"That's fine. One thing you should know: I hear Richard goes by Ricardo now. He might even have legally changed his name. You know why? He's a P-hound. Real liberal in that way, celebrates diversity and all that shit. Likes all the women, any kind of color he can get, long as it's pink inside. Asshole probably thinks he can score more Spanish pussy with a name like Ricardo. I mean, he's black, allegedly, but he doesn't look like any black guy I ever saw. Weird-lookin dude. With that fucked-up poof of hair he had, and his long nose. The guys used to call him Rooster."

"I'm guessing he didn't like that."

"Yeah, but fuck what he didn't like." Gibson killed his beer, caught the eye of the bar's sole waitress, and put up two fingers in the air. "One night Holley was Ten Ninety-nine in a patrol car over by Forty-second and Dix, near Fort Mahan Park." Gibson looked at Lucas's notebook. "Ten Ninety-nine means he was riding alone."

"I know what it means."

"This is what Holley told the investigators: He pulled over to speak to a young man who was sitting on a bench and looked suspicious. Holley exited his vehicle and

approached the subject. At that time, he said, he spotted narcotics and ancillary narcotic materials on or around the
bench and ordered the subject to stand. Holley said that
there was a flash of light and extreme pain in his hip and he
knew he had been shot. He went down, the subject stood and
fired twice more, Holley returned fire, and the subject fled."

"Holley was okay?"

"The round went in his side and came out his ass, but it
did some permanent damage. At the scene, Mobile Crime
recovered a vial of rock, an empty pint of Bacardi and a plastic cup, tinfoil, match pads, and a napkin."

"You got a good memory."

"I know. A daylight search of the area recovered a Charter
Arms five-shot thirty-eight with partially shaved numbers,
two live rounds, and one spent round lying under the hammer. The assault weapon. Holley said that he had an extended
mag in his service weapon. Twenty rounds, one live in the
chamber. But when the techs checked out his weapon, it was
fully loaded. No expended casings were found at the scene."

"So the suspect fired and only one round took effect in
Holley. Holley never returned fire like he said. Why would
he make up that story when it could be easily checked?"

Gibson shrugged. "To make it more dramatic. To say he
had more guts than he did. Or maybe because he's a professional fucking liar."

"Did they find the shooter?"

"I'm getting to that. I volunteered the services of my
squad. Even though Holley was an asshole, he was still
police, and when you shoot a police officer it's a hot case. We
wanted it."

The waitress arrived, placed two beers on the table, and picked up the empties.

"Thank you, darlin," said Gibson. He showed her his white teeth. When he looked back at Lucas he had lost the smile. "Fingerprints found on the objects at the scene were unusable, and the ATF search on the weapon was negative on account of the shave. Holley met with an MPD artist, and a composite drawing was made of the suspect. Holley said the shooter had a strong body odor, so we distributed the drawing to the area homeless shelters. The media, TV and the papers, they got it as a crime-of-the-week, which meant it was heavily publicized. I'd like to tell you that it was keen detective work that made the case, but as usual we were hoping for someone to come forward with information. The first tip we got was bullshit. A source said a dude she knew had bragged about shooting a police, but when we busted in his door in those homes down around Half Street, it was nothing but a pipe pad. We did find a nine-millimeter in the oven, but there was no link to this particular crime. Then, sixteen days after the event, we got a Crime Solvers tip that a guy named Curtis Dickerson had done the shooting. The source said Dickerson was staying in a crib down in Poto- mac Gardens. We do a little research, he's got hard priors, we get a photo, show an array of photos to Holley, he pops Dickerson out of the array. That night, me, Tim McCarthy, and this other detective, Ballard, we go to Dickerson's apart- ment. Dickerson's not there. We stake out the place from the parking lot; Dickerson doesn't show. It's late; we go home, plan to return with some heavy hitters."

"And?"

"We should've stayed."

"What happened?"

"The next day, we come back with a no-knock warrant. We didn't have to use a battering ram 'cause the door had already been busted in. Dickerson's inside, shot to death, facedown on his bed. One in the back of the head."

"You think what?"

"Holley somehow got hold of Dickerson's address. I think he killed him or had him executed by his neighborhood buddies. Holley ID'd Dickerson's corpse as the shooter. Homicide caught the Dickerson case, but it was never closed."

"Holley stayed on the force?"

"No. That bullet gave him a limp. He retired soon after all this went down. Shitbird gets a sixty-six-and-two-thirds disability, tax free, for the rest of his life. *God*, that eats me up."

"You don't mind my sayin so, you still seem pretty jacked up about all this."

"I made a mistake on that case, and I don't like that. More to the point, I don't like dirty police. I'm not talking about small stuff. This guy was all the way wrong. The fact that he wore a uniform and got away with what he did . . ."

Gibson's voice trailed off. He and Lucas took long swigs of beer.

"What about the son?" said Lucas. "Larry."

"I don't know much about him. There was a rumor that Richard's kid had joined the force. I heard he looks just like his old man. Other than that, not a thing. What's your interest in him?"

"I can't say for sure."

Gibson coughed into his fist. "Can't or won't?"

"Honestly, I don't have enough information to even talk about it. He kinda drifted into something I was working on."

"McCarthy said you do investigative work for an attorney."

"I'm solo on this one."

"And you can't tell me what it's about."

"It's better if you don't know."

Gibson sat back. "You think Larry Holley is connected to your case."

"In some way."

"You gonna shadow him?"

"That would be a start."

"Tailing a police officer on duty's a stupid game."

"I don't know any other way."

"It's better to look at him off the clock."

"How would I find him?"

"Not a problem," said Gibson. "I've got someone inside who can get me the information you need."

"Obliged," said Lucas. "Maybe I could get some current intel on the father as well."

"I'll get you that, too. It's a lead pipe cinch the father and son are sleeping in the same rotten bed." Gibson got up out of his chair. "I gotta have a smoke. You comin?"

Lucas followed him through the dark room. The music dimmed to nothing as the front door closed behind them. They stood on the sidewalk, facing Georgia, in front of the bar's plate glass window. Traffic rolled by, north- and southbound, but it was quieter out here than inside and pleasantly cool. Gibson flipped opened his hardpack lid and offered a cigarette to Lucas, who declined with a short wave of his hand. Gibson lit his smoke with a Zippo he produced from his slacks. He took that first good long drag and exhaled slowly.

"I used to like driving up Georgia Avenue," said Gibson. "Coming up it after I got off shift. All the neon liquor store signs. Beautiful."

"You were on nights, mostly?"

"I really loved working midnights. No brass to deal with. In those hours, just police and criminals were out on the street. The game was pure." Gibson turned his head and looked at Lucas. "I wish I knew what the fuck you were into."

"I wish I could tell you," said Lucas.

Gibson double-dragged on his Red and squinted against the smoke. "I got nothin going on right now. *Nothin*. Get it?"

"I'm sorry to hear that."

"You know, when I was tellin you that story in there...I think I got an erection."

"Every cloud has a silver lining."

"I miss those years. Odd to say it, but I never had so much fun in my life. I got up every morning and I couldn't wait to go to work. Does that make any sense?"

"It does," said Lucas.

"Gimme your phone number," said Gibson.

Lucas did it. Gibson gave him his.

FIFTEEN

PETE GIBSON had said that he had "someone inside" who could get Lucas the information he was looking for, and the next day Gibson made good on his claim. Lucas now had in hand the addresses of record for Ricardo Holley and his son Larry.

"I owe you," said Lucas.

Gibson said, "Stay in touch."

Lucas phoned Marquis Rollins and told him he had a little work for him, if he was interested. Marquis said that he was.

The following morning, Lucas and Marquis were having an early breakfast at the Tastee Diner on Cameron Street in downtown Silver Spring. Marquis was dressed conservatively: Adidas track pants and a matching shirt, with his usual New Balance sneakers. Lucas was in Dickies. Marquis was having eggs over easy with hash browns and a small steak; Lucas was enjoying his favorite Tastee dish, the chipped beef on toast.

Their roving waitress arrived, coffee pot in hand, and refilled their cups.

"*Habesha*, baby," said Marquis.

"You speak my language?" she said with a brilliant smile.

"Enough to let you know I care."

The waitress, still smiling, drifted. She held the smile as she filled the cups of a couple of Montgomery County police officers in a nearby booth.

"It's damn near all Ethiopians working here," said Marquis. "I mean they're all *over* this neighborhood."

"Eritreans, too," said Lucas. "They do work hard."

"I like the way the women look. They got that beautiful reddish skin, you know? Real nice complexions. But they won't give me the time of day."

"She smiled at you."

"She smiling at everyone."

"True."

"I can't get to first base with these Ethiopian gals."

"They can't *all* like you, man."

"I don't understand what it is. African women just don't want to get with African American men."

"Maybe you ought to call Al Sharpton. He could organize a protest or somethin."

"You got his number?"

"Yeah, we're tight."

Lucas and Marquis went to the register to settle up. It was time to get to work.

LUCAS AND Marquis drove over to a car rental lot on Sligo Avenue and got a couple of vehicles, a beige Buick Enclave for Marquis and a black GMC Acadia for Lucas. Same platform, different badges. Marquis got into the Buick and made sure that he and his prosthetic leg fit comfortably in the driver's seat. He said that he was good with it, and they went into the rental office, where a couple of Ethiopian men ran the paperwork.

On the way out of the office, Lucas said, "Aren't you going to comment on their complexions?"

Lucas got some equipment out of his Jeep and met Marquis by the rentals. There he handed Marquis a business-grade Motorola two-way radio, and an earpiece with an in-line mic.

"I gotta wear this thing?" said Marquis. "I'm gonna look like a newscaster."

"It's easier. Voice activated, so it leaves your hands free. You can keep one on the wheel and the other on your johnson."

"Thanks for thinking of me."

"I know you like to multitask."

They coordinated channels and frequencies, got into the rentals, and drove off the lot.

RICARDO HOLLEY'S residence was on 9th Street, Northwest, uptown between Tuckerman and Somerset. A middle-class neighborhood where teenagers attended Coolidge High, kids played ball down on 3rd Street, and adults got their beer and wine from the Safeway on Piney Branch Road. The block contained row houses mixed with detached houses in varying conditions. Quiet, most of the time.

Ricardo's place was an old one-story bungalow painted dark brown with black trim. It did not look inviting. The windows were barred, the grass was uncut, and there were no flowers or toys in the yard. A small alarm system sign was planted in the grass near the front steps. A Lincoln Mark V, white with a white landau roof and opera window cutout, sat out front.

Lucas and Marquis were parked nearby on different cross streets. Both of them had the bungalow in view. Lucas had a pair of Nikon 10x50 security binoculars on the bucket beside him, a bottle of water, and an empty piss bottle on the floor of the backseat. He and Marquis had been out here for an hour or so. It was now midmorning.

"Here he comes," said Lucas, speaking into the mic, his radio activated in the console cup holder to his right.

"I see him," answered Marquis.

Ricardo closed the front door behind him and limped onto the sidewalk toward his car, holding a manila envelope under his arm. He was wearing a black shirt and pants, a dark ensemble more suitable for night. Ricardo had a long thin nose. His hair was cottony and receding.

"Looks like that Jewish dude," said Marquis, "half of that old-time duo, you know those guys who sing those songs and, like, harmonize?"

"Simon and Garfunkel," said Lucas.

"Whichever one got the fucked-up hair."

"What do you think Ricardo is?"

"You mean, is he mixed? Shit, I don't know *what* he is."

"On the force they used to call him Rooster."

"I see it," said Marquis.

The envelope Ricardo carried bulged with weight. He popped the trunk on his car and dropped the envelope inside. Closed the lid, got into his Lincoln, and started it up.

"What you suppose that was?" said Marquis. "Paperwork, somethin?"

"He doesn't look like much of a businessman to me," said Lucas. "Could be cash."

"Car like that," said Marquis, "he's gonna be easy to tail."

"So let him get far ahead," said Lucas. "And remember, he's ex-police. He notices things."

"Right."

Ricardo stopped at the nearby Safeway for a Starbucks coffee, then drove south on Georgia. Lucas and Marquis took turns as the lead tail and kept well back. Mobile surveillance was easier on heavily trafficked streets than it was on side streets, and Ricardo did not stray. Down in Park View he stopped on the Avenue and went into a well-known establishment that featured pole-and-freak-dancing onstage.

"He's goin in that titty bar," said Marquis, driving past it.

"Might be in there for a beer or two," said Lucas, behind him. "I could use some lunch."

"Already?"

"We better fuel up. You know that place I like down here?"

"Got that sign, with the trout jumpin out water, a hook in its mouth. That one?"

"Yep. Get two fish sandwiches. Extra hot sauce on mine. I'll park on Georgia and keep an eye on the club."

They ate their sandwiches in their respective vehicles. Ricardo did not emerge from the club. Marquis told Lucas that he needed to piss, and Lucas said to go ahead, that he would use his bottle if he needed to and stay where he was. Marquis got out of the Buick and crossed Georgia, holding out his palm in a halt gesture to the oncoming traffic as he limped deeply over the asphalt and then the sidewalk, heading toward a gas station that had a restroom. He stopped to talk to a man outside a liquor store, a man he surely didn't know, a conversation that had probably started over spare change and had gone on to involve the Wizards and the Redskins and would eventually lead to God and church and some message involving a blessed day.

Lucas felt a rush of affection, watching his friend. Dipping down the sidewalk, trying to get from A to B. He'd be walking on a titanium shin pole and plastic knee for the rest of his life. But always positive, because Marquis looked for the good. A man with faith.

RICARDO CAME out of the bar around one o'clock in the afternoon and drove east, taking Irving Street to Michigan Avenue, then South Dakota Avenue to Bladensburg Road. Again, major roads, but with frequent stoplights, so they had to be cautious. Marquis offered to take the lead, reasoning that Ricardo would be less likely to notice a youngish black man driving a ubiquitous SUV in the city. Eventually they all appeared to be coming to some sort of destination in Maryland, out there near the Peace Cross, where Ricardo turned off Annapolis Road and headed into a commercial and industrial strip in Edmonston.

"Let him go," said Lucas, who knew the area from his frequent bike rides up along the nearby Northwest Branch trail. "That's Tanglewood at the end and nothing much else. He's got to be stopping. Bunch of little streets back there, but we can always make his Lincoln."

"Copy that," said Marquis.

They drove for a bit, then cut back on 450 and went down the road where Ricardo had turned, staying several car lengths from each other. Lucas in his GMC had taken the lead. They went by several fenced-in businesses. On the road itself Lucas noted that there were signs prohibiting stopping and parking. They did not see the Lincoln, and began to hit the side roads, the U, V, and W streets, the high forties on the cross. Finally, near a dead end, Lucas neared a business with a big sign that said Mobley Detailing, and he saw the white Mark V in its lot, young guys shining up a car, Ricardo idling, waiting to enter a cinder-block building before one of several bay doors that was coming up on its track, and Lucas said, "Go back." He and Marquis both reversed, swung around in driveways, and drove back to a place where there was something like a turnaround. They got nose to ass in their vehicles like police and talked to each other through open windows.

"Stay here," said Lucas. "I'm gonna walk down there and take a couple of photos."

"Seems kind of reckless to me."

"Parking on that road's illegal; we'd stick out. And I don't like that dead end."

"Whatever you say, cowboy."

Lucas found a spot to park the GMC, removed his headset, and got out of the vehicle. He nodded at Marquis and began to walk down the road. He looked like a working-class guy in his Dickies shirt and pants, young dude, short hair, nothing about him standing out among other guys who looked like him here, going about their blue-collar business in Edmonston. A jellybean Ford F-150 came up on him and passed, raising dust. There was no one else walking on the road, but that was all right. He pulled his iPhone from his pants pocket and touched the camera app, readying the device. He went by an auto body shop and was about fifty yards away from Mobley Detailing when he heard the rumble of a V-8 approaching from behind. As he turned his head there was a black Cadillac Escalade beside him, come to a crawl, and his stomach flipped as he locked eyes for a moment with the man behind the wheel, who was a younger version of Ricardo Holley. The Escalade accelerated and turned into the lot of the detail shop. Lucas spun around and walked back, his face flushed.

"Stupid," he said, and repeated it, muttering as he quickstepped down the road.

Marquis watched him approach, knew at once that something was wrong. He waited for Lucas to come up to the Buick.

"What happened?"

"I was burned," said Lucas.

"You sure?"

"Ricardo's son Larry."

"The police officer?"

"He stopped right beside me and looked straight into my eyes. I'm certain he knows who I am. He drove past me in his squad car last week when I was surveilling a house on Twelfth. Got my plate numbers, most likely. Him and whoever he's in with probably know where I live."

"What now?"

"I blew it," said Lucas. "Let's go."

*   *   *

LARRY HOLLEY had been let into the cinder-block building by Beano Mobley, who told him that his father was waiting for him in the office. Earl Nance and Bernard White were standing by their Tahoe, parked beside the Lincoln in the bay. Nance was smoking a cigarette, grinning at Larry as he approached. Larry did not acknowledge either of them as he went back to the office and knocked on the door. It opened, and Ricardo Holley stepped aside to let his son pass.

"Son," said Ricardo, regarding his offspring in his off-brand jeans, white T, and billowing windbreaker. The boy had no style.

"We got a problem," said Larry.

"Come on in and set."

Ricardo limped across the office and had a seat behind his desk. Behind him, the gun case and the door that led to the second office. There was cash money on the desk, stacks of it in twenties, tens, and fives. Larry eyed it warily.

"I said have a seat."

"I'll stand."

"What's on your mind?"

"Thought you said we were done with those two."

"Nance and White? I said we were done with 'em for *now*. Anyway, they're here for the same reason you are." Ricardo's eyes went to the money, then back to Larry. "To get paid."

"I thought they *been* paid."

"You know I like to parse it out a little bit at a time. Y'all might go on a spendin spree, attract some unwanted attention. I wouldn't like that."

"You're actin like you're the bank."

"I am."

"What about the rest of it?"

"What's left is safe at my spot. You don't need to worry. It'll come to you eventually. Your father ain't gonna let you starve."

"*Now* you're my father," said Larry.

Ricardo smiled. "You said you had a problem."

"*We* do," said Larry. "It's that Lucas dude. The one who's been camped out on Twelfth? I just saw him walkin down the road, not far from this shop."

If Ricardo was shaken he did not show it. "So?"

"What you mean, *so?*"

"What's he gonna do? He's not police. *You* are. You see what I'm sayin?" Ricardo gestured with his hand as if he were shooing away a fly. "I don't want you to worry over this. You ran his plates. *You* gave me his address. You did your thing and now I know where to find him. Let me take care of it."

"I told you, I don't want no more violence."

"Neither do I. I was thinking of setting up a meet. Whatever Lucas is looking for, it's got to involve money. That's true for every man, right? You of all people should know." Ricardo picked up a rubber-banded stack of cash and tossed it forward on the desk so that it landed within reach of Larry. "Speaking of which."

Larry hesitated. He picked up the cash and shoved it inside his windbreaker.

"Buy something for yourself," said Ricardo. "Maybe some new vines."

Larry looked at Ricardo, Bama material, wearing all black in the middle of the day, rayon shirt and slacks, looking like Zorro, telling him how to dress.

"Somethin funny?" said Ricardo.

"Nothin is," said Larry.

"You were grinnin."

"Don't lie to me again," said Larry. He walked from the room, closing the door behind him.

"Mother*fuck* you," said Ricardo, staring at the door. The light had left his eyes.

LUCAS AND Marquis dropped the rentals off at the lot on Sligo Avenue, then went to their own vehicles, parked near a corner Spanish market. Lucas took the radio and headset from Marquis, stowed it in the back of the Jeep, and pulled two water bottles from the cargo area. He handed one to Marquis. The two of them stood in the street and drank deeply.

"What's our next move?" said Marquis, wiping off his chin.

"You're out," said Lucas. "I don't like where this is going, and I don't want you involved with it anymore. I'll settle up with you for today when I get my cut."

"That's not why I asked. I know you're good for the money. I'm worried about you."

"I'll be fine."

"No doubt. But that look you got right now? I seen that in your eyes before. April twenty-six, two thousand and four, to be exact. In those houses on the edge of the Jolan graveyard."

Lucas nodded. "That was some day."

"The hajjis was comin in by taxicab and flatbed trucks. Must have been hundreds of 'em, wearing them checkerboard scarves."

"Kaffiyehs," said Lucas.

"You took point. I see that flashlight attached to the barrel of your M-Sixteen. I see you leading the way into those dark rooms, and the muzzle flash of those AKs, the walls just shredding from the rounds. I still dream all that."

And I see you sparing no one, thought Marquis. Emptying your mag into the heads and chests of the ones you put down. But then we all did that. When you kill a man twice, you know he can't get up and shoot at you again.

"It was somethin," said Lucas.

"All those bullshit movies about adrenaline-junkie soldiers and marines? I never served with anyone like that."

"Neither did I."

"It wasn't about thrill seekers. It was about emotion. We had a bond, man."

"We still do."

"But you can't say more than one or two words about it."

"What's to say? We don't have to talk about it, because both of us were there. To try and talk about it with someone who wasn't there...what's the point?"

"So, again," said Marquis, "what are you fixin to do?"

"I'm going back to that detailing shop on my bike. I can slip in there easier on two wheels. Take some photos, shit like that."

"You don't have your squad anymore."

"I won't take any unnecessary chances," said Lucas. "I want to live."

Marquis held out his hand. "Two-One, Luke."

"Two-One."

They tapped fists.

SIXTEEN

LUCAS CHANGED into black shorts, padded in the seat and lined with spandex leggings, a gray poly shirt that wicked, and gray shoes with steel-shanked soles. He carried his bike, an aluminum frame, gray Trek, down the stairs of his apartment and out to his Jeep. He dropped the back bench and slid the bike into the Cherokee, then checked to make sure he had his gloves, sunglasses, helmet, and phone.

He drove out to Hyattsville, Maryland, via Queens Chapel Road and Hamilton Street, and stopped in the lot of the 38th Street Park, through which ran the paved Northwest Branch trail. He got onto his bike and pedaled southeast, staying in the middle gears, through open fields, past woods, across Rhode Island Avenue, and finally across Alternate Route 1, navigating through fast vehicular traffic. He dipped down onto Tanglewood Drive, entered the industrial district of Edmonston, and cruised at a steady pace.

Winding around 46th and cutting off of Upshur, he took another high-forty street and crossed through the two-syllable, bottom-of-the-alphabet roads, Varnum, Webster, and Windom. He passed low-slung commercial buildings, many fenced in, many with security cameras mounted on their entranceways and walls. There were no other bikers back here, but with his gray-and-black clothing and gray bike he did not stand out. Also, his face was obscured by his helmet and shades. He slowed as he neared Mobley Detailing, seeing young men working on an SUV in its front lot, seeing no other vehicles. The employees were listening to go-go music coming from the SUV's open doors and they did not look up as he almost silently rolled by. He went to the end of the road and dismounted his bike. He walked it across the street and laid it down far back and out of sight of the Mobley lot, then he got his iPhone out of the small zippered pack fitted beneath the Trek's saddle. He walked along the stone wall of an elevated train track, behind a thin line of weed trees and brush, taking photos of the Mobley building and its geography, noting the fence topped with two strands of barbed wire, which could be easily climbed and jumped, noting that there were no cameras mounted on the building's face or above its front door or bay doors. The employees spoke to one another, joked and laughed, but never looked away from their task, and he made it easily behind the building, which was unfenced and bordered more thin woods and the train track wall, and he took photos of the rear of the building and its fortified back door.

His breathing was easy. He was in shape and he was calm. He'd barely broken a sweat.

INSIDE THE building, in the main office, Ricardo Holley sat behind his desk. Beano Mobley sat on the edge of the desk, a cigar butt lodged in the corner of his mouth. Earl Nance and Bernard White were seated on the couch. They were all having drinks, scotch for Nance and White, cognac for Holley and Mobley. The money had been cut up and distributed, and the atmosphere should have been celebratory, but the mood in the room was far from light.

"Your boy makes me nervous, Ricardo," said Nance.

"Ain't no need to stress," said Holley. "He's in now. He can't spill to no one and he can't walk. He don't even know what's going on, for real."

"Is he gonna get you more business?" said White.

"We don't need him to identify anyone else for the time being," said Holley. "We just gonna milk what we got for now and see how it goes. Make a few more pickups and move it on the wholesale level. There's cash in that. When it dries up, we'll regroup."

Holley and Mobley shared a look. Holley was being deliberately vague with the two hitters. They were on a need-to-know basis. Just like Larry.

"Larry don't like it that we did those boys," said Nance.

"He likes money," said Holley.

"What are we gonna do about that other thing?" said Nance. Holley had told him about Lucas when he'd poured them their drinks.

"What do *you* think we should do?" said Holley.

"Are you worried?"

"I'm not worried about him going to the police. He's motivated by cash. But that don't make him any less relentless. I don't think he's gonna stop comin."

"If you want," said Nance, "we'll just take care of it."

"Shit just got all complicated when we got into this marijuana thing," said Mobley in his gravelly voice. "I told you, Ricardo—"

"I know you did."

"Gun business just simpler. We should have stuck *to* it."

"Still, we got a problem," said Holley. "Hindsight ain't gonna make it disappear."

"It's about to be Saturday night," said Nance, fingering the wood crucifix hanging outside his shirt. "Young man like Lucas, you know he's gonna step out."

"You nominating yourself?" said Holley.

"Just me," said Nance. "Bernard might scare him off, seein as how he's a black dude with all that size."

"And you with no size," said White, amused. "He might not even notice your ass at all."

"Why you gotta say that, Bernard?" said Nance.

"'Cause you a pimp-squeak."

"It's pipsqueak, dumbass."

"See? You said it yourself."

"I don't want this getting back to Larry," said Holley. "We might still need his services."

"He won't know shit," said Nance. "I'll do it subtle. I won't even make any noise."

"Bernard?" said Holley.

"Man's got something to prove," said White. "Let him prove it."

The room went silent. Mobley glanced over at his partner, whose face showed no emotion.

"Well?" said Nance.

Ricardo Holley nodded. "Do what you do."

*   *   *

BACK ACROSS the street, from the side of an electrical supply house, Lucas watched as the bay door opened and a black Chevy Tahoe emerged. Behind the Tahoe, two figures followed on foot from the darkness of the interior bays: Ricardo Holley and a short, muscular, middle-aged man wearing a cap. Through the windshield of the Tahoe, Lucas saw a big black man behind the wheel, all neck and shoulders, and a much smaller white man in the passenger bucket, his face barely clearing the dash. As they drove out of the lot, Lucas took photographs. He could only hope that the stills would capture the plates. He watched as the short man said a few words to the employees and gestured at the SUV they were working on. Obviously this was a man in charge. Perhaps it was Mobley himself.

Ricardo and the boss went back inside the building. Lucas picked up his bike, fitted his left foot into the toe clip, swung his right leg over the saddle, and took off.

AS SOON as Lucas got back to his apartment, he sat down at the kitchen table and studied the photographs on his phone. He spread his fingers on the screen to make the photos larger. He opened his notebook and with a pen he sketched the Mobley Detailing building from various vantage points. He did not know how this helped him exactly, but it was habit, and sometimes when he looked at sketches he found that he could "see" things he could not see in photographs. But this did not happen now.

He got up and paced the room. He was amped up. He wanted a woman. He went into his bedroom and lay down on a camping mat and stretched and did crunches until his abs ached. He did six sets of pushups on his rotating stands, twenty-five reps, three sets normal hand-width apart, three sets wide stance. He did pull-ups on the bar set high in the door frame. He took a shower and dressed in jeans and a fitted black T-shirt; he felt clean, strong, and relaxed. He went out to his living room and sat in his reading chair and looked out the window. Dusk had arrived.

What did he know? He realized that he knew little for certain, but he had some ideas.

Larry Holley was in with his father, Ricardo, and the others at the detailing shop. Larry was in the Narcotics squad and had probably been tapped by his father to identify persons of interest and shake them down. Tavon and Edwin, under suspicion because of their involvement with known marijuana dealer Anwan Hawkins, were perfect marks. Looked at rationally, it was actually a good business arrangement. Assuming Tavon and Edwin were allowed to keep a cut, they had a lookout and protection in the form of police. In turn, Larry, his father, and their crew made money for themselves. Which was what was bothering Lucas. If it *was* all good, why were Tavon and Edwin killed?

The one thing Lucas did know was that he had been identified. Because Larry Holley was police, he could easily bring up all kinds of information on him. Where he lived, where his family lived, phone numbers, and more. The Holleys and their minions could get to him. They could get to his brother and his mom. The defense against this, he felt, was not in passivity but rather in aggression.

He fell asleep in his chair.

He was riding shotgun beside his father in the old man's truck, a two-tone Chevy Silverado. The Van Lucas he saw was around forty, big chested, a bit overweight, with a beard and a full head of curly hair. The windows of the truck were down, and from the dash tape deck the Stones were doing "Loving Cup," Mick singing, "I'm the man that brings you roses, when you ain't got none." His father was smiling, and through the windshield Lucas could see the people they knew in their neighborhood, the auto body guys and the Wanderer and the Hispanic workers standing by their 4Runners and the African barbers, waving at them as they passed. He saw his mother, also twenty years younger, walking their dog, Shilo, the animal stopping to pee in a bed of wild mint, and Lucas thought, That's nice, Shilo's alive. His father turned to him and asked, *"Thoolevis,* Spero?" the standard Greek man's question for his son, and Lucas said, "Yeah, I'm workin." When Lucas looked back through the windshield they were on Lincoln Road, Northeast, and with a sense of dread he realized where they were going and he said, *"No,* Dad, not yet," and his father pulled the truck over and kept it running. Nodding at the iron gate arched over the entrance to Glenwood Cemetery, he looked at his son and said, "Wanna come in?"

Lucas opened his eyes, startled. It was dark in the room and the streetlamps outside cast a pale yellow light on the darkened landscape. He sat in his chair, staring out the window, still hearing his father's voice. He wiped tears off his face.

Lucas stood. He felt like having a beer, but he didn't want to drink alone. The bar up on Georgia was as good as any. He brushed his teeth, washed his face, and came back out to the living room. He reached for the keys to his Jeep but picked up only his house key instead.

It was a nice night. He decided to walk.

LUCAS WALKED north on the Piney Branch Road that was not the same thoroughfare known by commuters but more like the urban-alley version of a country lane. He could hear cars moving to the west of him on 16th Street, but it was quiet back here tonight. A big engine moved somewhere behind him, and he turned his head and saw a flash of black vehicle on a cross street, and he kept moving his feet. He crossed Gallatin, then Hamilton, and made a right on the wide and majestic Colorado Avenue and headed northeast. Then he was in the small commercial district at 14th and Colorado. He walked by the Gold Corner Grocery, where he often bought beer, Louis' Barber Shop, Colorado Café, Florescence Beauty Salon, and the Ethiopian market called Mekides. He didn't have to look to recognize the business names because he knew them by heart. Many people, mostly black and Hispanic, were out. He walked by the beautifully maintained Longfellow apartments with their center-screened porches and iron balconies, and a man who smelled of alcohol walked toward him and said, *"Hola,"* and Lucas said, *"Hola, como estas,"* which was nearly all the Spanish he knew. At 13th Street he walked due north and crossed at the Missouri Avenue light. He approached Quackenbos Street, where he cut right as he often did and began to walk across the dark weeded field of Fort Stevens Park.

To his left were the historic fort, the trenches, ammunition bunkers, cannons, and flagpole. He stayed to the field and arrived at a gravel driveway that led up to the parking lot between the Methodist church and a four-square colonial with a wraparound porch, which was also church property and unlit behind its windows. Lucas often cut through the lot and descended the steep concrete steps that dropped down to Georgia Avenue. He passed a bucket truck and construction materials and went up a rise and came to the lot, lit faintly by a lamp hung on the side of the stone church.

In the lot stood a man.

Lucas stopped fifty feet shy of the man and studied him. His face seemed flat and his eyes were set wide. His skin was devoid of color in spots. His hair was lank. He wore jeans and a T-shirt rolled up at the sleeves to show thickly veined biceps. He was a small man, but he was strong and wired tight.

Lucas walked toward him.

The lot, empty of cars, was so greatly elevated that it was not visible from the heavily trafficked Georgia Avenue. Behind them was the darkness of the field. The man must have spied Lucas walking into the park and correctly surmised that there was but one way to the Avenue from there. He had left his vehicle down on Georgia, taken the steps up, and waited for him. He did not look like he had come to talk.

"What is this?" said Lucas, approaching the man.

The man said nothing, and as Lucas neared him he reached his left hand into his pocket and produced a knife. With a jerk of his wrist, a six-inch serrated blade sprang from its bone hilt. He held it loosely and correctly, palm up.

Now Lucas was just a couple of yards away from the man. They stood in the center of the lot. It was like a basketball court where they had come to jump for possession. Or the center circle of a wrestling mat.

"You know your Bible?" said the man.

Lucas did not answer. He stayed focused on the man's seemingly lidless eyes.

"John, Eleven-Ten. 'But if a man walk in the night, he stumbleth, because there is no light in him.'"

"Not this man," said Lucas.

They moved at the same time. The man swung the knife, and Lucas stepped out of its arc and back. The man swung again. His reach was not sufficient, and Lucas knew he would have to come in. The man flipped the knife, switching it to a down-grip, and brought it across from his right shoulder as if he were swinging a bat. He caught only air. He brought the blade back from the other direction and swung with a grunt, and it took him too far. Lucas stepped to the side, then came in quickly, grabbed the man's wrist, and struck a hammer blow to the knife arm's elbow. The man's hand opened like a stunned flower, sending the knife skittering across the asphalt. Lucas pushed him away.

The man looked at the knife, ten feet from his reach. He thought about it, and Lucas said, "You had your chance."

The man charged him. He drove his head into Lucas's abdomen and reached for the back of Lucas's thighs, and Lucas sprawled out in defense of the takedown. He grabbed the man's hair with his left hand, sprang forward, and with his right shot an uppercut into his jaw. The punch stood the man up and knocked him out of Lucas's grasp. He came in once more and threw a flurry of face and head punches that stunned Lucas and forced him to step back. He locked his eyes on the man. Lucas touched his thumbs, one after the other, to his nose. Now he knew where his hands were.

They circled each other in a slight crouch. In the man's eyes Lucas saw that he was about to move. The man feinted with his right fist and threw a wild roundhouse left that overshot the mark. Lucas ducked and came in, sliding one of his arms under the man's punching arm, forcing that arm up firmly, anchoring it with his hand on the back of the man's neck. Lucas slipped behind him and hooked his free arm around the man's neck and grabbed his own wrist and pulled tight. He had him in an air choke now.

He kicked the man's right heel out from under him and fell back, bringing the man down with him; Lucas hit the asphalt with the man on top of his chest. He scissored his legs around the man's waist and locked him up. Lucas violently tightened his grip on the man's neck and arched his back as he squeezed with his legs, squeezed the life out of the man who was writhing now in panic and pain and no breath. The man's feet kicked. He made a high-pitched, childlike sound. There was no mercy in Lucas and he squeezed with all he had. Something gave beneath the crook of his arm. He felt the snap of a bone. Lucas pushed the body off of him. He rolled away and stood.

He waited for his breath to even out. He looked down at the corpse. Urine staining the man's jeans, his eyes half open, saliva threading down from the corner of his open mouth, hands frozen and clawed. A broken string of beads and a crucifix lying crookedly on his chest. His face manne-quined in the pale yellow light.

Lucas felt nothing.

He reached into the man's back pocket and found his wal-let and opened it. He saw the driver's license that identified Nance, studied it carefully, and left it in its slot. He removed all the cash and credit cards and shoved them into the pocket of his jeans. He wiped the wallet off with his shirttail. He dropped the wallet on Nance's torso.

Lucas picked up the knife and pocketed it. He walked toward home and did not look back. He threw the credit cards and cash down various storm drains on side streets, and behind the Kingsbury School on 14th he broke the knife blade off on an alley floor and threw it in a stand of weed trees, then tossed the hilt into another drain.

Lucas entered his apartment, took a shower, got into bed, and fell to sleep. He had no dreams.

SEVENTEEN

THE BODY of Earl Lee Nance was found around sunup by an employee of the church arriving in advance of Sunday service. The Fourth District station sat one block south of the church, so uniformed officers quickly secured the scene. A homicide detective and mobile crime technicians arrived shortly thereafter. Parishioners who showed up later, unaware of the incident, were told that they could not park their cars in the lot, so they walked up the gravel road to the church on foot and, when given the reason for the police presence, tried to shield their children's eyes from the sight of the victim. But, being curious about death, as the very young often are, many children managed to get a look at the corpse, its head unnaturally angled, its hands clawed in the throes of death. Some of them did not think of it after that day. For a few unfortunate others, this twisted sight would visit their dreams for years to come.

In the morning Lucas went outside and picked up the two newspapers left on the front lawn of the house. He dropped one on Miss Lee's doorstep and took the other up to his apartment. Over coffee he read the Metro section of the *Washington Post*, guessing correctly that the event would not have made the morning edition. He went to his laptop and brought up the Crime Scene page of the *Post*'s website. There was a small item carrying the byline of veteran reporter Ruben Castaneda that told of the discovery of a body in the lot of Emory Methodist that was being treated as a homicide. No further details were available.

Lucas took a hot shower; despite the shape he was in, he had woken up sore. Afterward, he had a good look at himself in the bathroom mirror. The crook of his right arm was reddish and irritated. His face was bruised around his eye and temple where Nance had landed a particularly vicious blow. He expected to see his mother that day and would have to come up with a lie.

He dressed in a blue suit and drove across town to his church, St. Sophia, the Greek Orthodox cathedral at 36th and Massachusetts. He went through the narthex, greeting one of the board members who manned the inner doors, and found a spot in a pew on the left side of the nave, far in the back, beside a white-haired woman who had once been his Sunday school teacher. He spotted a couple of the guys with whom he'd played GOYA basketball, standing with their wives. He saw their parents and a few of their grandparents. He could see his mother, Eleni, standing beside Leo, center section, in one of the rows close to the altar. Leo brought her here nearly every Sunday. The good son, thought Lucas, without any feelings of sarcasm or rancor.

Lucas followed the liturgy in a book he found in a wood

box on the back of the forward pew. He recited along with the Creed, which he knew by heart, and the Lord's Prayer in English and Greek. He knew what was going on behind the sanctuary and in front of it because he had served as an altar boy at the age of fourteen and occasionally in the years that followed. He listened to the familiar voices of the priests and the beautiful singing of the cantor and her choir during the Communion Prayer, and when it came time to kneel and pray, he dropped the padded bar before him and got onto his knees. With his elbows on the pew lip, he put his cradled hands to his forehead and closed his eyes.

He would not ask forgiveness for the taking of another man's life. Just like those who had shot at him in Iraq, the man in the parking lot had intended to kill him. In fact, when Lucas prayed he never asked for anything. He had not even begged for a miracle while his father was dying of the brain cancer that had quickly claimed him. Instead, he silently said the same prayer he had always said in church, in the privacy of his home, and in the Middle East: *Thank you, God, for the gift of life you've given me, and the gift of life you have given to my family and friends.*

Lucas did not have the absolute faith his mother and his brother Leo possessed. He had seen too many bodies zipped into rubber bags, seen so much random death that he was no longer certain of an afterlife. But he did feel that the life he had, here on earth, was no molecular accident. It had been granted to him and it was a blessing. He came to church to give testimony to that, to express his gratitude, and to be a part of this community that had meant a great deal to him throughout his life. He saw his people here. In the fathers of others he saw his own father in the church.

Later, during a post-liturgy ceremony for a parishioner who had been deceased for forty days, Lucas did his *stavro*, the sign of the cross, three fingers for the Trinity touched to the forehead, chest, right shoulder, then left.

"...for there is no man who lives and sins not," said the priest.

And Lucas thought, *Amen.*

THE BROTHERS took their mother to brunch at a restaurant she liked, high on Wisconsin near a cigar store and the Gawler's funeral home. The food was in the French vein, the dining room was tastefully designed, and the service had a European elegance. Eleni ate a goat cheese omelet and her sons both had eggs Moroccan, served over easy with sausage and tomato sauce. Leo and Spero had juice; their mother was working on a chardonnay.

Spero had told them out on the front steps of the church that he had "had a few" the night before and walked into a door in the darkness of his apartment when he'd gotten home. Eleni took the story at face value, but Leo clearly did not. After they ordered, Eleni got up to use the restroom, and when she was out of earshot Leo brought up the bruise.

"What really happened, Spero? I know a door didn't hit you upside the head."

"I *was* a little wasted. I was in a place I shouldn't have been down around Petworth. Some guy standing next to me at the bar thought I looked at him funny or somethin and he just coldcocked me."

"Big strong guy like you?"

"Yeah, I know. You would have been proud of me, though. I didn't even retaliate. I let the bouncer get rid of him."

"What was the name of the bar?"

"Huh?"

"Place you were at had a sign out front, didn't it?"

"Man, I don't even know. I guess I was pretty gone."

"Uh-huh."

Eleni Lucas returned, sipped at her wine, double sipped. Spero shot a glance at Leo, but Leo didn't bite.

"My men," said Eleni, placing her glass on the table. "I'm so lucky to have you both here in Washington."

"We're not goin anywhere," said Leo.

"Your dad would be proud of both of you," she said, and Spero stared down at his plate.

"But a little more proud of me," said Leo. "Tell the truth."

"Well, you both have your positive attributes," said Eleni. "You are certainly different from each other, but your father loved you equally. Leonidas, he called you Cool Breeze—"

"Because it felt like a breath of fresh air when Leo walked into a room," said Spero, robotically repeating something he had heard many times before.

"Don't be jealous," said Leo.

"You did get the tightest nickname," said Spero.

"And your dad called Spero 'my *thereeyaw*,'" said Eleni. "Its literal translation is 'wild animal.' But he meant 'my wild one.' Your dad used to love to watch you wrestle. He said you had the killer instinct."

"Yes, ma'am," said Spero, still not looking in her eyes.

Eleni ordered another glass of wine. They quietly finished their meals.

BERNARD WHITE hadn't heard from his partner the night before, which he found strange. For White, doing jobs was just a way to make extra money, and he took no pleasure in the process. But Earl had pride in his work and he relished the details. He would've called Bernard after he'd done the dude, bragged on it, too. By mid-morning, White knew in his gut that the hit had gone wrong.

He got a call from Ricardo Holley on his disposable. Earl Nance was dead. The TV news was saying that it was a homicide committed during an apparent act of robbery. They'd found Earl in a church parking lot. Larry had gotten the unofficial word and told his father that Nance had died of asphyxiation and possibly a broken neck. Ricardo said that Larry was quite "upset."

Fuck that punk, thought White. He said, "What are we gonna do now?"

"Sit on it overnight," said Ricardo. "We need to think on this before we act. Come over to the warehouse tomorrow at lunchtime."

"Larry comin, too?"

"Think I'll speak to him alone," said Ricardo. "Look here: I'm sorry your boy got his self chilled."

"He knew the risks," said White, and he ended the call.

Bernard White sat in a big chair in his Marlow Heights apartment, a crossword puzzle and pen in hand, looking out the window. Thinking of the day ahead, and how empty it would be without his ugly little friend.

MOST OF the commercial and retail businesses back in the Edmonston industrial section were closed on Sundays, but Beano Mobley kept his place open, because working folks used their free time on the weekends to get their vehicles correct. Also, an open and active business meant less suspicion when one of his side customers came to call.

Mobley had been at the firearms thing for a while. Indirectly, it was how he'd met Ricardo Holley. He and Ricardo had struck up a conversation one night at the club out New York Avenue, the one near the dog shelter that had the best all-ass dancers in town. Ricardo had mentioned that he was looking for a heater, and when Mobley asked him if he was police, Ricardo said, "I used to be, but don't hold that shit against me." They ended up bringing a couple of the dancers back to Mobley's warehouse and partying in the far back room, where Beano poured mid-shelf liquor and Ricardo cut out lines of coke he had copped at the bar. Beano had put Brick and some Cameo, shit he liked from his day, on the stereo and cranked it up. Both of them were on the old side, but that night they tossed those freaks like they were young. The cocaine helped. Ricardo and Beano had the same taste in women—the bigger in the back the better. They liked them young, too.

Their friendship solidified, Ricardo began to talk partnership. He liked the fact that Mobley had real estate, a base of operations, and a gun thing that was recession proof. Ricardo would bring his knowledge of law enforcement and his ambition to the table. Both of them felt it was a good fit.

Lately, though, Mobley was beginning to wonder if he had made an error in joining up with Ricardo. Mobley had enjoyed a nice quiet run, selling firearms out the back of his warehouse to gangsters, studio gangsters, and plain old dudes who wanted protection for their homes and shops. He wasn't too worried about someone flipping on him because of the code. At first he was down with Ricardo's marijuana scheme, but when murder got attached to it, Beano wanted to walk away. Problem was, he couldn't.

Beano wanted his old life back. To own his detailing business, move a few guns now and again, drive his Cadillac DTS, watch his beloved Redskins on Sundays, party with women and girls in his warehouse when he could, and grow old with some kind of dignity. He wanted a divorce from Ricardo Holley, but he didn't know how to make it happen.

Mobley was outside standing in his lot, where his employees, a few ex-offenders he was trying to give a break to, were working on an SUV, when Larry rolled in, driving his Escalade. Dickless Larry, thought Mobley, watching as Larry's window rolled down, seeing that the boy was agitated.

"Where's Ricardo at?" said Larry.

"Waitin on you," said Mobley. "In the back."

Mobley watched with amusement as Larry got out of his ride and crossed the parking lot, trying to Walk Tall with an exaggerated swagger, a presidential candidate in elevator shoes and rolled-up sleeves, an actor trying to play a man. Larry, a tit with no milk.

"SIT DOWN," said Ricardo.

"I'll stand," said Larry.

They were in the main office of the warehouse, Ricardo seated behind his desk.

"You lied to me again," said Larry.

"No, I didn't. I kept you out the loop. That's not the same thing."

"You're always twistin your words around," said Larry.

"I have to, with you."

"How could you let this shit happen?"

Ricardo shrugged. "Earl thought he had a solution to our problem. I let him give it a go. Looks like the dude he tried to down was better than him."

"You're talkin about Lucas."

"Uh-huh."

"We got real trouble now."

"I expect we'll be all right, son."

Larry shook his head gravely. "Don't call me son."

"You're my blood."

"It's not like I'm proud of it."

"Neither am I. You look like me, but you ain't me."

"That's for *damn* sure."

As they always did, they came to a verbal stalemate. Ricardo leaned back in his chair. "Anything else?"

Larry's posture slackened. "No."

"If I need you, I'll call."

Larry left the room. Ricardo could only shake his head.

Beano Mobley entered the office shortly thereafter. "Your boy stormed out of here."

"What can I say? Larry's a woman."

"Do I need to be concerned?"

"I got him under control," said Ricardo. "But I rue the day I tapped that heifer he calls Mom."

"We all got regrets."

"Shoulda pumped my nut into a dirty sock instead."

"You can pick your nose," said Mobley, "but you can't pick your gotdamn relatives."

Feeling philosophical, Ricardo and Mobley met at the bar cart and poured themselves a couple of drinks.

LUCAS TOOK a long bike ride late in the afternoon and returned warily to his apartment. There were no patrol or unmarked cars on the street. He had not expected police to be waiting for him there, but he allowed that it might be a possibility. He was certain no one had witnessed the event in the parking lot, and though he had probably left DNA evidence behind, it would only be connectible if he was a suspect. It had been less than a day, but Lucas knew that if the MPD had made him, he would be in the box by now in 1D, being videotaped, answering seemingly polite questions, listening to the psychological head music that D.C. homicide detectives orchestrated so well.

Lucas went inside and took a shower. As the hot water calmed him, he speculated further: Ricardo Holley and his mob knew who had killed Earl Nance, but they wouldn't give that information up to the law. If Larry Holley was going to do his job as a police officer and turn in Lucas's name to

Homicide, he would have done so by now, but that would also incriminate him. Ricardo could plant an anonymous tip, but Lucas had the feeling that it would be emotionally unsatisfying on his part to set in motion such a cheap and cowardly resolution to what was becoming a game of wills.

If it is a game, thought Lucas, perhaps now is the time to step it up.

He had been hired to get the money or the product back. He had been sidetracked to a degree that he had stalled in achieving that goal. He had seen Ricardo leave his house on 9th with an envelope that appeared to bulge with cash. That same day, he had observed the man who could be Mobley, Nance, the big man driving the Tahoe, Ricardo, and Larry Holley all congregated at the detailing building, which perhaps also functioned as their base of operations. Since Ricardo had taken money there, the meet might have been for the purpose of a payday, set in a place where they could come together to cut it up. He assumed that Ricardo, being the senior member of the group, was in charge. Ricardo damn sure didn't use a bank. Ricardo distributed the cash from the reserve that he kept at his house. For Lucas, the next step was obvious.

He came out of the shower and dried off with a large bath towel. He put on some jeans, went out to the living room, picked up his cell, scrolled through his contacts, and found the friend he had last seen at the American Legion bar.

"Bobby Waldron."

"It's Spero Lucas."

"Hey, man."

"I could use your help."

"You need somethin?"

"For now I need you. I got a tail-and-surveil job."

"Thought you use Marquis for that sort of thing."

"His lack of mobility is an issue."

"I could use the work."

"You free tomorrow?"

"Affirmative."

"Let me give you some background."

Lucas told him some of it. They agreed to meet early the next day.

EIGHTEEN

BOBBY WALDRON was standing on Emerson, leaning against his Ford Lariat SuperCrew pickup, when Lucas came out of Miss Lee's house in the morning.

Waldron stood straight as Lucas approached. He wore cargo pants and a white T-shirt whose sleeves were filled with his bulging, Bengal-striped biceps. His left forearm was heavily dotted with shrapnel and ink. His hair, shaved back and sides, said military or police. A chaw of tobacco swelled his jawline.

Lucas wore dark blue Dickies pants, a matching blue long-sleeved Carhartt shirt, and black steel-shanked Wolverine boots. It was too warm for such an outfit, but any discomfort he would feel was necessary.

"My man Waldo," said Lucas.

"Sir."

"Knock that shit off."

"Yes, sir."

"C'mon."

They went to the back of the Jeep. Lucas lifted the tail-gate, exposing the cargo area, which he had loaded with tools and equipment. Waldron looked at a dark blanket covering several items and the thick pine handle that protruded from its edge.

"What is that, an ax?"

"It's a sledgehammer," said Lucas. "Haven't decided what I'm gonna use so I brought a racka shit." Lucas reached into a box, handed Waldron a two-way and headset, and a disposable cell. "Use the radio when we're in range. When we get out of range, use the cell. Here's my number." Lucas handed him a slip of paper. "You have the address of his house."

"I do."

"Park on Somerset or Tuckerman. Be aware that it becomes one-way on that strip due north. If our man is a creature of habit, he'll go right to the Safeway after he leaves his crib. He gets his morning coffee at the Starbucks there."

"Right."

"I'll be in the lot to make sure this is going as planned. From there you're on your own. Last time we tailed him he went to a pole-dance club deep down on Georgia. Look for him to go there or some other stroke palace and then over to his spot in Edmonston."

Waldron spit juice on the street. "Got it."

"He starts heading back to his house, hit me up." Lucas looked him over. "You got a long-sleeve shirt?"

"It's too hot for that."

"I know you're proud of your guns, but you do stand out with all your ink."

Waldron flexed, his stripes expanding. "Whaddaya think?"

"Tony the Tiger's jealous."

Waldron issued a lopsided grin. "I don't have a long-sleeve shirt with me."

"I'll get you one."

Lucas went back into his apartment and returned with a Johnson Motors long-sleeved T carrying a print of Bud Ekins riding his Triumph. Waldron examined it.

"Who's this guy?"

"McQueen's stunt double. He jumped the bike over the barbed wire in *The Great Escape*."

"Cool."

"My brother doesn't think so," said Lucas.

"He's overeducated."

They climbed into their vehicles and went to work.

LUCAS WAS far back in the lot of the Safeway on Piney Branch Road, waiting, when Ricardo Holley, in his white Lincoln, pulled in and came to a stop. Bobby Waldron's Lariat arrived shortly thereafter. His voice came into Lucas's headset.

"I'm here," said Waldron.

"I got you," said Lucas.

Waldron parked in another far corner. Holley stepped out of the Mark V and crossed the lot. He wore a purple shirt tucked into triple-pleated black slacks and a black bolo tie. His hair was large, puffy, and somewhat bronze in the sunlight.

"Where do you get that haircut in this day and age?" said Waldron. "And those clothes. Where do you *buy* shit like that? Seriously."

"Maybe he's got a time machine in his basement."

"Weird-lookin dude, bro."

"You think so?"

Soon Holley emerged from the Safeway with a cup of Starbucks in hand. He started up the old Lincoln and cruised through the parking lot toward the Georgia Avenue exit. Waldron ignitioned his truck.

"I'm on it," said Waldron.

"Switch over to your disposable."

"I will."

"He starts to head back to his house, you call me, hear?"

"Copy that."

Lucas watched Waldron follow Holley, Waldron spitting a stream of tobacco juice out the window. PFC Bobby Waldron, 2nd Platoon, 2nd Battalion, 503rd Infantry Regiment, had been stationed at a firebase in the Korengal Valley and had participated in harrowing recon patrols throughout his deployment. Lucas was not worried about his friend. This was butter for him. He'd do fine.

Lucas started his Jeep and drove toward Holley's residence.

AS THERE is with nearly every house in D.C., there was an alley behind Holley's house on 9th. Lucas drove through it, north to south, slowly. He noted the No Parking / Tow Away Zone sign, stopped his Jeep, and took several photos of the rear of Holley's bungalow. It was bordered by a cheap post fence one grade up from chicken wire that could be easily vaulted. It had a couple of windows that were probably locked and definitely hard to access, and an iron set of steps with a handrail that led to the wooden back door. Lucas saw no water dish, paw-dug holes, mounds of feces, or any other evidence of a dog. If Holley had one, he would mistreat it, and the animal would be mean. Lucas would deal with that if he had to.

He looked to his right. There was a commercial building on the west side of the alley whose windows faced north; its occupants would have no sight lines on the Holley house. Past the building was the busy Georgia Avenue intersection beyond which Piney Branch would soon become 13th Street.

Lucas drove out of the alley, went around the block, and parked on Tuckerman facing Georgia.

He examined the photographs he had taken on his iPhone. He stowed that phone in the glove box and slipped his disposable into his pocket. On his belt he wore a holster for a Leatherman utility device, which, assuming there was no safe to crack, had all the tools he might need, including a knife long enough to blind someone if properly stuck. He picked up a knit watch cap off the shotgun seat and fitted it on his head.

Lucas got out of the Jeep, went around it, lifted the tailgate, and pulled back the blanket in the cargo area. He looked at the sledgehammer and knew that it was too conspicuous and heavy. Beside it was a Stinger all-steel battering ram used by police that Lucas had bought off a website for two hundred and seventy-five bucks. It was not the monster hydraulic ram he had seen used to great effect on houses overseas, but it was sufficient and weighed only thirty-five pounds. He took it out of the Jeep and proceeded to the alley.

Walking south, he tossed the Stinger into Holley's yard

without breaking stride. At the foot of the alley he turned and went to 9th, then turned north. Now he was going by the front yards of the houses there. The street was quiet. A woman with a belly hanging over the front of her elastic-waist jeans crossed the street carrying a laundry hamper and went toward her car. She glanced at him for only a moment and walked on. He was a young white guy in a uniform and cap, medium height, solid build, no facial hair, no features to distinguish him, completely unremarkable and unmemorable, going about his business, which appeared to be some kind of official or blue-collar task. He continued up the sidewalk of the Holley residence, hearing the turn of an ignition behind him, going by the security alarm sign that he assumed would be bullshit. Now he was on the porch, hearing the car with the Laundromat-bound woman inside it going up the street.

Lucas stood before the door and pushed a button beside it and did not hear a bell. He knocked on the door and got no response. By now a dog would have come, but apparently there was no dog inside. He looked in the thin vertical window beside the bell, saw the messy interior, saw a plastic box hanging by the wall inside the door that showed a keyboard but had neither a red nor a green light, and he knew that it was a false security monitor that Holley had attached in a half-assed way.

He turned and walked off the porch, retracing his steps. He went back to the alley, and at the rear of Holley's house he vaulted the fence, picked up the Stinger off the ground, and headed for the back door. He looked to the right and left and saw no one and took the iron steps up to the door. With one hand gripping the rear handle of the ram and the other on the top handle, he swung the heavy steel bar with great force into the door a few inches from its lock, and he felt the door give. The sound did not seem alarmingly loud to him, and he swung the Stinger again, putting his hips into it, and the door splintered and moved, and Lucas kicked the heel of his right boot into the same spot with a grunt, and the door opened and he stepped inside. He closed the crippled door with his back.

Lucas was in a small kitchen with old appliances and a sink filled with dirty dishes. The room stank of unemptied garbage. He placed the Stinger ram on a cheap laminate countertop scarred by burn marks. He walked from the kitchen into the living room and did not stop to look around.

Lucas knew what every burglar knows: people, straight and criminal alike, keep their cash, jewelry, and valuables close to where they sleep.

There was no second floor, only a crawl space. He found the bedroom that looked to be Holley's by virtue of the fact that it held the largest bed. It was the master; there was a bathroom inside accessed from the room. Lucas went into the bathroom, saw men's toiletries, long black hair in the sink, a shower stall covered with mold. A tube of mascara and lipstick, no doubt left behind by one of Holley's tricks.

Lucas went back into the bedroom and surveyed it. An unmade king with no headboard; a cheap particleboard dresser with three drawers, an open cigar box doubling as a jewelry box atop it; a large velvet wall painting of a full-figured woman, naked, on her knees; a poster of the zodiac

signs showing men and women coupling in various posi-
tions; and a closet filled with shirts, slacks, sport jackets, and
shoes.

Lucas drew the blinds and closed the curtains. He got
down on his chest and looked under the bed. There was
nothing but dust bunnies there. He stood, threw the sheets
back, drew his Leatherman from its holster, and pulled from
it a small but very sharp serrated blade. He cut the mattress
open from head to foot and cut it crosswise and inspected its
stuffing and springs. Nothing. He went to the dresser and
pulled its drawers one by one, emptying them onto the floor,
tossing the drawers in a jumbled heap to the side. He looked
in the cigar box, saw several bolos, cuff links, and rings with
glass jewels, and he emptied this onto the floor as well. With
his hand he swept off whatever was left on the dresser and
felt his face grow hot. He removed the velvet painting
from the wall, held it aloft, punched his right fist through
its center, and dropped it. Lucas heard himself laugh.

That's for sending the little man.

He went to the closet, which had no door. He pulled all
the clothing out by the hangers and tossed it onto the bed.
There were many pairs of shoes lined up on the floor, side
weaves, fake gators, country-to-the-city, boat-to-America
shit, and Lucas kicked them to the side and got down on his
haunches and saw the plywood wall in the back of the closet
that was obviously false from the way it hung. He got a grip
on its edge and pulled it back and he smiled.

There were three ghetto safe-deposit boxes on the floor
behind the false wall, stacked on top of one another. Lucas
picked up the stack of Nike shoe boxes and put them on top

of the dresser. One by one he opened them, and inside he saw banded stacks of cash. Twenties, hundred-dollar bills, tens, and fives.

The cell rang in his pocket. He pulled it and answered.

"Yes."

"It's me," said Waldron. "Our boy came out a massage parlor ten minutes ago. I'm guessing he got his self yanked."

"And?"

"Seems to me he's headed back to his house. He just turned off Georgia onto Missouri."

"I need ten minutes," said Lucas.

"Copy that."

BOBBY WALDRON passed the Lincoln on the right, raced ahead, and got back into the left-hand lane. Now he was in front of Holley. They were on Missouri Avenue headed east. At the red light at the 9th Street cross, Waldron came to a stop. Ricardo Holley braked the Mark V behind him, his left turn signal activated. Waldron, wearing a pair of Bobster wrap-around goggles with amber frames, checked the rearview. He waited for Holley to look down at his cell, the modern habitual stoplight behavior, and when he did, Waldron put his truck in reverse and gave it a touch of gas. The Lariat rolled back slowly and tapped the fender of Holley's Lincoln. Waldron quickly threw the shifter into park and stepped out of his truck.

Holley got out of his Mark and limped forward, his face set in an angry frown. The light turned green and horns sounded as both men walked toward each other. The traffic on Missouri streamed by. Waldron and Holley met in the street, four feet apart. Holley towered over Waldron. Waldron spread his feet.

"What the fuck you think you're doin?" said Holley. "You backed into me."

"No, I didn't," said Waldron calmly. "You hit me."

"Motherfucker—"

"That's not necessary, sir."

"You—"

"I *saw* you, sir. You were looking at the screen of your cell phone. When the light turned green you came forward without observing that I was still stopped."

"That's not true. It's not."

"Is there any damage to your car, sir?"

Holley turned his head and inspected the bumper of the Lincoln. There wasn't a scratch on it.

"That's not the point," said Holley.

"Maybe you'd like me to phone the police."

"No, I *don't* want that."

"Then what do you want?"

"Motherfucker, I want you to *apologize*."

Waldron stared impassively at Holley from behind amber lenses and spoke in a monotone. "I told you, sir. That kind of language is completely unnecessary."

Ricardo Holley looked at Waldron, his redneck haircut, his redder than red sunglasses, his arms and shoulders stretching out the fabric of his long-sleeved shirt, had a picture of some white sucker riding a motorcycle. Holley had eight inches on the man standing before him, and reach, but

211

the short man had quiet confidence. And with that tree stump build of his, he would be hard to hurt. Still, if he were twenty years younger... but he was not.

"Apologize," said Holley, because he could not give it up.

Waldron said nothing. Holley's face darkened and he limped back to his car.

Waldron got into his truck and drove away. Down Missouri, near Kennedy, he phoned Lucas.

"He's one click away from his house," said Waldron. "He's on his way."

RICARDO HOLLEY pulled up in front of his bungalow and killed the Mark's engine. He was running a little late for the meeting at the warehouse, what with the extra time he'd spent with that Korean gal, but he decided to come back to his crib and pick up his bottle of high-dose naproxen, which he'd forgotten that morning. The prescription painkillers did help to soften the pain in his hip. Doctor said that the bone deterioration since his shooting all those years ago was "pronounced," and that he should think about getting the replacement surgery, that is unless he wanted to be physically impaired for the rest of his life. Holley knew what they did to you in that operation; they took a table saw or something like it to your ass. Just thinking of that saw cutting into his bone made him sick. He'd stay on pills and gut it out.

Holley got out of his vehicle, went up to his front door, turned the key, and stepped inside his house. Right away he sensed that something was off. He could smell the foreign perspiration in the room. The light was different than it should have been, straight back in the kitchen, for this time of day. He had lived here many years and he knew.

He moved quickly to the kitchen and saw that the back door was open and listing, its frame splintered. He looked out into the backyard. There was no one there, no cars in the alley. He turned and limped back through the house toward his bedroom, hearing his own heavy breathing, and then he was in the ruin of his bedroom and he knew he'd been violated and tossed.

For a moment he stood frozen, staring at the mess. His dresser drawers and clothing heaped on the floor, his mattress sliced both ways, his jewelry in various places about the room. That nice painting of the full-figured freak he'd bought at that flea market on Morrison, a hole punched through its center, its frame busted up.

He felt his hands shaking. He moved to the closet, empty of clothing. He knew before he saw the piece of plywood lying haphazardly on top of his best pairs of shoes. Knew before he saw the empty space where the Nike boxes had been.

He felt dizzy. He stumbled back and turned and made his way into the bathroom. He needed to run some water on his face. He looked at the mirror and saw the message, in big bright letters, written in red lipstick across the glass.

You Lose, Rooster

If the neighbors had been home, they would have heard Ricardo Holley's howl.

NINETEEN

LUCAS COUNTED the cash when he got back to his apartment. There was ninety thousand dollars, in various denominations, stacked in the boxes. He was on a high since he'd burgled Ricardo Holley's house and left the childish message on the man's mirror. And then, staring at the money, he grew puzzled.

Anwan Hawkins had told him that the initial theft of the first package had occurred several weeks before they'd first met. The second package, taken off Lisa Weitzman's porch, had disappeared a week before they met. Another full week had elapsed before Lucas began work on the case, due to some work he had previously committed to Tom Petersen. A third package was stolen in Northeast the day Tavon Lynch and Edwin Davis had been murdered. Three packages, worth roughly one hundred and thirty thousand dollars each on the retail level, which equaled close to four hundred thousand dollars. Even allowing for the six weeks that had elapsed, even allowing for the cutting up of the money, for the payoff to Holley's crew and to Tavon and Edwin, if they were paid at all, it was highly unlikely that there would only be twenty percent of the take left. Ricardo Holley did not seem to be the type to allow his minions to spend frivolously and potentially draw unneeded attention. The man himself drove a car that was twenty years old. Where had all that money gone?

It was curious, but it was less pressing than the problem at hand. He'd completed the task for which he'd been hired, which technically meant that he was finished. But Lucas knew that for Holley and his men, it couldn't be over. They'd come at him now.

Lucas counted out his forty percent, which came to thirty-six thousand dollars, then took a hundred-dollar bill from the stack and put it in his pocket. He stashed the rest of the thirty-six grand in one of the Nike shoe boxes he had taken from Holley's house. He placed the remaining fifty-four thousand dollars, which would go to Anwan Hawkins's ex-wife, in another shoe box. He tore up the third shoe box and threw it away. He carried the other boxes back to his bedroom and set them down. He went to his closet, where his shoes sat on a small throw rug, and he pulled the throw rug, carrying the shoes with it, completely out of the closet.

Beneath the rug was a cutout that Lucas had made in the floor. He had done a clean job of it, and Miss Lee would most likely never know. He pulled on a hinged ring he had set in a grooved-out section of the wood, and the piece came free. Beneath the cutout, in a solid-bottom frame, also constructed by Lucas, sat a steel Craftsman toolbox that had belonged to his father. Lucas placed the two shoe boxes on top of each other beside the toolbox. He replaced the wood piece, fitted it properly, put the rug and his shoes back over the cutout, and closed his closet door.

He locked his apartment, took the stairs down to his separate entrance, and went outside to try and find one of his neighbors, a young man named Nick Simmons. Simmons was on the street, standing by his Caddy. The car was parked in front of Nick's father's house, a wood-shingled colonial with a large front porch. Nick was working under the hood, rag in hand.

"Hey, Nick."

"Spero."

Nick Simmons stood to his full height. He was a tall man of twenty, had hang-time braids, was physically imposing but not aggressive, and wore a mustache, long sideburns, and some kind of business on his chin.

"What you up to?" said Lucas.

"Just checkin the fluids," said Nick. "Trying to beat those idiot lights."

He owned a rare and sharp 1990 baby-blue-over-dark-blue Eldorado coupe with gold spoke Vogue wheels. His father, Sam Simmons, who worked for the US Postal Service, had gone in on half of it and loved it as much as his son did. Nick's mother was deceased. The father had kept him in line and made him stay in school. He was in his second year at Howard. He was always broke.

"You about to find some work this summer?" said Lucas.

"I'm lookin."

"It helps to be clean shaven on job interviews."

"Thanks, Dad. You know, the Bible says that a man

shouldn't round the corners of his beard...or somethin like that."

"The Rastafarian Bible?"

"Leviticus," said Nick with a shy smile.

"Look, you need some pocket money, right?"

"Always."

"You have plans tonight?"

"I can't *go* anywhere without coin."

Lucas produced the hundred-dollar bill and held it out to Nick. Nick did not reach for it.

"What do I have to do?"

"I'm taking a young lady to dinner this evening," said Lucas. "While I'm out, I'd like you to sit on your porch and keep an eye on Miss Lee's house. If anyone comes around who you think looks suspicious, sits in their car too long, takes photographs, anything like that, I want you to call me. I'll give you my number. I don't want you to do anything but call, hear? Don't engage anyone in conversation or initiate any kind of conflict."

"I wouldn't."

"One other thing. If Miss Lee is outside of her house, and any suspicious type tries to talk to her or bother her at all, I want you to call the police. Don't even hesitate."

"You expecting something like that to happen?"

"I'm being cautious."

Nick took the hundred. "You got it."

"That's for tonight. I might ask you to do this again going forward, same pay. Until the situation changes."

"Sounds like easy money to me."

"Let's hope so." Lucas shook his hand. "Thanks."

"Good looks, man."

Lucas went back to his place, got out of his dirty work clothes, and ran a shower. He and Constance had a date.

THEY WERE in the original dining room of the recently expanded Mourayo, a Greek restaurant on the west side of Connecticut Avenue, above Dupont Circle. Lucas and Constance sat at a deuce by the opened front windows. The oppressive humidity of deep summer had not yet arrived, and a breeze came off the block. The sidewalks were heavy with foot traffic in this upscale neighborhood of retail, restaurants, and bars on the Avenue, old luxury row homes of brick and stone on the side streets. A mix of straight and gay, business suits and freaks. It had always been lively and offbeat here at night.

The dining room was airy, with warm wood trim, white walls, and hardwood floors. The busboys wore sailor shirts and fisherman caps. Lucas was wearing a fitted Boss summer shirt with vertical blue and white stripes.

"You blend in with that shirt," said Constance. "It looks like the Greek flag."

"I took a risk," said Lucas. "And as for you..."

"Please."

"You're beautiful."

"Thank you."

They had started with marinated anchovies, grilled octopus with a fava bean puree, sesame encrusted *haloumi* cheese with grapes, and a salad *voskou*, heavy on tomatoes, feta, peppers, and red onions. They were sharing a bottle of Boutari red, slightly chilled. The restaurant's owner came by and poured a few inches of wine into their glasses.

"Everything all right, Spero?"

"*Poli orayo*," said Lucas.

"*Kali oraxi*," said Natalie before moving on to another table.

"This is nice," said Constance after Natalie had gone away.

"Wait'll you taste the fish."

A short while later, the waiter brought Constance a whole branzino baked in salt and filleted it tableside. Lucas was having *soutzoukakia*, meatballs stewed in tomato sauce and served over rice.

"God," said Constance after taking a bite, "I'm glad I made that phone call for you."

"I am, too."

"It must have panned out for you."

"It did."

"You're in that mode tonight. It's like you hit the number or something."

"A ship came in," said Lucas.

They ate their meal. She talked about her initial intent to pursue a graduate degree in education and her decision to go to law school instead. She told him he would make a good high school coach, and he said it was too late for that.

"Tom told me your brother's a teacher," said Constance.

"Yeah, Leo's over at Cardozo," said Lucas. "He's doing good work."

"You've got other siblings, right?"

"Allegedly. My sister's an attorney in California. We don't hear from her much. Got a brother named Dimitrius I haven't seen in years. He's in jail somewhere for all I know."

"Your family sounds fractured."

"Somewhat."

"Is it—"

"Because the kids were adopted?"

"I'm just curious."

"Irene wasn't adopted. My mom had a rough pregnancy with her and was advised not to have any more kids. So my folks built the family another way. I don't know what Irene's malfunction was. She was always unhappy. Dimitrius, I look at him basically as being defective. Those two were older than me and Leo, and when they left home it all got better."

"The pressure was off. I had an older sister who put my parents through the wringer. When she went off to college, it was like the clouds broke over our house. Everyone was relieved."

"You'd like my mom," said Lucas, softening. "And my father was..."

Constance set her fork down on the plate. "I know you miss him."

He reached across the table and laid his hand over hers. "You about ready?"

"Yes."

Lucas paid for the meal in cash.

AT NIGHT, most of the Edmonston commercial district was church quiet. Back in the corner of the small street that dead-ended at the elevated railroad tracks, the lot of Mobley Detailing was lit by a single floodlight centered over its bay doors. The fenced gate to the driveway entrance was closed and locked.

Inside the building, parked in the bays, were Beano Mobley's DTS, Ricardo Holley's Mark V, and a gray Ford Expedition that Bernard White was renting. The Tahoe that he and Earl Nance had driven, registered in Nance's name, had been impounded on Georgia Avenue after Nance's murder. White had been questioned by homicide detectives at the car dealership service department where he and Nance worked. The detectives were apparently satisfied with his answers, as they had not returned.

Further inside, in the main office, Ricardo Holley sat behind his desk, wearing the same purple shirt and triple-pleat black slacks he had put on that morning. The clothing and Holley stank of perspiration.

Mobley and White were also in the room. Mobley was perched on the edge of Holley's desk, a stub of a dead cigar between his fingers. White was on the couch, depressing it. All of them smelled of alcohol. They had been at the hard liquor for a couple of hours. They had drinks in their hands now.

"The man must have known I'd be gone," said Holley.

"Someone followed you more than one time," said Mobley. "They knew your routine."

"So there had to be two of them," said White. "One to keep an eye on you and one to toss your house."

It came to Holley then that the short muscled-up redneck who'd backed into his Lincoln at the stoplight might have been both the tail and the decoy. He had a soldier's haircut. He *could* have been in on it with Lucas. But Holley couldn't remember much about the dude except that he drove a Ford truck. This inability to recall the details frustrated him. He shouldn't have drunk so much so fast. He couldn't seem to focus. He noticed that his glass was empty and he got up out of his chair and limped across the room to the cart. He poured four fingers of off-brand scotch out of the Johnnie Walker black bottle. He inspected the level in his glass and poured some more.

"We sure it was Lucas?" said Mobley.

"Goddamn right I'm sure," said Holley, his face twisted. "Who else it's gonna be?"

"I'm just askin," said Mobley, who seemed to grow calmer and more reasonable the more he drank.

Holley went back to his chair and settled in.

"I know you're angry," said Mobley.

"*Shit*. He trashed the bedroom where I sleep. He busted up this real nice painting I had, too. I feel like I was... What's that word, Bernard?"

"Violated," said Bernard White helpfully.

"Yeah, like some pork got pounded up in my ass."

"We did try to murder him," said Mobley.

"What's your point?"

"He came back at us. You can almost understand it. Got his little bit of revenge and got the money he was after, too." Mobley looked at Holley meaningfully. "And you know we gonna get some of that back eventually."

Holley drank scotch and placed the tumbler on the table. "Say what you tryin to say, Beano."

"This is over if we decide it's over," said Mobley. "Lucas got no cause to bother us no more. If you want to keep going with this weed thing, we can. There's money to be made, quietly, if we go back to our business and forget about Lucas and what got done."

"I can't forget," said Holley.

"Neither can I," said White.

"All right, then," said Mobley. He relit the cigar, got the draw going, and tossed the spent match into a tire ashtray set on the desk. He stood to his full five foot six inches and walked to the corner of the room, where the smoke would not bother Holley or White. "Let's be smart about this. Take the emotion out of it."

"Well?" said Holley.

"What do we know about this dude?" said Mobley.

"What do I know?" said Holley. "He was in the military. Served over there in *I*-raq."

"What else?" said Mobley. "We know how to find him, right?"

"Larry crossed the phone numbers out of Tavon's cell," said Holley. "We can call him. We know where he stay at, too."

"I'll do the motherfucker where he lives," said White.

"No," said Mobley. "I said, be smart."

"Okay," said White, his face strained, thinking hard. "If he's local, he's got family. Maybe he got a mother or father he cares about. A little sister or sumshit like that."

"No *again*," said Mobley, growing impatient with White, one step up off a special-bus kid. "You kill a Caucasian in this town, you make the front page. 'Specially a square or a child."

"We could take someone in his family," said White. "I'm sayin, kidnap someone he loves."

"That's worse," said Mobley. "Then you make Fox News."

"What about that kid on Twelfth?" said Holley. "The one who saw Larry make the exchange? Lucas been talkin to that kid, too. You remember his name, Beano?"

"I don't," said Mobley, too quickly. It was a lie.

"Ernest somethin," said Holley, opening his desk drawer. "I got it here somewhere." His fingers spidered through the papers there.

"I could scoop him off the street," said White. "He knows too much anyway."

"Then we tell Lucas we got the boy," said Holley, warming to it. "We tell him we'll exchange this Ernest for the money. Tell him to bring the money here."

"And then?" said Mobley.

"We down the dude," said Holley, as if he were explaining it to a child. "Take the boy out, too."

"Lucas might try to go hard," said White.

"He can try," said Holley, and he and White smiled.

Mobley dragged on his cigar. He didn't like where the conversation had gone.

"Ernest Lindsay," said Holley, finding the piece of paper he was looking for.

"You gonna tell Larry?" said White.

Holley shook his head. "He don't need to know just yet."

It seemed to Holley that there was a ringing in his head. White got off the couch and fixed himself another drink.

Holley said to White, "Fetch me some of that, too."

THEY CAME back to his place, smoked a little weed, and opened a bottle of Worthy Sophia's Cuvee, an excellent Napa Valley red from the Axios label that he had been saving for a night like this. Lucas put Augustus Pablo's *King Tubbys Meets Rockers Uptown* on the stereo, lit some candles, and killed the lights. He and Constance made enthusiastic, energetic love on the edge of the bed and atop the sheets, the cascading, rhythmic dub swirling around them, the sound of a hard rain tapping on the roof. When they were done they were exhausted and slick as seals, and they took a long shower together and made it again.

Afterward, Lucas asked Constance to spend the night, but she declined. He put on a pair of jeans and phoned for a cab, and when it arrived he walked her downstairs. The street shone with the storm that had come and gone.

"You could sleep over once," said Lucas. "You never do."

"That's not what this is," said Constance, her face close to his in the doorway, her breath warm on his face.

"You mean it's not that serious."

"Some things are better unspoken." Constance kissed him softly on his mouth. "Thank you for the wonderful night, Spero."

He watched her get into the cab, which then rolled east toward 14th. He stayed in the doorway, looking at the Simmonses' house next door, its darkened porch, the familiar cars parked on the street. Seeing nothing unusual, Lucas went back up to his apartment and fell asleep.

TWENTY

LEO LUCAS stood at the head of his class, wearing a crisp blue oxford shirt, a red-and-blue rep Ralph Lauren tie, plain-front khakis, and Clarke desert boots. His ID badge hung on a chain over the shirt. The boys in the room, in uniform, wore purple and white polo shirts, and khaki pants.

In Leo's hand was a slim Avon paperback of a novel called *The Hunter.* Its author credit read "Donald E. Westlake writing as Richard Stark." The cover art collage featured a red scarf, red pills spilling out of a vial, playing cards and chips, and a stainless steel .38 revolver with wooden grips.

"Okay," said Leo. "When we first meet Parker, who I'll call the antihero of this book, he's walking across the George Washington Bridge. This is from the first page: *Office women in passing cars looked at him and felt vibrations above their nylons. He was big and shaggy, with flat square shoulders and arms too long in sleeves too short. He wore a gray suit, limp with age and no pressing.* What does that tell you, in shorthand?"

"The ladies want to do him," said a boy.

"Yes, women do find him attractive," said Leo. "But not in a boy-next-door kinda way."

"He's too big for that suit," said Hannibal, known as Balls.

"Hold that thought," said Leo. He looked down at the open book. "This is also from the first page: *His hands, swinging curve-fingered at his sides, looked like they were molded of brown clay by a sculptor who thought big and liked veins. His hair was brown and dry and dead, blowing around his head like a poor toupee about to fly loose. His face was a chipped chunk of concrete, with eyes of flawed onyx. His mouth was a quick stroke, bloodless. His suit coat fluttered behind him, and his arms swung easily as he walked.*" Leo closed the book. "What does this say about Parker? How does it make you feel?"

"He's like an animal or somethin," said a boy named Mark Norman.

"Way his hands are swinging," said another, "it's like he don't care about nothin."

"He doesn't belong in that suit," said William Rogers, aka Moony.

"Exactly," said Leo. "The suit doesn't fit him, both literally and metaphorically. It's a costume to him. He'd be more comfortable walking naked through a jungle. The Parker books are crime novels, but they're also about a man whose physicality stands in contrast to a working world that, at the time, had become increasingly mechanized and deskbound."

"I don't get what you're sayin, Mr. Lucas."

"Parker is a man of action. He's defined by what he does rather than what he says."

"We gonna see the movie?" said Moony.

"Yes," said Leo. "When we're done reading this, I'm going to show you *Point Blank*, the classic film that was made from this book. You'll see how Lee Marvin embodies the loose-limbed description of Parker that I read to you. He plays him like a big cat."

"You mean like a panther."

"Right," said Leo.

"They made another movie with that character, too."

"That Mel Gibson joint," said a boy. "It was crud."

"Y'all haven't even seen the best one they made," said Ernest Lindsay, speaking up for the first time because the discussion had veered toward his interests. "It's called *The Outfit*."

Some of the boys in the class looked at him and then at one another. They didn't begrudge Ernest his knowledge, but felt he was somewhat strange, being into the old-time stuff that no one else cared about. He didn't seem to pay much attention to sports, music, video games, or girls. They felt he lived in a fantasy head, when they were more concerned with the real.

"I'm not familiar with it," said Leo.

"I stayed up till three in the morning once to watch it on AMC. Robert Duvall, Joe Don Baker, Robert Ryan... Parker was called Macklin in that movie."

The room grew quiet. Ernest, at first proud, now embarrassed, slumped in his seat.

"What do you all like about this book so far?" said Leo, breaking the tension.

"It's short," said Hannibal, and a few of the boys laughed.

"Yeah, *thank* you," said Mark Norman.

"We're at the end of the school year," said Leo. "I gave you guys a break."

The too-loud voice on the intercom boomed suddenly and statically in the room, telling the boys it was time to go to their next class. They got up boisterously, clumsily pushing chairs against chairs, making unnecessary noise.

My pups, thought Leo.

"Read this book before the next class," he called out, and got some groans in return. "Come on, fellas, we want to go out strong. Participation is a large part of your grade."

As they filed out, Leo reached out and stopped Ernest with a hand on his arm.

"You need me?"

"Stick around for a second," said Leo. He waited for the others to leave and sat on the edge of his desk. Ernest stood before him, a book bag slung over his shoulder.

"What's up?" said Ernest.

"Just want you to know, you add a lot to this class. When you speak on things you're passionate about, it gets everyone up, even if they don't show it."

"They think I'm a rain man or somethin. Soft, too."

"No, they don't. They respect you because you're smart." Leo looked him over. "You get out in the world, what you know is going to set you apart from other folks. But first thing, you got to get that higher education."

"I know it."

"Did you fill out the college application yet?"

"I didn't get to it."

"Thought your mother was going to help you."

"She is," said Ernest. "But she went away this week with her man. Took a vacation with him, like."

Leo caught the distaste in Ernest's voice. "Look, we've got applications in the office. Come past after school today and I'll help you knock it out."

"I don't want to bother you."

"Just come by," said Leo.

"Thank you," said Ernest. "And tell your brother I said thanks, too. He gave me a couple of movie books that were tight."

"What'd he do that for?"

"I helped him out with somethin, is all."

Leo digested that but asked nothing further.

"Okay," said Leo. "I'll see you after school."

"Bet," said Ernest.

Leo waited for a long while that afternoon, but Ernest did not return.

BERNARD WHITE and Beano Mobley were parked on 12th Street facing north, White under the wheel of the Expedition and Mobley on the other side of the console, seated in the shotgun bucket. White thinking, Mobley's small, like Earl. But Mobley seemed bigger, because he was an endomorph. Meaning Mobley was round and muscular, and Nance had been skinny and wiry. Had the body type they called ectomorph. Those were good words. White had written them down and put them in a file he kept at home.

The Tahoe Bernard White and Earl Nance used to drive was large, but the Expedition was like a bus. No one in the city needed a vehicle this huge, but people wanted to own the biggest SUV on the block. That name, Expedition, it suggested adventure, a safari, the discovery of new worlds. Lewis and motherfucking Clark. But all Bernard ever saw behind the wheels of these beasts were fat brothers and sisters holding cell phones and white middle-aged fathers with beer guts and goatees. If they ever went off-road, it was an accident when they'd drunk too much. Highlander. Pathfinder. *Expedition*. To where, the Walmart? That shit liked to kill him, man.

"Kids got out," said Mobley, looking in his side-view, seeing students coming from Cardozo in groups. "You see him?"

White glanced in his mirror. "No. He'll be along."

They had been sitting on the street for hours. That morning, after the Lindsay boy had gone to school, they watched as the boy's mother and a middle-aged man who had the sour, baggy-eyed look of a mean drinker, left out the row house they stayed in and, carrying a couple of suitcases, got into a VW Cabriolet and sped off. Had to be her car, 'cause a man wouldn't own a Cabriolet. White had laughed out loud at their good fortune. Obviously the adults of the house weren't coming home that evening at least. Now was the time to steal the boy.

"They're all wearin the same shit," said Mobley with that sandpaper voice of his, observing the sea of purple and white polo shirts. "Why the school make them put on those shirts?"

"Regimentation," said White.

"What?"

White knew he'd get Mobley on that one. He surprised Ricardo and them when he threw in a word they didn't know. They thought he was stupid. Everyone did, going back to his mother, his uncles, his teachers, the other kids in his neighborhood. He was always way big for his age, six foot two by the time he turned twelve, and big to them meant dumb. Played football for the Marlboro Mustangs in the peewee league, then later at Largo High. The coaches yelling at him, *Hit somebody, son!* And he did, with fire. Broke this one boy's neck with a helmet-to-helmet thing, got him while his head was turned toward a pass, running a sideline pattern. He could have hit him low, but hey. White had a powerful feeling when he saw the kid lying there, eyes all wide and scared, his head taped to a gurney. He apologized for the unfortunate hit: he didn't mean to hurt no one, football was a contact sport, etc. It was called a tragic accident and largely forgotten. The boy never did walk again.

Yeah, he put some hurt on those kids, and if they looked at him wrong or called him a retard, he gave them double hurt. That is, until he dropped out. He didn't get past the tenth grade, but that didn't mean anything. He read bodybuilding magazines and did crossword puzzles. He could break down an engine. He was smart.

White had liked using words to fuck with Earl. Like saying Earl was compensating when he really meant *over*compensating. By doing this, he could get Earl to admit that he was touchy about his lack of size. He did it all the time to Earl when they were working in the service bays. Earl talking about women, and how he was small of stature but plenty big "down there," "thick as a can of Mountain Dew," and how he liked to use it, though White had never seen him with a girl. White saying, "You just a diminutive fellow, is all you are," Earl saying, "Huh?"

Earl Nance was a funny little dude to hang with. Even when they murdered together, after it was done, the back and forth they had, what was called the *banter*, was fun. He wished Earl was still sitting next to him, instead of this bad-tempered, Have-a-Tampa-smellin old man. He'd give it to that Lucas dude fierce when he had the opportunity. It wouldn't bring Earl back, but it would make White feel good.

"*Regimentation* mean they like to keep those kids in order," said White.

"That so," said Beano Mobley.

Some time must have passed while he'd been, what was that word, *ruminating*, because when White looked in the side-view again, most of the schoolkids were gone. Except for one, a tall, thin boy with braids, coming down the block on foot. He was kind of looking around, taking his time, his mouth moving though there was no one with him. Had to be the Lindsay kid, since he was slowing down near the steps that led to the Lindsay row house. He was coming closer, damn near right beside their vehicle.

"That's him," said White.

"Who don't know *that*," said Mobley. He had already opened his door.

ERNEST LINDSAY had lingered in the library after the last bell. He'd flirted with going by the office to pick up that college application, but in the end he had decided against it. He didn't like to leave Mr. Lucas hanging like that, but he didn't feel like spending the time with it, and figured that he could apply to UDC some other day. This was what he told himself, but deep down he knew why he was putting the process off. He was scared.

Ernest had a comfort thing where he was at. He had lived in the same row home with his mother his whole life. He had walked to all of his schools. This was a big step for him, having to go across town to an unfamiliar neighborhood, face a new challenge, interact with strangers, faculty and students alike, people he wasn't sure he could trust. And the aspect of it that he could not even admit to himself: he was afraid to fail.

Ernest had this dream of making movies, but how could he ever make it real? How could a dude from D.C. who had never been out of the city, except to go to amusement parks and such, how could he make that leap from stoop boy to someone who worked in a fast and glamorous business, an *industry*, one of polish and glamour, personal assistants, *conference calls?* His dreams were his everything. If he were to lose them, if he were to know for certain that these dreams were never going to be realized, what would he have left?

Ernest went down the dark interior stairwell of his school, the stone steps beneath him worn in the centers from almost a century of use. He passed through the lobby, where the police and security were stationed, and exited the building. Out in the sunlight, he walked toward 12th.

It's just a few people who work in that business get to direct, thought Ernest. They got carpenters, folks who set up the lights, location scouts...I could do something like that. But I bet those folks don't have that cinema knowledge I do. I know how to look at a film. I like to read about movies, and I like to talk about 'em, too. I could teach.

He realized he was talking to himself and he stopped. Up ahead, a small, strong, older guy was getting out of a big Ford SUV.

Ernest wouldn't mind standing in front of a classroom, turning students on to film. He was still learning. He had been reading the thick biography that Spero had given him. He was in the middle of the chapter on the making of *The Good, the Bad and the Ugly*, which in Italy was called *Il buono, il brutto, il cattivo*. He liked those kinds of facts. Ernest felt this was Mr. Sergio Leone's masterpiece. He was especially into that scene toward the end where the Eastwood character performs an act of kindness for a dying Confederate soldier and gives him a last smoke. There was hardly any dialogue in that scene. What Leone put into the shot, what he left out of it, the framing, the acting, the beautiful music, were all in harmony. That scene right there, Ernest got chills when he watched it. He had bought the soundtrack off a U.K. website using his mother's credit card, and when it arrived at his house he saw that it had the song titles listed in Italian. He had asked his teacher what *"Morte di un soldato"* meant, and Mr. Lucas told him it meant "death of a soldier," and Ernest knew that he had bought the right CD. If he became a teacher someday, he would show the students the film and then play the cues from the soundtrack for them as well. That perfect blend of image and sound.

"Ernest Lindsay," said the short man who had gotten out of the big SUV. He stood before Ernest now, blocking his way. He had an unlit cigar in the corner of his mouth. He wore a jacket in the heat. His hand was in the jacket pocket.

Ernest nodded. He couldn't even raise spit.

Mobley made an eye motion toward the back door of the SUV. "Get in the back, son."

Ernest's head moved birdlike as he glanced around the street. Mobley stepped forward, pulled his hand from his jacket, and pressed the barrel of a revolver hard against Ernest's stomach.

"You'll be all right if you do it," said Mobley, his breath foul. "Otherwise...Look, I'll just go ahead and shoot you right here. I don't even care."

Ernest got into the backseat of the Ford. Mobley slid in beside him.

The big man in the driver's seat said, "You *know* he's got a cell."

A few minutes later, going north on 11th, Mobley tossed Ernest's cell phone out the window. Ernest heard it break into pieces as it hit the street.

TWENTY-ONE

LOQUACIA HAWKINS lived with her son, David, in a clapboard colonial on Quintana Place in Manor Park. It was not far from the community garden on 9th and the Fourth District police station, where huge radio towers landmarked the neighborhood and loomed over the landscape. David and his friend Duron had stolen the Denali on Peabody, in the shadow of the towers.

Lucas parked his Jeep on Quintana and grabbed a black Patagonia pack off the seat beside him. He slung the pack over his shoulder and walked down the sidewalk, glancing at the parked vehicles, looking for a law car and seeing none. He noticed a shiny Range Rover HSE, black with sand leather interior and spoke alloy wheels. It looked brand-new. No city dweller needed an eighty-thousand-dollar luxury off-road vehicle like this one, but it was beautifully designed and crafted, and Lucas admired it as he passed.

He stepped up onto the porch of the colonial and knocked on the front door. Soon the door opened, and a tall, handsome woman, strong boned and well proportioned, stood in the frame. She was in her thirties, had liquid ebony eyes and smile lines parenthesizing her mouth. She wore indigo jeans, ankle-strap shoes, a faintly patterned cream-colored shirt that looked expensive, and a small crucifix on a simple gold chain.

"Loquacia Hawkins?"

"I'm Loquacia."

"Spero Lucas. I have something for you."

"Come in."

Lucas stepped into a foyer that opened into a kitchen and family room. Both held nice furniture, built-in appliances, and custom cabinetry. The latest wide-screen technology hung on the family room wall. The house was not new, but its interior spoke of money.

"Is your son here?" said Lucas.

"No, he's out."

He handed her his backpack. "Here you go."

She took it by its strap. "Should I—"

"Yes. Count it out so there's no misunderstanding."

He followed her into the kitchen. She extracted a manila envelope from the pack, which contained cash held together by rubber bands. She removed the bands and counted the bills out carefully on the granite counter. When she was done she counted the money again and said, "Fifty-four thousand."

"Then we're good," said Lucas.

He and Loquacia shook hands.

Lucas walked to the front door, stepped outside, and stood on the porch. When he turned to say good-bye she was next to him.

"I want to thank you," she said.

"Just honoring my agreement," said Lucas.

"I'm not talking about what you brought me today. I'm speaking on what you did for my son."

"I caught a little luck," said Lucas.

"You and that jury gave him another chance. I don't want to say he made a mistake, because what he did, he committed a crime. But he saw how it tore me up, and he knows he did wrong. David learned. He's not gonna go there again."

"They're kids. They stumble."

"Yes, they do."

"If Tom Petersen's successful, David will have his father back in his life again."

"We don't need Anwan," she said, her tone suddenly grim. "Me and David are doing just fine."

I'll say, thought Lucas. He nodded toward the new SUV parked in front of her house.

"Is that your Range Rover?"

"It is."

"How do you like it?"

"It's real nice," she said.

Their eyes locked and she held his gaze. Maybe he'd make another comment about her expensive new vehicle, or the clothes she wore. Her furniture, her richly appointed kitchen.

But Lucas wasn't about to judge her. If her hands were unclean, then his were, too.

"Have a good one," said Loquacia.

"You do the same."

*   *   *

IN THE back of the Mobley Detailing warehouse, past the main office, was the second room, the one Ricardo Holley and Beano Mobley used as a fuck pad and playhouse when they entertained women and girls they brought back from the clubs.

There were two large beds in the room, taking up much of the space. Sometimes Holley and Mobley liked to do it to women in the same room at the same time, like they imagined fraternity brothers would, even though they were both deep into middle age. On the walls were posters of women in thongs and a couple of framed, infamous photographs of Darlene Ortiz in her white body thong, front view and back, holding a pistol-grip shotgun, from the cover of the Ice-T album *Power.*

Like the office, the room had a portable bar. Atop it were several cognacs that Mobley claimed were expensive but were just top-shelf bottles refilled with rail yak. Also in the room were a beat-up stereo system and a couple of comfortable chairs. A round table strewn with porno mags. A filthy bathroom with a toilet and no shower. A mirror with the Jack Daniel's logo that was frequently taken off the wall and used to track out lines of coke.

Ernest Lindsay sat in one of the chairs. He was leaning forward and looking down at the linoleum tiled floor, his hands clasped tightly together. The windows had outdoor bars and interior curtains. Through the thin white curtain Ernest could see that it was night.

Fluorescent light fixtures hung from the drop ceiling, but their tubes were not illuminated. A man had come into the room and turned on a floor lamp with a tasseled shade.

"Ain't you gonna eat that food I got you?" said the man. Tall, with puffed-out copper-colored hair and a long thin nose. He looked strange and familiar, but Ernest didn't know why.

"No, thank you," said Ernest. "I'm not hungry."

It was Chinese from one of those Plexiglas-wall grease pits, and that garbage gave Ernest diarrhea. Even if he wasn't so nervous he wouldn't eat it. His mother had taught him early on not to touch it.

"You want a drink?" said the man. "I got liquor."

Ernest nodded at a dirty plastic cup of tap water he had set on the floor. "I'm fine."

The man limped toward Ernest and stood over him. He spoke in a soothing way. "Look here, son. You just sit tight and behave yourself, and you're gonna be fine. I don't want nothin from you. A man took something from me, and when he gives it back, you're gonna be free to go. It's not on me to decide when you walk out of here. It's on him. Until that time, you're my guest, hear?"

"Yes."

After a long silence, the man said, "The color purple."

"Huh?"

"Do you like it?"

"The movie?" said Ernest, meeting his eyes directly for the first time.

"I'm speaking on your shirt. Purple happens to be my favorite color, too."

"This is my uniform for school." Ernest knew the man was trying to act nice, but it was false. There was no kindness in his eyes.

"Don't expend no energy with the back door," said the man. "It takes a key to unlock it." He went to an interior door that led to another room and put his hand on the knob. "You just relax. Knock if you need somethin. My name's Ricardo."

He walked out, closed the door behind him, and latched it.

Ricardo.

Ernest's stomach turned. He felt like he was going to vomit. The man didn't care if Ernest knew his name.

RICARDO HOLLEY walked into his office, opened his desk drawer, and dropped a ring of keys inside. His son Larry, seated before the desk and in uniform, watched him. Ricardo settled into his chair.

"The boy's all right," said Ricardo. "I talked to him in a real nice way. Made him feel comfortable."

Larry stared at him, disbelief in his eyes. He found it hard to speak.

"Just tryin to keep you in the loop, young man."

"A little late for that," said Larry, his voice unsteady.

"We're men. We make decisions and we act on 'em. We don't need to form no committees."

"You might have spoken to me first before you went and did something like this. You and your low-ass crew."

"I don't need permission from you to do any goddamn thing. You perform a service for us and you're well paid. But you're not my partner. I told you that before. I guess I need to make it clear again."

"*You,*" said Larry.

Ricardo got up and fixed himself a brown liquor drink, no mixer, no ice. He brought it back to his desk and sat in his chair.

"Now, let's talk about this rational," said Ricardo. "I'm gonna call Lucas. Tell him that he needs to bring me the money he stole in exchange for the Lindsay boy. When he comes, we'll take him out."

"What about the boy?"

"What do you think? He *saw* you, Larry, in uniform, taking that package and puttin it into the trunk of an MPD vehicle. It's you who brought this on him."

"This isn't a marijuana transaction, or receiving stolen property. It's even bigger than moving guns. This here is a capital crime."

"It's not *any* kind of crime if no one finds out. We'll do the both of 'em right here and bury 'em in pieces out in the woods somewhere. You don't even have to get your hands dirty, Larry. Bernard will take care of it. He *wants* to."

"I'm out."

"Uh-uh." Ricardo wagged a finger at his son theatrically. "That's not an option. Besides, what are you gonna do? Go to IAB and make a confession? You wouldn't just lose your job. You'd go to prison, boy. You know you ain't built for it."

Larry stood up abruptly. His fists were clenched. Tears had come to his eyes. He hated himself for it, but he couldn't control his emotions.

Ricardo smiled. "Look at you. You about to cry."

"Least I feel something."

"I can't even believe you're my blood."

"I wish to God I wasn't," said Larry. "I *hate* you, man."

"So?"

Ricardo laughed. Larry turned and walked from the room.

TWENTY-TWO

SPERO LUCAS woke up the next morning without any plans. It was unusual and discomforting for him to have no immediate goals. The euphoria of the money and the satisfaction of having completed his task had worn off, leaving him with an unfamiliar feeling of having been tainted by the job. He'd done this kind of work for a while now, for Petersen and on his own, and his methods had often been questionable and occasionally beyond the law. But he'd never experienced this kind of foul aftertaste. There was dirt in his mouth and he couldn't spit it out.

It wasn't the murder of Nance; despite the fact that he could have spared his life, Lucas had convinced himself that he'd acted in self-defense. The retrieval of marijuana money didn't bother him on the moral level, either. He believed that marijuana prohibition was hypocrisy. He saw nothing wrong with it. He smoked weed himself.

But the violent deaths of Tavon Lynch and Edwin Davis were harder to bear. It wasn't that he felt personally responsible. They had lied to him, but they were decent young men who had not fully understood the consequences of the game. What touched Lucas like a cold finger on his shoulder was that he had done nothing about their murders. And there was his professional curiosity, too. The question still nagged at him: why had they been killed?

Lucas walked to the living room window and looked up at the sky. It was a glorious day.

He changed into swim trunks, a T-shirt, and waterproof sandals, and packed a lunch. He went to the back porch, lifted his kayak off the ceiling hooks where it hung, carried it through his apartment with his hand gripping the cockpit lip, and walked it carefully downstairs and out to the street. There he strapped it to the crossbars of the Jeep's roof, distributing its weight on foam pads. He loaded his gear into the rear deck, and drove out of the city and into Maryland via River Road.

A half hour later, twelve miles north of the Beltway, he pulled into Riley's Lock, high on the Potomac above Great Falls, along the C&O Canal. He unloaded his kayak and other items from the back of the Jeep. He drove up a rise and parked in a lot, removed his T-shirt, then returned on foot, where he locked together the two pieces of his paddle, fitted his life vest under the deck rigging, pulled free the stern hatch, placed his soft cooler in the bulkhead, and dropped a large container of water behind the cockpit's seat. He dragged the kayak to the public boat ramp, put it partially in the water, steadied himself on both sides of the cockpit lip, and lowered himself into the seat. He adjusted the slide locks of the foot braces so that his legs were slightly bent and his thighs fit firmly against the foam pads.

He shimmied into Seneca Creek and slowly paddled west. He passed under one of the two remaining arches of the Seneca Aqueduct and entered the Potomac River.

The river was wide here, with a relatively smooth surface due to a nearby dam. It was a weekday, which meant there was very little water traffic, save a John-boater and his yellow Lab, and a sole kayaker going south. He had the river virtually to himself. A pair of hawks circled above the trees. To his right was the state of Maryland; the left bank was the commonwealth of Virginia. He began to paddle upstream, against the current and into the wind.

He used a high-angle paddle technique for a faster, more powerful stroke. He pushed rather than pulled. When he found his rhythm he began to move at a steady clip. The air in the bulkheads maintained ballast; he was on the river's surface and also a part of it. He began to sweat. He could feel his whole body—shoulders, abs, and legs—working. His goal was an island a mile or so upriver.

The sky held brushstroke clouds and full sun. The sun's rays lightened the water and illuminated its depths. He saw many smallmouth bass, brown with dark bands, the females larger than the males. His hands grew slightly cramped and he pushed on. As he neared the island he cruised into the shallows, where catfish lurked in the undulating river grass and in the crevices between boulders. He made a final push and lifted his paddle and let himself glide into the bank of the island. He got out of the cockpit and pulled the kayak up on shore.

Lucas drank water until it dripped down his chest. He retrieved the soft cooler, in which he had stored an ice pack, a turkey-and-provolone with sliced pepperoncinis, an apple,

and a bottle of Stella, out of the stern's bulkhead. He sat on a
log facing the Virginia shoreline and ate his lunch. A red-
winged blackbird flew across his sight line, and a juvenile
osprey lifted off the water's surface and headed toward shore.
Ants tickled his feet, and a ruby-throated hummingbird fed
from the flowers of the island's trumpet vine. He ate his
sandwich and apple. He swigged from the green bottle,
drinking deeply in the midday sun, and marveled at the
beauty of the living things around him. And he thought: my
father is here, too.

HE STRAPPED his kayak back atop the Jeep, unlocked his glove
box, retrieved his iPhone, and scanned it for messages.
There were none.

He checked the kayak to make certain it was secure and
stood shirtless behind his vehicle, its tailgate up, drinking
the remainder of his water. His phone rang. The call-in
number on display was unfamiliar. He slid the answer bar
from the left to the right.

"Yes," he said.

"Spero Lucas. My *man*."

"Who am I speaking to?"

"It's Rooster." Ricardo Holley chuckled. "You know, ain't
nobody called me that for twenty years. And even then, no
one had the guts to say it to my face. I'm curious, though:
who told you to use that name?"

Lucas did not reply.

"I guess it doesn't matter," said Holley jovially. "Here's
why I called: you know that young man Ernest Lindsay?
Lives on Twelfth? Well, we got him."

"What do you mean, you've *got* him?"

"We took that motherfucker off the street. Gonna hold on to him until you and me settle up."

"Settle up how?"

"Bring us the money you stole out my house. I'll give you the boy. I believe you took ninety thousand dollars. That sound right?"

"It's thirty-six now."

"Then bring thirty-six."

"You just gonna accept that?"

"Fuck do I care? I can *get* more money. Anyway, this really ain't about money anymore."

"You got that right."

"Got *that* right. My, you do talk tough. Big tough marine. Breakin up my bedroom into pieces, leaving lipstick messages on mirrors like some fifteen-dollar trick. But what you gonna do when you come up against men, for real?"

"Nothing," said Lucas. "This'll be a simple one-for-one. The money for Ernest. I don't want anything to happen to him."

"Come on, then. You know where we're at. You been here, after all."

"I have."

"Hurry up. Ernestine's lookin a little frail. He hasn't touched a bit of food. I'm afraid he's gonna starve."

"I'll call you when I'm on the way," said Lucas, struggling to steady his voice.

"You done captured my number now."

"Yeah, I've got it."

"We'll be waitin on you, Spero. And make sure it's you

alone. You bring someone with you, I'll spill that little nigger's brains when you walk through the door."

Lucas ended the call. He closed the tailgate, got into the Jeep, and dropped his phone on the passenger seat. He gripped the wheel. When the tightness in his chest went away and his breathing settled, he turned the Cherokee's ignition and drove back toward D.C.

LUCAS PARKED illegally on Clifton Street, got out of his Jeep, and jogged down 12th to the Lindsay residence, where he took the steps up to the porch. He knocked on the door, rang the bell, and fist-knocked so hard the frame shook. He looked in the living room window and saw no signs of life. Clearly Ernest's mother and her boyfriend were not home.

He moved quickly to the porch of Lisa Weitzman's row home. He was fairly certain she would be at work, but he knocked on her door anyway and got no response.

Spero went back to his vehicle and phoned his brother. Leo picked up on the third ring.

"What's goin on, Spero?"

"Can you talk?"

"I'm in the teachers' lounge."

"Come outside, man. I'm on Clifton. "

"Now?"

"I need to see you, Leo."

Leo heard the desperation in Spero's voice. "Is Mom all right?"

"Far as I know, she's fine."

"Gimme a minute."

It didn't take much more than that for Leo to emerge

from the school, neatly dressed, his ID badge hanging out over his chest. He scanned Spero, standing by his Jeep in a no-parking zone, the kayak lashed atop it. Normally he would have said something smart, called him Jeremiah Johnson or "pilgrim," but he saw the muscles bunched on Spero's jawline.

"What's wrong?"

"Did Ernest Lindsay come to school today?"

"Matter of fact, he wasn't in class. That's unusual for him. Why?"

"Could he be somewhere with his mom?"

"He told me that his mother and her boyfriend went on some kind of vacation. He didn't mention that he was going with them. I asked you, why?"

Spero stared down at the asphalt. "There's a problem."

"Tell me what's happening," said Leo, trying to get his brother to meet his eyes. "*Look* at me, man."

"I messed up," said Spero. "Ernest helped me out with something and now I think he's in trouble."

"You mean you pulled him *into* something. *And* you mean it's serious. Don't call it trouble when it's more than that."

"Leo, I—"

"This is about that job you took, right?"

"Yeah."

"A job you took for money."

"I work for money," said Spero. "Same as you."

"Bullshit." Leo stepped forward, grabbed a handful of Spero's T-shirt, and got close to his face. They had fought many times growing up, and neither of them was afraid to go. But Spero kept his arms at his side.

"Let go of me," said Spero quietly.

"I don't know what you do or why you do it. But don't tell me we're about the same thing. I put you up with one of my students, and now that boy's in some kind of danger. You need to tell me right now how you're gonna resolve it."

"Let go."

Leo loosened his grip and stepped back.

"He'll be all right," said Spero. "I promise you."

"You should call the police."

"I can't. And I can't tell you why."

"Then what're you going to do?"

"Pick him up from where he's at. It's a simple exchange."

"Simple."

"I've *got* this," said Spero.

Leo nodded. "You better call me when it's done."

A SIMPLE exchange.

Lucas had lied to his brother. There would be nothing simple about what was going to happen.

He knew too much about these men, and so did Ernest. They would kill Lucas as soon as he gave them the money, and they would kill the boy. And if he managed to rescue Ernest, or if Ernest escaped, it could perhaps go somewhere that was much worse. They knew where Lucas lived. Larry Holley, a police officer, had access to all kinds of information, so it stood to reason that they could easily get to his mother and to Leo as well. They had killed Tavon and Edwin without thought. He couldn't stand to think of what they might do to his family.

Lucas knew what had to be done. But it was anything but simple.

He stopped by his place to offload his kayak and gear, and to grab some cash. He phoned Bobby Waldron and drove out of the city once again.

WALDRON LIVED with his folks in a vinyl-shingled rambler off upper Veirs Mill Road in Rockville, past the Twinbrook shopping strips. Waldron's father was a master plumber and his mother was retired from the Montgomery County school system, where she had worked in various cafeterias. Their home was small and old but well maintained. Bobby kept the lawn mowed to within an inch of its life. What with his ever-dwindling security work, he didn't have much else to do.

Lucas parked and went up to the front stoop, where an American flag hung above the door. He rang the bell. Presently, Rosemary Waldron appeared in the frame, a bottle of Miller High Life in hand.

"Spero," she said. Rosemary was a good-time redhead in her late fifties, fifty pounds bad for her heart, with a gone-to-hell belly and the straight-out missiles that some women get in their middle age.

"Miss Rosemary," said Lucas, stepping into the house as she moved aside. He was still in his swim trunks and T.

"Would you care for a beverage?"

"No, thanks. Is Bobby around?"

"He's in the basement. C'mon."

With Rosemary accompanying him, he walked through a living room that showcased framed photos of the Waldrons' only son in dress and combat uniforms, and with his fellow soldiers in Afghanistan. Bobby's medals and commendations, mostly for sharpshooting, were also framed. They moved around the furniture that crowded the room and came to a kitchen and an open door that led downstairs. Rosemary yelled into the space, "Spero's here," and motioned for him to go ahead.

Lucas took the wooden steps to the basement, finished and carpeted with knotty pine walls and a matching bar. Bobby Waldron got up off a sleeper couch that was set before a TV on a stand. He was playing the latest Madden on his Xbox. His video games were aligned in a cheap bookcase beside the television. The room was clean, orderly, cool, and dark, and smelled of cigarettes. Curtains were drawn on the small casement windows.

Waldron was shirtless and in skivvies, displaying his build and tiger-stripe tats. They shook hands.

"What do you think?" said Waldron, looking at his right biceps, then his left, flexing each.

"If you ever get drafted by the Cincinnati Bengals, they won't have to issue you a uniform."

"Har har."

From upstairs, they heard Waldron's mother's voice. "Would you guys like some sandwiches?"

"No thanks, Mom!" shouted Waldron. To Lucas he said, "Let's go to my room."

They entered Waldron's bedroom, which Lucas guessed had been framed out and finished by his father. It was just as orderly as the rec room. Waldron's shoes were neatly lined up along one wall, his clothing, shirts and trousers, even T-shirts, on hangers in an open closet. There was a low-watt lamp on beside his bed, which was a simple mattress and box spring sitting frameless on the floor. There were no windows. Bobby closed the door and locked it.

He picked up an old JanSport day pack that sat against a wall. He unzipped the main compartment and pulled out a gun wrapped in an oiled rag. He unpeeled the fabric. In it was a Smith and Wesson five-shot Special .38, blue steel, short nosed, with rubber grips. He handed it to Lucas butt out.

"That's what you lookin for?" said Waldron.

Lucas broke the cylinder, spun it, looked through its empty chambers. He jerked his wrist and snapped the cylinder shut. "Yes."

"I don't know what you need it for..."

"As it should be."

"...but I would be concerned for you if I thought that was all you had."

"This is insurance. Revolvers don't jam."

"There's no paper on it. I got it at a show. Shaved the numbers for you, hombre. I hope that's not a problem."

"It's not."

"Hollow points and a clip-on are in the bag. You can keep the bag, too."

Lucas reached into the back pocket of his swim trunks and pulled out his wallet. He handed Bobby the cash they had agreed upon and something extra.

"That's a thousand too much," said Waldron.

"It's for the surveillance job," said Lucas. "You did good work, and you saved my ass."

"I'm always available." Waldron's close-set eyes flickered. "For this, too, whatever it is."

"I'm good, Bobby. Thanks."

A few minutes later he was walking through the living room, the day pack slung over his shoulder.

"That was a quick visit," said Rosemary Waldron, seated in a recliner, a fresh bottle of beer in hand.

"I just came by to borrow a few video games," said Lucas.

"You're always welcome here, Spero."

"I appreciate it, Miss Rosemary."

Lucas tossed the bag onto the rear deck of his Jeep and covered it with a blanket. His blood ticked electric through his veins. The feeling was familiar and right.

TWENTY-THREE

LUCAS TOOK a shower and changed into jeans and a white T-shirt. Out in his living room, he studied the sketches he had made of the Mobley Detailing building in his notebook. He looked at the front facade, the entrance door and bay doors, and the rear, its windows and back door. He went through the photos he had taken from his iPhone, and the ones he had shot of the surrounding landscape. After a while he had the external layout committed to memory. That was all well and good, but the interior was a complete unknown. Lucas had no idea where Ernest was being held inside those walls. If in fact Ernest was in that building at all.

He needed help, but he didn't want Marquis Rollins or Bobby Waldron further involved. He thought of Lieutenant Pete Gibson and his longtime hard-on for Ricardo Holley. Gibson might want in. But that wouldn't work, either. What Lucas was about to do had to stay with him alone.

The room had darkened by degrees. The day was bleeding off.

Lucas sat at the kitchen table, his notebook and phone before him. He was staring at a wall meaninglessly when the phone began to ring. His young next-door neighbor Nick Simmons was on the line.

"Nick, what's up?"

"Thought you might like to know, there's a police officer out on Emerson, standing by his car. He's lookin up at your windows."

"Where are you?"

"Inside my house."

"Hold on."

Lucas got up and went to one of the windows that fronted Emerson. He stayed back in the living room, just far enough so he couldn't be seen. Larry Holley, in blue, was out there on the street beside an unmarked black Crown Vic that was obviously an MPD vehicle. He was standing with his arms crossed, leaning against the rear quarter panel. He seemed to be waiting.

"I guess I'll go out there and see what he wants," said Lucas.

"Okay," said Nick.

"If you see something going down —"

"*What?*" said Nick. "Call the police?"

"That is a problem," said Lucas.

"I would say so."

"Forget it," said Lucas. "Just draw your blinds and go about your business."

"I can do that, too."

"Thanks for the heads-up."

Lucas ended the call. He was barefoot, so he found a pair

of shoes and put them on. He walked downstairs and out of the house. He crossed the lawn and the street. He neared the Crown Vic, and Larry Holley stood away from it and uncrossed his arms.

Lucas stopped, staying out of Holley's reach. He put his weight on his back foot.

"You looking for me?"

"Maybe we ought to take this someplace else."

"I'm not going anywhere with you."

Holley looked at Lucas's defensive posture, the veins popping out on his biceps. "You're a little jacked up."

"I guess I am."

"Why come outside, then?"

"You're every citizen's bad dream. A bent cop can do whatever he wants. I can't really hide from you, can I?"

"I came to see you for one reason only: to speak with you."

"That's it?"

"Yeah."

"You're on duty?"

"I'm Ten-Seven."

"If you're here to take me down—"

"Told you, I'm not."

"If you *are*, let me make this clear: if anyone has an idea about fucking with my family, they better rethink it. I've got everything documented and in the hands of an attorney. Your name, too, and your involvement in this. Everything. Something happens to someone I care about—"

"What about *your* involvement?" said Holley. "You put the part about killin Nance in those documents, too?"

"That was self-defense."

"What I heard, his hyoid bone was broke. Seems to me you coulda just choked him out. With your military background, you must know how to render a man unconscious without ending his life."

Lucas said nothing.

"We all got dirt on us," said Holley. "Don't try to act like you're clean."

Lucas's anger drained away. He studied Larry Holley's face. He was the younger, mirror image of his father, but they were different in a crucial way. There was vulnerability in the son's eyes.

"How'd you get involved in this?"

"Can't say, exactly," said Holley. "I'm not claiming I'm innocent. When my father approached me, I could have said no. I *took* that step. I wanted to please him, see? But I never thought it would end up in all this death."

"What did Ricardo ask you to do?"

"Identify targets. That's what I did with Tavon and Edwin. Boys in the game think they got it all figured out, but they never do. I tailed them in my personal vehicle and rolled up on them at a Brookland home when they were picking up a package. I told them how it was gonna be. Fifty percent to us, fifty to them. They didn't have a choice."

"You took the package right there?"

"I delivered it to my father and Mobley. They wholesaled it, I guess."

"What do you mean, you guess?"

"My father keeps me in the dark about damn near everything having to do with the business side. I was told to have the boys lie to their man Hawkins. To tell him the product got stole so the pie didn't have to get sliced up too deep. They went along with it. They were too scared not to."

"Because you were police."

"Yes," said Holley quietly.

"If they went along, why were they killed?"

"I don't know," said Holley. "I *don't*. We had done two other retrievals, one on Twelfth Street, and the last one in Northeast. It was time to pay the boys off. I was there that night. I was supposed to watch the transaction and make sure it went down straight. The idea being, a patrol car idling on the street will keep all the other knuckleheads away. But I got called off by my father. I didn't know Nance and Bernard White were gonna do what they did."

"White's the muscled-up dude?"

"Yeah. Him and Nance were partners. Amateur hitters. Trash."

"And now they've got Ernest Lindsay."

"Ricardo, Beano Mobley, and Bernard. That's right."

"You left your name off the list."

"I'm not with 'em anymore."

"How're you gonna break off from your own father?"

Holley shook his head. "Did you have one who loved you?"

"I did," said Lucas.

"That's all I ever wanted, man. I waited my whole life to meet up with my pops. I dreamed on how that reunion was gonna be. Ricardo only reached out when he found out I was MPD. And that was just to plug me in to his scheme."

"Do they have Ernest at the building in Edmonston?"

Holley nodded. "There's an office, and another room behind it that leads to the back door. He's in that room."

"Tell me more about the interior."

Holley went through it, room by room. The doors, the windows, the vehicles that would be parked in the bays. Lucas tried to see it in his head.

"What're you gonna do?" said Holley.

"I've got to get him out of there."

"They'll kill you soon as you give them the money. The boy, too."

"We'll see."

"You're not gonna make it."

"You're forgetting something,"

"What's that?"

"I've done this before."

In the fading light of dusk, Lucas's eyes were bright.

LUCAS AND Larry Holley spoke for a little while longer and exchanged cell numbers. Holley drove off in the black Crown Victoria, and Lucas went back up to his apartment. In his bedroom he pulled the throw rug and his shoes out of the closet. He freed the wood cutout in the floor and reached down into the hole and from the framed basket retrieved the steel Craftsman toolbox that had been his father's. He opened the lid and removed the top tray. In the main compartment he found what he was looking for: a pistol, a holster and belt, and two fifteen-round magazines holding metal-jacketed rounds.

Lucas moved to his desk, where he had placed the .38 Special, now loaded with hollow points and seated in its holster. He examined the gun he had taken from the toolbox. It was a double-action semiautomatic Beretta, an M-9 with a steel body and black checkered grip. It was similar to the side-arm Lucas had carried in Iraq. He had replaced the military-issue magazines with those manufactured in the Beretta factory because he felt they were more reliable. The previous owner had been left-handed, and Lucas had switched the safety for right-hand use. It was not a perfect weapon, but he was comfortable with it and in his grip it felt right.

Sitting at the desk, he picked up the Beretta and, with the gun pointed sideways, pulled back its slide several times. This would allow any rounds left in the chamber to fall free; none did. With the slide locked out, he looked through the chamber and determined that it was clear. He pointed the weapon at the floor and he dry-fired and heard a click. He then palmed one of the magazines into the gun and racked the slide. With the safety on, he fitted the gun into the holster and belt. He slipped the second magazine into one of the pouches of a black nylon mesh pistol vest that he had laid out on his bed. He put all of his gear and a couple of bottles of water into a medium-sized duffel and placed it by his front door.

He phoned Ricardo Holley. Their conversation was pointed and short.

Lucas changed into a black T-shirt. Without introspection he went to his door, picked up the duffel bag, took the stairs down to the exit, and walked to his Jeep. Full night was on the street.

TWENTY-FOUR

LARRY HOLLEY dropped the Crown Vic off in the lot behind the 4D station, switched over to his black Escalade, and drove through the northeast quadrant of the city and into Maryland. He pulled over to the shoulder on a side street in the industrial section of Edmonston and killed his engine. He had stopped several commercial buildings short of the Mobley Detailing lot. Larry got out of the SUV and left it unlocked.

He walked down the street. No one was out, and there seemed to be no activity in any of the properties he passed. It was dead as a graveyard back here at night.

He was in blue. Not a patrolman's uniform but the uniform of his squad. On the back of his shirt "Police" was spelled out in big white letters. His Glock 17 was holstered on his side. In an ankle holster he had fitted an old Armscor six-shot .38 revolver. He had found it under the seat of a suspect's car and now it was his throwdown. Larry did not expect or want to use either of the guns. He had never even

264

drawn his service weapon except in front of a mirror. Violence wasn't in his nature, but in the event that it transpired, he was fully armed.

He walked across the Mobley lot. He reached into his pants pocket and took out his cell and called Beano Mobley on his.

"Mobley speaking."

"It's Larry. I'm on my way in."

"Wasn't expecting you, man."

"I'm here, Beano, right out front. Let me in."

Larry always phoned Beano, and Beano was always the one who opened the door. As he neared it, he heard the dead bolt turn, and Larry walked right through as the door swung open, Mobley behind it in his white guayabera shirt, the stub of an unlit cigar wedged in the corner of his mouth. Mobley looked around the edge of the door before closing it.

"Where your 'Lade at, Larry?"

"On the street. I don't want anyone to know I'm here."

"You ashamed?"

"Close the door, Beano. You're gonna catch cold."

Mobley laughed huskily. Of Ricardo's associates, Larry disliked him the least. Beano was crooked but likeable in a drunken-uncle kind of way. Larry thought: too bad about him. Righteous fire burns all.

Mobley closed the door and threw the dead bolt. "The fellas is in the back."

The Expedition, the DTS, and the Mark V were parked in the bays, with the big SUV taking up much of the space. Larry walked under a flashing fluorescent light, through the narrow opening between the Lincoln and the Ford, and when he came to the office he knocked on its door and turned the knob at the same time. He walked inside and Beano Mobley came with him.

Bernard White and Ricardo Holley were standing by the steel gun cabinet behind the desk. A couple of the pistol compartments were open, the red felt lining of their interior cavities visible. Bernard White wore an oversize T-shirt with cutoff sleeves and work pants. He held a Heckler & Koch 9mm auto-pistol loosely in his hand. Ricardo was in the process of slipping a Glock under his shirt. The 17 had been his sidearm when he was on the force, and he was fond of it. A large tumbler half-filled with whiskey sat atop the desk. Also on the desk, Ricardo's keys.

"What you doin here?" said Ricardo, his eyes unfocused. His shirt was bright purple silk, buttoned to the neck and decorated with a bolo tie. He wore billowing black slacks; on his feet were black side-weaves. "Thought you were through."

"I am," said Larry. "But you still owe me money."

"What I tell you, Beano?" said White. "Man acts all high and mighty, but he still wants to get paid."

"I don't have the cash," said Ricardo. "You know this. Lucas took it."

"When you're gonna get it?"

"Lucas called me a little while ago. He's comin here tomorrow morning, ten A.M. Says he's bringin the money."

"And you're gonna do what?"

"Take it," said Ricardo.

"I mean after."

"That ain't none of your business anymore," said Ricardo.

"It is if it comes back on me," said Larry. "You kidnapped a minor. I got a right to be concerned."

"Oh, you *concerned*," said Ricardo.

"The boy's all right," said Mobley. "He's scared, is all."

"Lucas is a grown man," said Larry. "He knew what he was into. But the boy—"

"You don't like it," said White, "but you're too weak to try and stop it."

Larry didn't respond.

"Larry got a gun, but he don't like to use it," said White, giving him a slow going-over with his eyes. "You do look resplendent in that uniform, though."

"What's that mean?" said Mobley.

"Means our man Larry is like a peacock." White smiled. "Got real colorful feathers. *Don't* you, Larry?"

"I'm confused," said Larry. "You askin me to dance?"

"Pretty peacock," said White.

"Y'all run your mouths too goddamn much," said Ricardo. "In my day we'da gotten to it by now."

"I can do that, too," said White.

"Save it for Lucas," said Ricardo. He picked up his tumbler and drained it. He limped to the bar cart and poured more scotch.

That's right, thought Larry. *Drink up.*

"Let's go," said Ricardo, making eye contact with Mobley and White. "We need to go out to the bays and strategize. You, too, Larry. We'll see your ass out."

The four of them walked from the office, Ricardo mumbling, limping deep. Larry lagged behind. He was unsteady on his feet. He would be all right if he could just get outside. He wanted to run.

You're too weak to try and stop it.

Larry felt his cell vibrate in his pocket, heard that little chime sound it made when a text message had come in. He drew the phone and read its screen.

I'm here. Get him out.

"*Fuck* me, man," said Larry, staring at his phone. The others stopped and turned to look at him. "That's my lieutenant. I need to call in."

"You're off duty," said Ricardo.

"I'm *never* off duty," said Larry.

"Call in, then," said Ricardo.

"Not in front of y'all," said Larry.

"I bet this motherfucker got to pee sittin' down, too," said White, and Ricardo laughed.

Larry looked at his father. He felt nothing, not even hate.

"Take your privacy," said Mobley, pointing back at the office. "Go on."

Larry's long strides got him back to the office quickly, where he closed the door behind him. Now he was committed. He was sure.

He picked up the ring of keys off the desktop and dropped them into his pants pocket. He opened the desk drawer and rummaged through it. He found the piece of paper with Spero Lucas's name and contact information written on it, along with all the names and numbers taken from Tavon and Edwin's cell, and he folded the paper and slipped it into his back pocket. He flipped the dead bolt on the door that led to the back room, opened the door, and stepped inside. He shut the door softly.

"Ernest," said Larry.

Ernest Lindsay got up out of his chair as if sprung. "*You.* You're—"

"I know who I am," said Larry. "I'm about to get you out of here. C'mon, boy, *move.*"

Larry went to the rear door, read what was etched on its lock, and searched on the ring for the Schlage key that would match it. There were two possibilities and the second key fit. Larry turned it and opened the door. Ernest was right beside him.

"Listen up," said Larry. "Get yourself to the wall of the tracks and follow it to the street. You'll see a black Escalade parked about a hundred yards away. It's open. Get in the backseat and lie down on it. I'll be out there in a hot minute."

"Why don't you come with me?"

Larry put his hands on Ernest's shoulders and gave him a little push. "Go."

He watched as Ernest took tentative steps, then quickened his pace as he walked into a stand of weed trees that led to the wall. Ernest was swallowed by the darkness. Larry thought for a moment, then closed the door and locked it. He slipped the keys into his pocket.

He went back to the main office, opened the door leading to the bay area, and shut it behind him. He stepped quickly across the bay floor, passing under the buzzing, flashing fluorescent light that no one had ever thought to change, moving through the narrow space between the Expedition and the Mark, his eyes on the front door of the building, where the others were now grouped.

"Where you goin so quick?" said Mobley in that rasp of his, and Larry said, "Something came up; I gotta go back in," and he kept on walking without breaking stride or looking at the man who was his father by blood only. Larry opened the door himself and heard it shut behind him.

He breathed fresh air as he moved across the lot. On the street he broke into a run and reached the Escalade. He got behind the wheel and looked over his shoulder. Ernest was lying down across the backseat.

"Stay like that," said Larry.

He retrieved his cell and put it on the console, found his ignition key and fitted it, and fired up the SUV. He pulled away and when he got to the top of the cross street he braked and picked up his cell. He looked in his rearview mirror and waited. Soon he saw a man in dark clothing cross the street on foot, then pass through the open gate of the Mobley Detailing lot. Half a minute later, the text chime sounded from his cell. Larry looked at the screen.

Make the call.

Larry dialed Beano Mobley's number.

"Mobley speaking."

"It's Larry. I'm comin back in."

"What the fuck..."

"I left my car keys back in the office. C'mon, Beano, open that door up, man."

"Yeah, okay."

Larry ended the call and tossed the phone onto the seat beside him. He gave the Escalade gas, turned right, and gunned it toward 46th Street. He could smell his perspiration. His shirt was damp and it clung to his back.

"You can get up," said Larry.

Ernest got himself to a sitting position and wiped sweat off his face. He took deep breaths and let them out slowly. Larry looked in the mirror. Their eyes met.

"*Thank* you," said Ernest.

"This didn't happen," said Larry. "None of it. Anybody asks you where you been, your mother, your teachers, your friends...tell 'em you been shacked up with some girl. I reckon you're gonna see something on the TV news tomorrow, or read about it in the paper. You're not to speak on this, *any* of this, again. You understand me, young man?"

"Yes, sir."

"Relax," said Larry. "I'm taking you home."

LUCAS HAD parked the Jeep one street west of Mobley Detailing. Standing behind it, its tailgate up, he slipped on his pistol vest and belt, the holstered Beretta on his right hip, the clip-on holding the .38 on his left. He took a short drink of water from a bottle, dropped the bottle on the cargo deck, and closed the tailgate.

He hugged the wall of the elevated tracks until he came to the adjacent street. He crossed the street, keeping low.

He swiveled his head and saw the Escalade idling up at the cross. He went through the open gate of the detailing lot. There was a light over the front door, but its wattage was weak and it did not illuminate the entire lot. He crouched against the fence in shadow and pulled his cell from one of his vest pouches. He hoped Larry Holley had the kid. If Holley had lost his nerve...But it didn't matter now. He looked at the phone's keyboard and he punched in the words *Make the call* and he hit "send."

Lucas slipped the cell back into its pouch and velcroed it shut. He drew the .38 from its holster and the M-9 off his right hip and thumbed off its safety. He walked forward, snicking back the hammer on the .38 and locking it into place.

His heart rate was up and he could feel its hammer. In Fallujah his platoon had fought in two-man teams. He had paired up with Marquis Rollins, and after Marquis was injured it had been Jamie Burdette until Jamie's death. Going into houses together near the Jolan graveyard, facing the unknown, jacked up on energy, ambition, and confidence, because your partner was with you and he had your back.

But now Lucas was alone and at the door.

The door opened a crack, and he felt a violent surge inside his chest. He kicked the door open, moved through it, and looked left. A short man in a white shirt was falling from the force of the contact. Lucas fired the .38 three times rapidly into his torso just as he hit the floor, and his shirt tore apart and bloomed deep red.

He saw movement in his peripheral vision on his right, heard a gunshot, and felt the air move past his head. He dropped. In the prone position, one arm extended, he saw a big man in a cutoff T-shirt backing up between two vehicles, holding a gun, pointing it at him and firing, and he saw the muzzle flash and the floor before him spark, and Lucas rolled and got to his feet. He took cover behind the tail of the Expedition. He looked through its windows and saw the big man moving along its side, and he stepped back and straightened the arm holding the Beretta and he fired off two rounds into glass and the glass shattered, and in the rain of it he saw the man crouch down.

Lucas spun off the tailgate and shot the big man as he was struggling to stand. The round hit the man in the groin, and as he staggered, his arms pinwheeling, a look of surprise on his face, Lucas moved forward and buttonholed him with a shot to the chest and one to the throat. The man flopped onto his back, jerking wildly. He released his gun and grabbed weakly at his open neck. Lucas stood over the man and shot him twice in the face. He dropped the revolver, now empty, on the body.

A light flashed and buzzed overhead. Lucas heard a door slam in the back of the warehouse. He walked forward between two vehicles, the automatic in hand.

Beano Mobley at the door, Bernard White lying by the Ford, both dead. Ricardo Holley in one of the back rooms. Five shots expended from the .9's fifteen-round mag. These were Lucas's thoughts as he approached the main office, its walls once glass, now wood panels, just as Larry had described it. The door was open.

Lucas stood beside the door, gun arm out. He cleared it and walked into the office. He knew from the sound he'd heard that Ricardo had entered the far back room.

Lucas passed a gun case with open compartments, went to the door at the back of the office, and stood beside it. Pressed against the wall, he reached over to the dead bolt and flipped it. Three shots punched through the door, missing Lucas. He crouched down, turned the knob, pushed the door open with the toe of his boot, and whirled into the space, firing his weapon twice at the purple shape in the center of the room. The sound was sonic, and he saw a tall man topple over a table and upend it and come to rest on his back. Lucas walked through smoke, the Beretta pointed at Ricardo Holley. Holley's Glock was beside him. Lucas kicked it across the floor.

Holley looked up at Lucas with dying eyes. One slug had caught him square in the chest. A pool had rapidly spread beneath him and darkened his coppery hair. The jacketed round had exited his back, and he was bleeding out. Holley's bright purple shirt was flapping at the entrance wound and it was black there.

"Larry did this," said Ricardo weakly. "He trapped me."

"Why'd you kill those boys?" said Lucas.

Holley's lips twitched into a smile. His teeth were stained red. "You don't know shit, *do* you? You took that money just to give it back."

"*Tell* me what I don't know."

"You killed me, man. Now you want me to..." Holley's eyes closed, then opened. He was smiling still.

"Say it," said Lucas.

"Come close," said Ricardo softly.

Lucas holstered his gun, got down on his haunches, and put his face close to Holley's.

"*Fuck* you," said Holley, with a chuckle that was a sickening wheeze.

He thought he would go out that way: laughing. But his smile became a grimace as he began to cough, and a great stream of blood spilled from his mouth. Fear came to his face. In its grip he stared at the ceiling. His body shivered in spasm and his eyes faded. Then his eyes were black buttons in a cardboard mask.

Lucas found Holley's cell phone in one of his pockets. He put it in a pouch of his vest. He collected the cells of Mobley and White, picked up his spent .38 off White's corpse and holstered it. He left the building quietly through its front door. He heard no approaching sirens and made it to his Jeep and took off his vest and unarmed himself and put everything in the duffel bag and covered the duffel with a blanket.

He headed into D.C., staying within a ten-mile range of the speed limit, careful not to drive too slowly. He went through neighborhoods where normal citizens were sleeping, or making love to their spouses, or lying in bed worrying over their children, or sitting in their favorite chair, having a last, late-night drink. He passed bars where young people stood out on the sidewalk, talking to one another and smoking cigarettes. He found himself on M Street in Southeast, and he followed it to where it seemed to end but in fact continued along the Anacostia, past old marinas partially hidden in the trees. He parked down by the river, under the Sousa Bridge, where there was no one. There he retrieved his guns from the back of the Jeep and hurled them, one after the other, out into the water. After the second muted splash he got back into his vehicle and went north.

He made one more stop, on 12th Street, Northwest. A light was on in the living room window of Ernest Lindsay's place. Lucas made a call to his brother, and when it went to message he said, "Ernest is safe."

Lucas's hands, tight on the steering wheel, relaxed at once. He drove home.

TWENTY-FIVE

FOR THE next few days, Lucas stayed in his apartment. He tried to read a novel and watched bits of old movies and sports on TV, but he couldn't focus on any of them. His work was done, but there was no satisfaction. He felt, somewhat, as he had upon his return to the States: no duties, no mission, no cause.

The killings did not make the morning *Post*, but broke instead on its crime-related website. Many firearms had been found at the scene, implying business-related violence perpetrated on the participants of a criminal enterprise. He scanned the initial story but did not bother with the print or web follow-ups. If he was a suspect, if the police were going to question him or arrest him, so be it. He wasn't going to turn himself in, and he wasn't going to run.

His one possible link to the murders would come from Tim McCarthy in IAB and former MPD lieutenant Pete Gibson. McCarthy had taken his request for a background check on Larry Holley and referred him to Gibson. Both had tried to nail Ricardo Holley twenty years earlier. They must have known immediately that Lucas was, in some way, involved in Ricardo's death. They could have been weighing their options. Perhaps they considered the demise of Ricardo Holley, Beano Mobley, and Bernard White to be justice, what some D.C. police call a "society cleanse." At any rate, the law did not come.

His brother Leo phoned him the afternoon following the shootings.

"Ernest showed up for school today. Made it back for the last day of class."

"Yeah?"

"Claims he went off with some girl. That would be a first, far as I know."

"Even a nail gun like you had a first time, Leo."

"It wasn't pretty, either."

"Neither was she."

"I just wanted to say thanks."

"For what?"

"Play it like that if you feel the need to."

"Okay."

"You wanna go over to Mom's tonight and have dinner? We could sit and watch a game on the wide-screen."

"I don't think so," said Spero.

"She's been asking after you."

"I'll get over there."

"You go to the graveyard more often than you go to see Mom. You know that?"

"Let me get off this phone."

"Something wrong, Spero?"

"Not a thing."

"Whatever it is, I still love you, man."

"I love you, too," said Spero.

"I mean it."

"So do I."

"Okay, *malaka*," said Leo. "You need me, I'm here."

Spero Lucas had no doubt.

YOU TOOK *that money just to give it back.*

As Lucas paced the floors of the apartment, Ricardo Holley's words would not leave his head. And then something came to him, a bit of information that Tavon and Edwin had given him the first time they'd met. Lucas was coming to it, though the answers to his nagging questions were irrelevant now. Still, he had to know.

He got dressed in blue pants and a blue shirt, left the apartment, and drove to the D.C. Jail. By process of observation and elimination he located a lot where prison guards and DOC employees seemed to park their cars. He waited there for several hours, reading a novel behind the wheel, using the piss bottle he kept in his vehicle as needed. At the end of the day shift a tall, handsome woman in uniform walked across the lot.

Lucas got out of his Jeep and moved toward her. She was turning the door key on her Mercury when she noticed his approach. She stood straight and faced him.

"Cecelia Edwards?" said Lucas.

"You are?" she said, confident and not entirely unfriendly.

"Spero Lucas. I'm an investigator. We've met before."

"What can I do for you?"

"I'm looking for a little bit of information," said Lucas, extending his hand for a shake.

Cecelia Edwards took his hand. Her eyes briefly examined the folding money that she now held. There were three hundred-dollar bills there, and she slipped them into her pocket.

"I was hoping we could be friends," said Lucas.

"Sugar," she said, "we are now."

THE NEXT day, he returned to the D.C. Jail.

After going through security, where he showed his ID, signed in, and was wanded, he went to the visiting room and had a seat in a hard plastic chair set before a heavily smudged window. Soon Anwan Hawkins appeared in an orange jumpsuit and took his place on the other side of the glass. His hair was down and his braids touched his broad shoulders. He snatched the phone out of its cradle, and Lucas took his receiver out of a similarly mounted cradle and put it to his ear.

"Spero Lucas," said Hawkins, his voice husky and riddled with static. "Mr. Petersen said you'd be stopping by. I never did get a chance to thank you for visiting my wife. You do good work."

"You didn't really need me, though, did you? You would have gotten your money regardless."

"Huh?"

"I *know*, Anwan."

Hawkins nodded. A glint of gold showed in his wry smile. "You wired up?"

"No."

"You wouldn't be. That's not your style. But then again, you can't rightly go to the police."

"No."

"On account of you're a murderer. I'm not just talkin about that little white dude, either. I get word in here. Holley, Mobley, and White. That was you, wasn't it? Had to be."

"Your business associates," said Lucas. "Ricardo told me, in so many words. That I was giving the money back to the same people I stole it from. Meaning you."

Anwan stared at him dead-eyed.

"But you *hired* me," said Lucas. "Why?"

Anwan said nothing.

"You *know* I can't hurt you," said Lucas. "I can't speak to anyone on this."

"But you're the curious type," said Hawkins. "Relentless, too. Once I let you loose, I didn't know how to rein you back in. I tried to warn you off of it. I did try." Anwan shook braids away from his face. "When I hired you, I had the need for your services. But you took a week to get started."

"I had to complete a job for Petersen."

"That was crucial."

"It was the week that Ricardo Holley visited you here in jail. Twice. It's in the logbook, Anwan. You have to show your photo ID and sign your name to get in. It's damn near impossible to falsify that."

"You got a DOC in your pocket, too," said Hawkins, with something close to admiration.

"I'm guessing that Ricardo told you that he and his crew were shaking down Tavon and Edwin."

"Yeah. And they were paying those boys fifty percent of the package."

"Ricardo came to you because the deal with them was finite," said Lucas. "Tavon and Edwin told me themselves that they didn't know the identity of your connect. Only you did. So if the financial relationship was to continue, Ricardo needed you. He didn't need those boys anymore."

"Eliminate the middleman."

"You ordered them killed."

"Had Tavon and Edwin come to me right away, told me that they were being stepped on by those men, it wouldn't have happened. But they decided to keep the full fifty. I regret it, but it had to be done."

"You said you weren't about that."

Anwan shrugged. "They stole from me. I can't have that perception gettin out there on the street telegraph. The idea that I'm weak. I didn't get up here where I am by being soft."

"Up where?" said Lucas. "You're in prison."

"Today I am."

"You're looking at long time."

"I got the best lawyer in town. I'm gonna walk. Bet it." Hawkins studied Lucas's narrowed eyes. "Don't be angry, Spero. I got paid and so did you."

"I fucked up," said Lucas, more to himself than to Hawkins.

"You're a bull, son," said Hawkins. "It's your nature. You walk into a room and you just break shit. But don't be getting on your high horse with regards to Anwan Hawkins. You can't fix it. And you can't do a motherfuckin thing about me." Hawkins leaned forward. "You got your cut. There ain't nothin more to say."

Lucas quietly hung the phone in its cradle. He stood and walked from the room.

LUCAS SPENT the next few days quietly, going out occasionally, wary when he came back to his apartment, expecting the law to be there, waiting for his return. But it did not happen.

He passed an evening with Miss Lee, playing Scrabble in her first-floor living room, and on Sunday he went to church and said his customary prayer of thanks, and something extra. Afterward he went to Glenwood and lay roses on his father's grave.

On Monday he visited Ernest Lindsay at his house to make sure that he was settled and okay. They talked about the books Lucas had given him and the movies described within their pages, but they did not discuss the events that had led to Ernest's capture and rescue in Edmonston. The mother's boyfriend was there and the atmosphere was tense. Ernest seemed relatively fine, with the resilience of youth on his side, and Lucas promised himself as he left the house that he would stay in touch with him.

Outside he saw Lisa Weitzman sitting on her porch. He visited with her, intending to stay for a minute or so, and right away he remembered the fun they'd had and their easy conversation, and he asked her if she was free for dinner. The two of them had drinks in the downstairs bar of Café Saint-Ex, on 14th, then drove north and dined at Sergio's, in his old neighborhood, in a hotel on Colesville Road, where the veal scaloppine's tomato-based sauce was exquisite, and afterward they went to back to his apartment and made love as reggae music played through candlelight, and he was reminded of how good it was to be young and alive.

The next morning, he phoned Tom Petersen and asked him if he could come in.

"YOU'VE COME far, pilgrim," said Petersen.

"You sound like my brother," said Lucas.

"You do have a bit of a beard going there."

"I shaved a few hours ago. It's my two o'clock shadow."

"The testosterone levels are off the charts at your age. I'm sure it speaks volumes to the ladies."

Lucas, in Carhartt, was seated before Tom Petersen's desk. Petersen, big, shaggy, and blond, wore a wide-striped shirt, open collar, jeans with a thick brown belt, and side-zip boots. He looked as if he had just stepped out of a shop on Carnaby Street.

"What can I do for you, Spero?"

"Just wanted you to know I'm back in circulation and available."

"You're done with side work?"

"For now."

"Excellent. I can use you."

Lucas nodded, said nothing.

"Is there anything else?" said Petersen.

Lucas leaned forward. "Can I ask you something?"

"Ask."

"Hypothetically…"

"Go ahead."

"You're defending a drug dealer. Jury trial. You know he did it, and the law and prosecution have all their bases covered. What's your strategy?"

"In general?" Petersen tented his hands on his desk. "If it's a black defendant, if he grew up disadvantaged, if he's a nonviolent offender, and *if* I get the right jury? I argue, artfully I might add, against putting another young black man in prison for political reasons related to a costly and ineffective drug war. I talk about the disparity in sentencing along racial lines, if I can get away with it. I only need one juror who's willing to acquit, and in D.C. that's not too difficult. It's your basic nullification argument."

"What if your defendant was a violent offender? I'm talking about a stone killer."

"I would prepare a different defense. But I'd know that from the start."

"But what if you found out about his acts after you'd taken on the case?"

Petersen didn't answer right away. He was trying to read Lucas.

"I defend murderers often, Spero. You know that. It's what I do."

"You don't take on everyone who offers you money."

"True," said Petersen. "I've refused clients before simply because I didn't like them. Because there was no conscience or humanity in their eyes. On occasion I've quoted outrageous fees to clients, knowing they couldn't afford them or wouldn't pay that kind of highway robbery on principle. It's the easiest way to say no."

"You're missing my point."

285

"I'm *not*," said Petersen.

"Have you ever deliberately tanked a case?"

Petersen smiled and shook his head. "I've *lost* cases. I've lost them because I was insufficiently prepared, or I underestimated the prosecuting attorneys, or a witness underperformed on the stand. I've lost cases because..."

"What?"

"Because I wasn't feeling well. Because my rhythm was off in court. I've lost cases, Spero, because I simply had a bad day."

They sat there in the office, looking at each other, saying nothing. Neither of them cut his eyes away.

Lucas got up out of his chair. "Thanks for listening."

"Do me a favor: when you're working for me, make sure you shave. You'll make a better impression out on the street."

"I will, if you comb your hair and put on a tie."

"I do, when I'm in court."

"Were you mad when Mick and Keith kicked you out of the band?"

"Brian Jones. Very funny, but I've heard that before. Are you a Stones fan?"

"My dad was. He used to play *Exile on Main St.* front to back when we were riding around in his pickup truck."

"Good record."

"Listen, is Constance around?"

"No. She's waitressing this summer. Said she needed to make some money for a change. I think she was trying to convey some sort of point."

"Which restaurant?"

"You want the truth? She asked me not to tell you."

"Why?"

"I don't know for sure. She said something about treating people right. She said you needed to learn."

"I'm young," said Lucas.

" 'Drink in your summer, gather your corn.' "

"Inspector Clouseau?"

"Jagger/Richards," said Petersen. He reached his hand across the desk. "Glad you're back."

"Call me," said Lucas. "I'm ready to work."

OVER THE summer, Lucas did a couple of small, simple jobs for Petersen and one that involved murder and conspiracy charges that was much more intricate. Between his work and his physical routine, the daily bike rides and afternoons with his kayak on the river, he stayed busy. He bought a second vehicle, had it registered under a false name with the assistance of one of Nick Simmons's friends, and kept it in a garage he rented with cash in one of the old alley dwellings east of the Hill. He bought a GPS Internet tracking device that he could access from his laptop or phone. He bought a carton of disposable cells. He was getting smarter about the way he worked.

There was a day trip to New York, organized by Leo, in which the brothers accompanied Ernest Lindsay on his first major excursion out of D.C. Their intent was to take him on an informal tour of the film school at NYU, where they hoped he would apply the following year. He had enrolled at UDC, but they felt that he needed to ultimately get out of Washington and broaden his world. He was smart enough, he had the grades, and he qualified for various minority grants and scholarships. Spero told Leo in private that he might be able to help out if there was a shortfall in the tuition; he felt he owed the young man at least that much. On the Acela ride back, Ernest could not stop talking about the city and the school.

Lucas had not been contacted by Larry Holley since the night they'd worked together to rescue Ernest Lindsay. A query e-mail to Tim McCarthy in IAB prompted a terse response sent from McCarthy's personal account: "Larry Holley resigned from the MPD a month ago." Lucas never learned where he'd gone.

In August he received an envelope in the mail with no return address. Inside was a faded trading card of Foghorn Leghorn, the oversize rooster from the Warner Brothers cartoons, with a slash of red Magic Marker through the character's throat. On the back of the card, a note was written in block letters: *Heard he got scratched. Nice work.* The postmark told Lucas that the card had been sent from Frederick, Maryland, the hometown of Pete Gibson.

One humid night toward the end of the season, Lucas was riding his bike uptown, cycling past Wonderland, the bar at the corner of 11th and Kenyon, when he saw Constance Kelly seated at one of the outdoor tables, drinking beer with two other young women. Lucas turned around, cruised back to the patio, and came to a stop alongside her table.

"Hey, Constance."

"Hi."

She smiled. She didn't seem mad at him, nor did her demeanor give him hope. She was simply being polite.

"Can I talk to you a second?" he said.

"Sure."

He walked his bike along Tubman Elementary and she walked beside him.

"Where you been?" said Lucas.

"Working. I made a couple of trips down to the ocean. But mostly work."

"Me, too." Lucas caught her eye. "I called you a couple of times."

"I know."

"My phone takes calls, too."

"Must be a real fancy one."

Lucas stopped. "So what did I do wrong?"

Constance shrugged. "It wasn't a long-term thing. We both knew that."

"Something must have made you get off the bus."

"I saw you one night, Spero, at the downstairs bar at Saint-Ex. You were with a woman. You were looking at her the exact same way that you looked at me when we were out and having a good time. And it came to me that I was nothing special to you. I was just one of many."

"That's not how I feel, though," said Lucas. "You're exactly the kind of person—"

"Please. Don't do that."

"I'm trying to figure things out, Constance. I missed out on the good part of my twenties. When everyone else was in college, going to parties and whatever, *being young*, I was in the desert. Now I'm here, catching up. I told you once before, I'm not ready to make plans."

"I wasn't looking for a commitment," said Constance. "Just some courtesy."

She went back to join her friends. Lucas swung onto the saddle of his bike and pedaled uptown, not yet understanding what he'd lost.

THE ANWAN Hawkins trial began late in August. Lucas did not speak to Tom Petersen during the proceedings, but he read about them daily in the *Washington Post*. Because the marijuana legalization movement was making inroads in D.C., the chronicle of this high-profile, high-volume weed dealer and his possible conviction made timely copy. The day after the jury reached its unanimously guilty verdict, the *Post* reporter assigned to the story quoted an unnamed courtroom witness: "It seemed to me that the defense's closing arguments were oddly dispassionate and, at times, clumsily delivered." Tom Petersen, normally light on his feet, had forgotten how to dance. He'd had a bad day.

ONE SUNDAY early in October, Lucas went to church. He took his seat beside the white-haired former teacher, noticing many of his friends and their families in attendance, and Leo and his mother front and center, in place. He recited the Creed and the Lord's Prayer, followed along with the liturgy in the book, and when it was time he kneeled and gave his usual thanks, and added a prayer for the dead.

After the service he bought a dozen red roses and drove over to Glenwood, passing under the arched gate. He negotiated the twisting lanes and went along the stretch of mausoleums, where a blanket of scarlet leaves had fallen on black asphalt, and continued on to the section of headstones at the

ACKNOWLEDGMENTS

I'd like to thank Larry Nathans, Jon Norris, James Grady, Quintin Peterson, and Nick Pelecanos for their help with this novel; the sources on both sides of the law who spoke to me with candor and wish to remain anonymous; Sloan Harris and Alicia Gordon for their friendship and guidance; Michael Pietsch, Marlena Bittner, Tracy Williams, Heather Rizzo, Karen Torres, Miriam Parker, Betsy Uhrig, and everyone who has worked so hard on my behalf at Little, Brown over the years; Jon Wood, Malcolm Edwards, Susan Lamb, Gaby Young, Sophie Mitchell, and the kind staff of Orion Books in the U.K., and Robert Pepin in France. Proudly, this is my first book published under the imprint of my longtime editor and friend Reagan Arthur. A special shout-out to Emily, Nick, Pete, and Rosa, and to all the readers who have come along with me on this excellent trip.

west edge of the cemetery, which gave to a view of the Bryant Place row homes and North Capitol Street.

Standing before his father's grave, he made the sign of the Holy Trinity with three fingers of his right hand and did his *stavro*. He stood there, feeling the energy around him, listening to the call of sparrows, watching a gray squirrel scamper up the trunk of a tree, breathing the crisp fall air. He looked at the flowers he held by his side.

Lucas returned to his Jeep. He drove north, crossing over the District line at Georgia Avenue and into the neighborhood where he'd come up. He saw one of the barbers standing outside of Afrikuts, and the man shouted out a greeting as Lucas went by in his vehicle, and Lucas waved. He passed a couple of Guatemalan housepainters standing by an old 4Runner, a ladder lashed to the crossbars of its roof.

Driving down his street, Lucas punched in a number on his cell. When the call was answered he said, "Just wanted to make sure you were home."

"I'm here, honey."

His mother was standing outside the front door, waiting for him. He met her there and put the roses in her hands.

IN THE evening, in the stillness of his apartment, Lucas grew restless. He decided to go up to the bar on Georgia that had the quiet patrons and the eclectic juke. He left his place, went out to his Jeep, and looked up at the hunter's moon and clear sky. He'd walk.

He took Piney Branch to Colorado, east to 14th Street and its small commercial strip, and followed it to 13th, where he turned left. Down at Quackenbos he cut into the weedy field alongside Fort Stevens, and he traversed it, going up the gravelly road to the parking lot of the Emery Methodist Church, where he'd fought Earl Nance.

He'd killed many men. Some, like Ricardo Holley and Bernard White, had been murderers themselves, and others, like Beano Mobley, had been dirty, in the wrong place, and had simply caught his fire. And then there were the men who were fathers, sons, and brothers, fighting in their homeland. Men he'd ended because they'd tried to kill him.

He stood on the edge of the lot and stared into its shadows. Close to the church's north wall, where the light from the moon was obstructed, the night was very dark. He walked through it and took the steps down to Georgia Avenue. He crossed the street and headed for his bar.

Lucas was thirsty. He wanted a beer.